ADVANCE PRAISE FOR WHO LIES IN WAIT

"Who Lies in Wait, Brenda Chapman's riveting new Hunter and Tate mystery, opens at night in a frozen forest outside Ottawa. You can almost feel the frost as Detective Liam Hunter and his partner view the body of a murdered woman. Chapman's evocation of winter is so vivid that it's almost a character. The story is littered with red herrings and unexpected twists. There's a family of siblings with motives for murder, a subplot involving a young woman trafficked for sex, the fraught sexual tension between Hunter and crime blogger Ella Tate, and a bevy of characters to embrace. This compulsively readable tale will keep you up past your bedtime as you try to unravel the mesmerizing mystery."

- **Don Butler**, author of *Norman's Conquest*

"With WHO LIES IN WAIT, Brenda Chapman's fourth novel in her Hunter and Tate mystery series, the Ottawa author has crafted a twisty, expertly plotted page turner, grounded in a wonderfully evocative sense of place, with richly developed characters that confirm Chapman's place as one of Canada's doyennes of crime fiction."

- **John Delacourt**, author of *The Black State*

"The story is complex and compelling while further developing the various characters and their arcs. So, well done!"

- **Allister Thompson**, editor

PRAISE FOR Fatal Harvest

"With lots of suspense, some great interplay between characters (among the police as well as civilians) and a couple of great twists, this is a terrific read with some intriguing storylines that intertwine and lead to a satisfying ending."
   – **Lis Angus,** author of *Not Your Child*

"Chapman's gripping, emotionally resonant third Hunter and Tate mystery quickly grabs readers' attention … Standout procedural of a cop and podcaster chasing a killer and a missing boy."
   – ***BookLife***

"The story is riveting and keeps you on your toes."
   – ***Kitchissippi Times***

"… compelling characters, an interesting plot and a conclusion that one does not see coming."
   – ***Glebe Report***

PRAISE FOR WHEN LAST SEEN

"...wows with well-crafted tension and original characters. In a genteel Ottawa neighborhood, ...Literary sleight-of-hand comes naturally to Chapman, and the culprit could be one of many poker-faced or temperamental suspects as in any worthy mystery-thriller. A tryst with an escort, a traumatizing roofie, a naive vigilante, and plenty of delectable surprises make *When Last Seen* a treat for mystery readers."
   -***BookLife***

"WHEN LAST SEEN is a descriptive and compelling novel showing the fractures in a family when the worst occurs, and the strength and resilience of those who push forward to seek the truth."
   -Fresh Fiction

"The dynamics between Hunter and Tate – true friends and colleagues without being lovers – forms the heart of this intricate, riveting tale of a missing child, family jealousy, business skullduggery, and the deepest sort of betrayal. Hunter and Tate are a duo to root for. I'm looking forward to their next outing."
   – **Vicki Delany**, national bestselling author and recipient of the 2019 Derrick Murdoch Award for Contributions to Canadian Crime Writing

PRAISE FOR BLIND DATE

"…a well-crafted page-turner that explores the evil lurking in the shadows of the nation's capital."
   – ***Ottawa Citizen***

"A credible, well-crafted story that will keep readers turning the page and when finished, thirsting for more. Highly recommended."
   – ***Ottawa Review of Books***

"*Blind Date* will hook you from its early pages and reel you in, holding on until its final page."
   – ***Glebe Report***

WHO LIES IN WAIT

A HUNTER AND TATE MYSTERY
BOOK 4

BRENDA CHAPMAN

This is a work of fiction. Names and events described herein are products of the author's imagination, or used fictitiously. Any resemblance to actual events, organizations, or persons, living or dead, is entirely coincidental.

Title: Who Lies in Wait / Brenda Chapman

Names: Chapman, Brenda, 1955 – author

Description: Series statement: A Hunter and Tate mystery - #4 Edited by Allister Thompson. Cover Design by Laura Boyle Published by Ivy Bay Press, First Edition May 2025

ISBN Trade Paperback: 978-1-0691842-2-1

ISBN E-book: 978-1-0691842-1-4

Dedicated to my good friend Janet Bowick. Your kindness and strength inspire me every day.

The third day comes a frost, a killing frost

— Shakespeare, *Henry VIII*

CHAPTER 1

Detective Liam Hunter stepped out of his car onto the snowy country road and shivered at the thought of the misery waiting for him out of sight somewhere past the black ridge of trees. He took a moment to lean his head back and breathe, attempting to detach himself from what was to come but unable to rid himself of the hollow feeling in the pit of his stomach that had worked its way into his chest. A quarter moon glowed milky white against the dark sky, the light hazy through the gathering clouds, their bellies low and swollen with moisture. A sharp blast of wind blew shards of ice against his face, and he hunched into himself, attempting to find warmth where there was none.

This is a desolate place to die.

The thought depressed him. He hoped that when his time came he'd be tucked up in a warm bed having just drunk a shot of whiskey, not in a location as isolated and frigid as this. Whoever was lying dead in these woods had not been given a choice.

His partner, Julie Quade, was already striding toward the entrance to the trail cordoned off with bright yellow police tape, her matching neon vest a bright smudge against the trees. She stopped and aimed the beam of her flashlight down the path, waiting for Liam to join her.

"I could have done without this tonight," she said when he moved alongside. She yanked the hood of her parka over her springy mass of black hair with a gloved hand and tucked her chin into the scarf wrapped around her neck. "Really could have done without this."

"You had plans?"

She snorted. "Needed to call my ex to pick up the kids, and he gave me an earful as per usual. The three of us had just settled in with a movie and popcorn, then the scramble to collect all their stuff and get them out the door. I wonder sometimes if they'll ever forgive me for this hellish, workaholic life. Damn, it's cold."

He knew she didn't expect him to comment. Already she'd turned and was crunching through the snow ahead of him toward the sound of activity deeper into the woods. "Did dispatch tell you anything about the victim?" he asked, raising his voice to be heard above the gusty wind.

"No, just that a guy's dog led him to the body. Apparently, he drives here daily to exercise the hound. I don't know how we'd find half the bodies we do without dogs off-leash."

A hundred metres into the woods, Liam heard the voices of officers up ahead. He rounded a corner in the path and saw the sharp glow of lights set up to illuminate the site. The track had widened into a small glade, and the body lay at the farthest corner next to a border of sumac bushes. Coroner Brigette Green looked up at him and Quade as they approached from where she crouched in the snow.

"It's okay," she said, motioning them closer. "We've already done a search of this part of the terrain. Jane Doe was found deeper into that bit of brush just over there, but we moved her so I could undertake an examination once photography was completed."

"You made it here fast," Quade said, squatting down next to her. "What have we got then?"

"A woman I estimate to be in her late twenties to early thirties. She hasn't been dead long."

"So, time of death…?"

"Now, Detective Quade, when have you known me to give you that at the scene?"

"Hope springs eternal."

Green's smile lasted as long as it took for her gaze to travel from Quade to the body. Her gloved fingertips gently brushed the woman's cheek. "Strangled, I'd say within the last several hours from the state of bruising on her neck, if I were forced to guess. The snowfall a few hours ago was light, but it coated her in a layer that also filled in some of the footprints. The wind gusts haven't helped." Green's voice was matter-of-fact, but Liam had worked with her long enough to know that the detachment was surface-deep. "I can't ascertain yet if she was raped, although her clothes are all accounted for. After a cursory inspection I can tell you that she's wearing lacy lilac underwear, but that might mean nothing."

"She could have been meeting someone. Women often wear flimsy undergarments for an assignation. I used to before I got married." Quade's voice was wistful.

"She's not wearing a wedding or engagement ring; however, she might simply enjoy the feel of lace." Green stood and stretched out her back.

"You need thermal undies on a night like tonight. Any sane woman in Ottawa knows that," Quade said.

Liam shuffled closer, and Green bent to pull back the woman's collar with gloved fingers to show the angry, purplish marks on her neck.

"Has she got any ID?" he asked, his eyes moving to encompass her length.

She lay on her back, short, layered hair framing a narrow face. Crystals of ice clung to her eyelashes and strands of hair that were likely a lighter shade of blond when dry. Some of the snow had been removed from her clothes as a result of Green's examination. An unbuttoned, grey wool coat revealed a green sweater and black pants tucked into knee-high leather boots. Her clothes were well cut, expensive. His eyes travelled back to her face. He wondered what colour her eyes were and whether her face had lit up when she smiled. He took a step back and swept his gaze past the brightened section of the glade into the darkness of the trees. This place was within city limits but out of the way. Isolated, except for dog walkers and cross-country skiers, but they tended to stay on the main trail that led to the river bay. The choice of location to conceal the body leaned toward a local who knew the area. It was a more popular spot in the summer and fall, when paddle boarders and other watercraft set out from the short stretch of beach nearby.

"No ID or purse." Green bestowed a half-smile upon him. "You'll have work to do figuring out who she is, Hunter, but I imagine someone will be missing her.

By the quality of her clothing and haircut, she certainly wasn't homeless. I believe she was killed in a different location and moved here, but the autopsy will confirm my assumption."

"Someone could easily have driven into the lot and carried her to this spot. It's isolated enough."

"I agree. She's not an overly large person."

"Jewellery?"

"None. There's a dove tattoo on her left wrist." Green turned over the woman's arm for them to see.

Quade stood. "That should be helpful. I'll check with HQ to see if anyone has reported her missing and get them to be on the lookout if nothing yet. I'll also have a unit canvass the neighbourhoods, although there's none close by. Not near enough to have seen or heard anything, anyway."

Liam nodded. They'd decided on the way over that she'd take the lead. He offered to brief their staff sergeant Kurt Auger, but she shook her head. "You don't need to protect me from him," she said. "I can handle myself."

"I was thinking of protecting him from you." Liam grinned, and her face relaxed. She'd been grumpy since giving up the acting position to Auger, who'd wrangled the job out from under her. Auger had officially become their boss a month earlier, and the entire team teetered on the edge of revolt, waiting for him to begin making changes. Their loyalty to Quade ran deep.

"Keep your enemies closer." The determined look on Quade's face sent a ripple up Liam's spine that had nothing to do with the frosty night and the plunging temperature. He couldn't shake the feeling that their unit was headed for trouble. He wanted to counsel her to be patient, but she'd already yanked her phone out of a pocket and stomped toward the edge of the tree line.

"I'll have the body moved now," Green said and waited for Liam to signal his assent. "The autopsy will be tomorrow morning if I can fit it into the schedule. This week for certain."

"I'll let Quade know."

Green nodded, one sharp movement of her head. "This could end badly," she said. Her gaze moved past him to focus on Quade. "It never should have happened."

He knew she wasn't speaking about the dead woman but pretended he'd misunderstood. "Hopefully, we'll figure out her name by morning. One of us will sit in on the autopsy."

"Sure."

He left her and trudged past Quade toward the road, inky blackness swallowing up the light several metres down the path. He stopped and turned on his flashlight, swinging the beam back and forth as he walked, shadows and creaking boughs unsettling his sense of safety the farther he got from the site. A branch cracked like a gunshot somewhere to his right, and he stilled, shutting off the flashlight and listening in the darkness, his heart thumping hard. The wind soughed overhead through the conifer trees, but the forest cocooned and protected him from its bitter bite. He cocked his head as if this would help him to hear better, but whatever had snapped the branch was quiet now, and he relaxed the hand that had reached inside his jacket for his service revolver. He flicked on the flashlight and continued to the entrance of the woods, relieved to see a CBC van parked behind his car, engine running, headlights casting their beams across the road. Two men stepped out to meet him, and the creepiness of the moment was quickly forgotten as they greeted him. He recognized the reporter, Derick Bukowski.

"Can you tell us anything about the victim?"

"It's a woman, but that's all I can say at this point. We don't have a name."

"Has she been there long?"

"Nothing has been corroborated."

Bukowski's colleague had been filming the interaction, and Liam moved past them. He wouldn't be drawn into being the spokesperson. He got into his car and turned on the engine in an attempt to get warm. The two CBC reporters crossed over to stand next to the police tape. Quade exited the path and spoke with them for a moment before striding toward the car. She heaved herself inside, bringing with her a blast of frigid air before she slammed the door shut. "There's got to be a mole in our unit," she said. "How else did they get here so damn fast?"

"Don't look now, but a CTV van just pulled up."

"We don't even know how Auger wants the media handled." She tugged at her seatbelt, cursed, and wrenched harder. "I phoned and filled him in a few minutes ago, so the ball's in his court. Not my problem anymore. What in the hell is wrong with this damn thing?"

Liam started to reach over to help, thought better of it, put both hands on the wheel, and stared straight ahead until he heard her belt buckle click into place. Snowflakes had begun drifting down like icing sugar and melting on the windshield. He'd have believed it too cold to snow.

Two men from Forensics stepped out of the woods carrying a stretcher with a sheet covering Jane Doe's body. They hurried toward the waiting ambulance while Brigette Green kept the reporters busy and prevented them from following. She'd left behind a team who would scour the woods for another hour or two. They'd be back in the morning to canvass the site during daylight.

He would have texted Ella Tate to join the media throng if they'd been on speaking terms. She'd dropped off his radar since baseball ended for the season in the fall and he'd begun dating Georgina. There hadn't even been any murders since autumn to make their paths cross. It would be good if her editor at *The Capital* assigned this case to her. The thought sent a rush of pleasure through him that he didn't allow himself to think about too deeply.

He put the car into gear and made a U-turn. They should be at HQ within the half hour, and they'd be working into the wee hours. So much for dinner plans. He'd message Georgina when he got to his desk. He hoped she'd understand once the case overtook his life and all else became secondary. Already a rush of adrenaline had kicked in as he contemplated the night's work ahead. These were the days he lived for, the challenges that gave his life meaning. He began making a mental list of what needed to be done as he drove slowly up the snow-packed road toward the highway into the city.

CHAPTER 2

Ella Tate waited out of the wind in the doorway of a closed flower shop. The snowfall was picking up speed, and she was chilled to the bone. As the frosty air seeped through her parka and the pain in her feet intensified, she realized that her contact wasn't coming. Still, she was loath to leave. She'd give her ten more minutes before getting out of this icebox. Otherwise, the last two hours would have been a complete waste. Make that the last three days that she'd spent tracking down this woman and convincing her to meet. The woman who'd made initial contact through Ella's podcast website with a blockbuster story about an illegal business with untold victims. No further details. Ella had responded through email with her phone number and an invitation to text or call anytime. She was eager to follow up. The woman had signed off as Sally when texting Ella after a one-day silence to say that she was having second thoughts. She feared for her own and others' safety. Ella's spidey sense told her this was a story worth pursuing, and she offered to meet anywhere, anytime. After some back and forth and more lengthy silences, Sally had agreed to this quiet street at nine o'clock in the evening after the stores closed. If she felt secure, they could grab coffees in the café on the corner. Ella should have insisted they meet in the coffee shop when she saw the weather report, but she'd been scared of spooking her.

A car eased past, and Ella moved forward, craning her neck to see inside. A man sat at the wheel, not her Sally deep throat, and she stepped back into the shadows. She jumped up and down and flexed her fingers inside the leather gloves, trying to stay warm. After fifteen minutes, she decided the woman had bailed. She took one last look up the road before jogging back to her car. She started the engine and put the heater on high, willing the blast of cold air to turn hot before she lost feeling in her feet and hands altogether. Shivering, she fumbled to open her phone and check messages. Nothing from Sally, which worried her slightly. Despite her eagerness to meet the woman, this entire enterprise had her on edge. She only hoped that Sally's absence didn't mean something terrible had happened since she last made contact. Likely, though, her feet had turned as cold as Ella's were now.

The snow began in earnest by the time Ella turned onto Percy Street in the Glebe neighbourhood. Four blocks farther on, she paused at the bottom of the driveway to her house. A black Jeep with British Columbia plates sat in her usual spot behind Tony's car. She steered next to the curb, the tires crunching through a drift that had accumulated with the swirling wind. She slammed the gear into park. "Tonight of all nights," she muttered before opening the door and fighting to keep it from blowing out of her grasp in a sudden gust. She stomped across the street and let herself inside the three-storey brick house. After kicking snow off her boots, she stood still and listened. All was quiet in Finn's bottom-floor apartment, but she heard male laughter coming from Tony's floor above. She took the stairs two at a time and pounded on his door with the side of her fist. Tony pulled the door open, holding a martini glass, dressed to entertain in a purple velvet lounging jacket, Aladdin-style gold pants, and leather sandals. A man she'd never seen before stood behind him at the entrance to the living room.

"Do you own a Jeep?" she asked, looking straight past Tony at the stranger. "Because one is in my spot."

Tony half-turned. "Tell me you didn't."

"I should have checked with you, Tony. Sorry about that." The man looked past Tony and gave her an amused grin that had likely charmed many a heart. Ella decided right then that hers would not be one of them.

Tony spun back to face her while saying over his shoulder, "You'll have to park your wheels at the high school and hope the beast doesn't get towed. If you park on the street, it will be hauled away for certain because of the snowfall. I'll make arrangements for a spot at a friend's place tomorrow."

"Cool, I'll get my coat." The man disappeared into the living room.

"Ella, stop in for a drink after you move cars, and I'll introduce you properly." Tony waved his martini glass in the air. "Shaken with a twist. It'll warm the cockles of your cold, cold heart."

Ella scowled. "More like the bunions on my frozen,

frozen feet. Tell your guest that I'll be waiting in my car for him to get out of my parking spot."

She thumped down the stairs and crossed the street to her vehicle. Barely any heat remained inside, and she once again turned on the engine and jacked the level to high. She also punched on the radio before wrapping her arms around herself and shivering. It was the top of the hour and time for the local news. Lede story: a woman's body found at Shirley's Bay in the woods. She immediately thought of Sally but gave her head a shake. Just because she'd been worried about the woman's safety and she'd missed an appointment didn't mean she was dead… No, that was crazy thinking.

Ella glanced across at the house, but the man had not come out yet. "Take your sweet time. Don't worry about me sitting here freezing my ass off." She turned on the windshield wipers to clear the snow before pulling out her phone. Sherry picked up on the first ring.

"You on the story about the body found at Shirley's Bay?"

"Hi to you too, Tate. I'm attending the media briefing tomorrow. Why, you want in?"

"Sorry, I'm having a cranky evening." She took a deep breath and told herself to lower the frustration level. "I'm available if Canard wants me."

"I'll let our fearless editor know."

"Thanks. Any idea yet who she is?"

"Nope. Cops are being close-lipped for now."

Ella spotted the front door of her house open. Tony and his friend stepped outside. "Listen, I gotta go. Be in touch."

"For sure."

She watched Tony climb into the passenger seat while his buddy started the Jeep before cleaning off the windows with a snow scraper. When did Tony buy that floor-length fur coat that looked toasty as hell? Had he finally gotten over his last long-term relationship and met someone new? Her emotions ping-ponged from pleased for him to morose for her. She liked having his undivided friendship but knew he needed more to be fully happy. This fellow appeared to be Tony's type: muscular physique, square-cut jaw, good hair, and interesting eyes. Hell, he was her type too if you overlooked his overbearing cockiness.

Finally, the guy backed his vehicle onto the street and continued on toward the school two blocks over. Ella took the opportunity to slide into the vacated space, scoot inside the house, and hurry upstairs to her apartment, forgoing the offer of a drink. She needed to connect with Sally now more than ever and had no desire to play third wheel tonight.

———

Nicola stepped out of bed and picked up her silk robe from the chair next to the wardrobe. The man watched her with appraising eyes, and she gave him a coy smile before slipping both arms into the flimsy covering and tying it at the waist. She felt his eyes follow her into the ensuite and tossed him a smile over her shoulder before shutting the door. Her expression in the mirror flipped from sultry to anguished. The hatred she felt for the man in the other room was getting harder to conceal.

She used a washcloth to clean between her legs, letting the warm water run while she leaned on the counter and took deep breaths to steady herself. He'd left the syringe, packet of heroin, foil, and lighter on the shelf above the toilet, his payment to her for taking away her freedom. She prayed he'd leave two more packets in the bedroom before going. That would mean he didn't intend to return for at least a full day, and she'd have time.

She turned off the tap and picked up the heroin. It didn't take long for her to empty it onto the foil and get the lighter going underneath. The urge to fill the syringe and inject its contents into her arm sent a momentary surge of adrenaline through her, but she rested the filled needle on the edge of the sink and opened the cupboard door. She crouched down and pulled a tampon box out from behind the row of cleansers, reaching until she extracted the small bottle tucked inside. Straightening and checking that he hadn't gotten off the bed, she unscrewed the bottle and emptied the syringe. It only took a few seconds for her to tighten the cap, put the bottle back in place, and return the tampon box to its hiding spot. She set the empty needle on the shelf next to the piece of rubber she would have tied around her arm if she'd injected herself as in days past.

A longer delay would have him on alert, so she opened the door and clicked off the bathroom light, returning to lie next to him. She lay on her back and pretended to watch a film running inside her head, careful not to let him sense that she was wide awake and cognizant of her surroundings. She slowed her breathing as if she was going to sleep. Not even five minutes later, the mattress shifted as he rolled to a sitting position and set his feet on the floor. His phone blared out Russian rapper Allj, and he answered before standing.

"Yeah, I'm on my way. Just finishing up here." He laughed, and she imagined the man on the other end joining in. A shared moment of lightness between two predators.

He lit a cigarette after signing off and blew the smoke across her face. She kept her eyes closed and lay still with a smile on her lips to make him think she was enjoying her trip. He leaned down and squeezed her breast, but she forced herself not to flinch.

"If I only had more time," he said. "Well, you'll be here when I get back, and we can take up where we left off." He laughed again, and she heard him putting on his clothes. He took his time leaving the bedroom, but at last the condo door opened and shut, and he was gone.

She sat up and listened ten minutes longer to be certain he wasn't returning. He'd left three packs in the bedside table drawer. She grinned. He'd be gone tonight and tomorrow.

Not much longer, she thought as she stood to get dressed, *and this life will be in my rear view.*

She put on the warmest clothes she had, which were anything but: a short skirt and pantyhose, black bra. She dug around in the drawer and came up with two silky shirts that she wriggled into, one overtop the other. Not practical in the least, but the best she could do. She'd shoplifted a ratty second-hand coat that covered her rear end from a thrift shop on her first time out and pulled this from the last hanger in the closet where she'd hidden it. She'd also stolen a frayed red and black toque that she yanked over her cascade of black hair, effectively disguising her unless someone looked closely.

Finally, she tugged on the unlined white leather boots that hopefully would keep her feet from getting wet because they sure wouldn't keep them warm.

Her captor had placed a camera in the kitchen angled toward the hallway and the front door as a deterrent. Getting past the camera had proven to be the most worrisome obstacle, taking her a while to negotiate the first time she got up the nerve. She'd been lucky several times since and hoped today would be no different. She dropped to her hands and knees and propelled herself to the far side of the hallway, only standing and pressing herself into the wall where she knew the camera angle would miss her. Night had fallen, and the light in the hallway, while enough to illuminate her, wasn't as clear as during the day. She stepped behind the coat rack and reached a trembling hand to turn off the alarm system that he set every time he left her. He had no idea she'd figured out the code — she'd overheard him giving it to a client when he thought she was out of it. Then she turned the deadbolt before easing the door open a foot and slipping outside. He hadn't checked the camera feed closely on her other trips out of the condo — because why would he? He believed she was in no condition to leave, and he'd been correct at the beginning, before she found the free clinic and the methadone that helped her to kick the drugs. She hadn't trusted anyone enough to help her get away from him, though. The pimp network had eyes and ears everywhere downtown. Since she had no idea whom she could trust, she trusted no one. However, the window for her to bide her time and finalize a plan was closing. It was now or never.

The hall was clear, and she hastened to the exit, steering clear of the elevator, where she knew another camera was mounted near the ceiling. She climbed down twelve flights, relieved when nobody else entered the stairwell. The door opened next to the back exit, and she stepped outside into the frigid winter night. She welcomed the blast of bracing air that enveloped and accompanied her away from the confines of her prison as euphoria filled her like bubbly champagne. She'd arrived in this city three months earlier on another stormy late-fall day. It was fitting that her escape from this hell should end on the same wild note.

CHAPTER 3

The Grady family awoke to an uneasy dawn, not unlike every morning beginning five weeks earlier, when Peter Grady had moved girlfriend Marnie Vaughan into his house. Today was Friday, the eve of Peter and Marnie's wedding, and everyone except the two of them was dreading the impending ceremony. Cassie Grady had flown into Ottawa from Vancouver Wednesday evening, when she'd met Marnie — her soon-to-be stepmother — for the first time. Cassie had smiled and congratulated her, all the while mortified by the relationship: her dad marrying a woman young enough to be her sister. The entire length of the courtship clocked in at less than four months with a rushed, obscene feel that hung over their union like a bad smell.

Cassie sighed and rolled out of bed, not eager to get the morning underway.

Please let the next few days unfold without drama.

She put the thought out into the universe, not expecting to be rewarded. Her three brothers and two sisters-in-law were not known for their tact. But one of them was going to have to take their dad aside and ask if he'd thought this marriage through. It couldn't be her; she'd been living on the other side of the country for too long. No, one of her brothers — Foster, Gordon, or Mick — was going to have to take on the task.

Foster had promised to arrive after breakfast to hang out with their dad, and he was the most logical one to broach the subject, being the eldest son and CEO of their father's architectural firm. Yet Cassie worried the marriage preparations had moved too far along to turn back now. Foster's wife Deirdre had conveniently flown to Toronto on business around suppertime the evening before and would miss the Saturday nuptials. She'd skipped out on the girls' luncheon at the Viv bistro yesterday as well, leaving Cassie and Gordon's wife Khloe to spend an awkward couple of hours with Marnie, toasting her upcoming marriage to Cassie's dad over mimosas and eggs benedict. They'd pretended to welcome her into the family, but Cassie suspected Marnie hadn't been fooled. Deirdre's absence had spoken volumes. Marnie had offered to drive Cassie to lunch in the silver BMW her dad had bought her as a wedding gift, but Cassie had declined. She'd borrowed her father's Aviator instead to avoid being alone with Marnie any longer than necessary.

Mick, her youngest brother who was all of twenty-one, had spent Thursday night at Gordon and Khloe's after driving up from university residence in Kingston that afternoon. None of her brothers had made plans to spend the previous evening with their dad and Marnie, and while it pissed Cassie off, she didn't blame them. In the end, she'd gone out with two girlfriends she hadn't seen in three years, deciding to take a break from the family drama. And now it was Friday. Two days down and two to go before she could fly home to her empty apartment.

Cassie showered and dressed in a red wool dress, black tights, and suede ankle boots, ready for today's festivities: a trip to the spa with Marnie and Khloe, followed by a catered dinner back here at her dad's Rockcliffe house. Saturday's wedding would be held at noon in the back sunroom because Marnie wanted to keep things simple. She wasn't even inviting any friends or family, something Cassie found odd until Marnie explained that her parents and brother lived overseas and would come when the weather turned nicer. She didn't want their visit during the dark, winter months when there was so little time for sightseeing. Marnie had only arrived in Canada a few months before she met Cassie's dad and didn't have any close friends in the city, only acquaintances and ex-work mates, nobody she wanted at her special day. Cassie had no idea where Marnie had worked before quitting to marry her father and reminded herself to ask later.

She heard voices in the kitchen as she passed through the dining room and imagined Wilma had arrived early to cook breakfast before making a final pass at cleaning the house. She'd wanted some time alone with Wilma to get her opinion on Marnie and her father's relationship but hadn't found a spare moment. Was Wilma as distraught about the impending marriage as the rest of them? She'd worked for her parents the last fifteen years, from the time Cassie turned fourteen, and had become like one of the family. She'd gotten them through her mother's sudden death from an aggressive cancer four years after she took up the position, her silent strength keeping them centred. Wilma used to live in an apartment closer to downtown but had moved into a spare bedroom in the house soon after Cassie's mother's passing to keep the household running and to be home for Mick, who was only six years old and in grade one at the time. Cassie had started at Queen's that September and made the trip home most weekends to find comfort with her dad and brothers as she worked through her grief. Those days seemed like a dream to her now.

Wilma had found her own apartment the week after Marnie moved in. It was odd to have Wilma leave the house in the evenings after she'd cleaned up the dinner dishes. Cassie wondered if her father minded this change to his routine.

Mick's face lit up when he spotted Cassie in the doorway. He crossed the floor to give her a hug. "You're looking terrific," he said before holding her at arm's length. "Glad you made it for this awkward occasion. Sorry we didn't get over last night, but Khloe said you had a good time at lunch." He rolled his eyes.

Cassie grinned. "It wasn't that bad."

Gordon stepped forward and enveloped her in another embrace. "Been too long, sis. How's life in Vancouver?"

"Lovely. Warmer than here." She hugged him back before Foster took a turn wrapping his arms around her. His embrace was light, with barely any pressure. Of her three brothers, she and Foster had always had the most distant relationship. He dropped his arms, and Cassie looked around the room. "Where's Wilma?"

"We were going to ask you that," Gordon said. "We

also wonder where Dad and Marnie have gotten to. Shouldn't they be seeing to last-minute details for the regrettable event?"

"Is that what we're calling it? I imagine Wilma is handling the odds and ends. Perhaps she's driven into town to pick up the flowers. Marnie and Dad are likely still upstairs."

"Seriously, what's Dad thinking? He could have shacked up without making anything legal. We wouldn't have cared." Mick's expression was troubled. "Why the rush?"

"Marnie's got him wrapped around her ring finger," Foster said. "Gordon and I worry she's a gold digger, although Dad won't hear a word against her."

Cassie tried to put herself in her father's shoes. "She's young and vibrant, gorgeous, really, and seems attracted to Dad. In all fairness, I think we'd have a hard time accepting any woman replacing Mom."

Gordon snorted. "You always see the best in people. I like to think we all do, but there's a cunning about her."

"I can't put my trepidation into words, but it grows every time I see them together. Plus, the age difference. Gawd, it's unseemly," Foster added.

"Does anybody even use that word anymore? Unseemly. It's sounds so theatrical, darling." Cassie delivered the last sentence like an upper-class Brit.

"You would know." Foster punched her lightly on the shoulder.

They all turned their faces toward the entrance to the kitchen as footsteps clattered down the hallway. A moment later, their father entered and searched with anguished eyes around the room. "She's not here then?"

"We think Wilma's gone to the flower shop," Cassie said, taking a step toward him.

"Not Wilma. *Marnie.* She didn't make it home last night and isn't answering her phone. I'm worried sick and have called the police."

"That seems premature, Dad," Foster said. "She probably met a girlfriend and lost track of time. She'll be coming through the door at any moment."

"That's not something she would do. She had a hair appointment this morning and didn't show up to that either. I checked."

Cassie could have pointed out that none of them knew Marnie well enough to know what was abnormal behaviour, even her father, but she thought it best to stay silent. The front doorbell rang at that moment, seemingly on cue. As wedding lead-ups went, this was turning into high drama, almost like Cassie had tempted the gods. It might have been amusing to watch the scene unfold except for the very real pain Marnie was causing her dad. Cassie would have a difficult time forgiving her for being so careless with his feelings. And where the hell was Wilma when they all needed her so desperately to keep this day from sliding completely off the rails?

———

LIAM AND QUADE glanced at each other before following Peter Grady into the foyer of his Rockcliffe mansion. It was unlikely this elderly man's missing fiancée was the young woman whose body had been found several hours earlier, so they'd be dealing with a missing person case on top of the murder. Liam placed Peter in his early to mid-sixties — fit for his age, but the white hair and creases around his eyes told the tale. He and Quade would get the details about the missing woman before turning the case over to another team. It could be that his bride-to-be had dementia and had simply wandered off. Hopefully she'd found a place indoors to spend the night. They'd need to mobilize to find her quickly.

Peter led them into a living room the size of Liam's entire townhouse. The furniture included two couches and coffee tables positioned on a thick beige carpet under the casement windows lit by pale winter sunlight. Several plush armchairs arranged invitingly around a large stone fireplace sat strategically placed beneath oil paintings that added pops of colour to the background of muted sand and ivory walls. Large flower arrangements of yellow and pink roses and baby's breath brightened the coffee tables. Peter indicated two chairs for them to sit in while he took the one facing them. A slender woman entered and took the seat next to him.

"My daughter Cassie," he said by way of introduction. "Home from Vancouver for the wedding."

"My brothers are making coffee. They'll be in momentarily."

Her deep, honeyed voice could be on stage in Stratford. Liam imagined the camera would love her angular face, black hair, and wide brown eyes. He might have seen her in a series drama on Canadian television but couldn't remember which show. He felt Quade's interest perk up next to him, her gaze focused on Cassie.

Three young men entered together, one carrying a tray with cups, cream, and sugar and another holding a carafe. They poured and handed out cups and invited Liam and Quade to doctor their own. Liam took the opportunity to study each of the brothers in turn. The youngest, named Mick, dressed in a burgundy Queen's University sweatshirt and jeans, appeared in his early twenties. He had the same dark colouring as Cassie and equally arresting features. The older boys, Foster and Gordon, took after their father, tall and ruddy-faced, with fair hair and blue eyes. Gordon was the heavier set of the two, with a footballer's stance while Foster's lean face and hooked nose stuck Liam as aristocratic. Mick pulled over a chair to sit next to Cassie while Gordon and Foster leaned against the wall on either side of the fireplace like near-identical bookends.

"When's the last time you saw Marnie, Mr. Grady?" Liam asked.

"Yesterday around 11:00 a.m. She drove her car to a luncheon with Cassie, where they met up with Gordon's wife, Khloe. Marnie planned to run some errands after the meal. We agreed to meet late afternoon. I left phone messages when she didn't show up, but she never replied."

"Do you know the licence plate, make, and model of her car, by any chance?"

"Certainly. It's a black BMW X3 SUV, licence plate DWL 950. This year's model."

"How would you describe her mood?"

"Upbeat. Happy. She was looking forward to our wedding tomorrow."

"Does anyone have more to add?" Liam's eyes swept the others.

Cassie looked at Mick and then the detective. "I met her for the first time Wednesday evening, and she appeared eager for the marriage and honeymoon. She and Dad are planning two months on the west coast and leave Sunday morning. Nothing unusual happened at lunch on Thursday before we separated. She was excited and happy, as Dad described."

The other three shook their heads. "I haven't met her yet," Mick said. "I spent Thursday night at Gordon and Khloe's, arriving around suppertime. The family festivities were starting today."

"You've never met her?" Quade asked with a surprised note in her voice.

"That's right. I've been away at school. Their courtship was … sudden."

Foster nodded. "As for me, I was working until I drove Deirdre to the airport at around four o'clock. She flew to Toronto on business. She's a recruiter for the University of Ottawa. Neither my wife nor I saw Dad or Marnie yesterday."

"Do you have any photos of Marnie that we could circulate?" Quade asked.

"Of course. I'll get my laptop." Peter stood and hurried from the room. Liam heard his footsteps on the stairs.

"You're away at school then, Mick?" Liam asked.

"Queen's. I'm living in res."

"Not that far to make a trip home to meet your dad's girlfriend."

All four of the grown Grady children exchanged looks, so quick and furtive that Liam would have missed their interaction if he hadn't been watching closely. Foster, whom Liam realized was the eldest, spoke for all of them. "They've only gone out a few months, and she moved in with Dad after Christmas. The engagement was … unexpected."

"Did you like her?" Liam sensed a direct approach would be the best way to get answers.

"As my sister, Cassie, pointed out this morning, my mother is a hard act to follow. She died when Mick was six, so a few years have passed, and you'd think we'd be ready. My dad's happiness matters more than how I feel about the woman." Foster looked at the others, but their faces were closed off, unreadable.

Peter Grady entered holding his laptop. Liam wasn't certain how much he'd overheard of his son's response. He opened the screen and turned it in Liam and Quade's direction at waist level. "I snapped this picture a few days ago."

Liam's eyes took a few seconds to focus. He and Quade went still as the smiling face of the woman found dead in the woods the evening before stared up at them. She'd raised her left hand to brush a strand of hair from her face, revealing a dove tattoo on her wrist. Her clear blue eyes stared directly into the camera. Seeing the murder victim alive and vibrant struck home the pathos of her loss. Liam looked closer at the photo. The woman seemed vaguely familiar, but he couldn't place where he'd seen her before. There was no doubt, however, that this Marnie Vaughan was their deceased Jane Doe.

How are we going to break this news? Liam thought. *How do we tell this man his fiancée is dead, and the eve of their wedding day marks the start of an investigation into her murder?*

Quade knew him well enough to take the lead. She cleared her throat and raised her eyes to Peter Grady. "We have some terrible news," she said. "I'm gutted to say the worst possible news."

CHAPTER 4

Ella woke late and jumped into the shower. She'd only finished soaping her hair when the lukewarm water turned blistering cold. She shrieked and stepped out of the direct stream. "Damn it, Tony," she yelled at the wall. He and his new friend had drained the tank, annoying her right where they'd left off the evening before. She rinsed at warp speed and wrapped herself in a towel, muttering curses to herself the entire time. The hair dryer on high warmed her, and she calmed down once her teeth stopped chattering. She picked an oversized sweater and jeans from her dresser and added the thickest wool socks she owned to prepare for another chilly day working in her apartment. With the kettle plugged in, she checked her phone for messages while waiting for the water to boil.

Nothing from Sally.

Someone knocked on her apartment door, and she hurried down the short hallway. Tony's friend stood smiling on the landing when she pulled the door open. He handed her a mug of coffee and toasted her with his own cup. "Tony will be up shortly with muffins hot out of the oven."

"Blueberry?"

"Raisin bran. A peace offering for my thoughtless parking in your spot."

"Come in then. There's no point pretending I can resist his baking."

He followed her into the cramped living room and stood in the doorway, surveying the space. "You don't need much, do you?"

She shrugged. "Does anybody?" She motioned toward the one decent chair. "Take it before Tony gets here. He's not fond of sitting on my old couch." She smiled and dropped onto her desk chair, spinning around to face him. "So how did you and Tony meet? Online is my guess. He's so busy with work these days, I can't imagine him finding time otherwise."

"You think…? No, that's not…" He laughed. "Tony's my brother."

"Tony has a brother? He's never mentioned you." Tony had never spoken about any of his family, come to think of it. She studied him more closely and saw no similarity to her downstairs neighbour except that they were both unnaturally attractive. He flinched under her stare.

"Yeah, I can see you don't believe me. My name's Decker Kincaid, and we're not blood brothers. For one thing, I don't have his Italian genes. Tony grew up with my family after his father went to prison and his mother took off."

"Say what?"

"He hasn't confided, I see."

"No, but——"

She stopped talking as Luvy barked and scooted across the floor and under her desk with Tony close behind, holding a tray of muffins.

"What have I missed?" He offered around the food and snapped his fingers for Decker to move over to the couch so he could have the leather chair. Decker stood and grinned at Ella as Tony took his place. "Good lord, girl, did you hear the weather forecast? We're in for another wallop of snow. Why do we continue to live in this godforsaken city? Ella, can you point that space heater in my direction?"

"So, you two grew up together?" Ella asked. She decided the questions about Tony's parents needed a less direct approach. She bent down to adjust the heater, and Luvy licked her hand.

"We did. Decker is the family success story. Self-made man."

Decker shook his head. "Not exactly. Tony tells me you're a true crime podcaster and sometime reporter for the city paper."

"I am, but we were speaking about you. What is it you do exactly?"

Tony waved a hand in the air. "Decker hates talking about himself, so let me."

"Enough," Decker said, cutting him off. "Have you got a story on the go, Ella?"

"Not exactly, but a woman's body was found last night on a trail at Shirley's Bay. Have you heard anything, Tony?"

"No. How awful. Are you assigned to report on the case?"

"Sherry Carpenter has the lead, but I'll give updates on my podcast."

"So, you're essentially covering … a murder?"

"Looks like it."

"Well, I have the week off work and will happily be your backup."

"Count me in too," Decker said.

"Do you have experience in sleuthing, Decker? Police work? Investigations?" Ella asked, still fishing for information.

Decker grinned. "Not especially, but I like a challenge. Speaking of which, we're on the hunt for Beluga caviar and duck *foie gras* mousse to go with the wine I brought as a house gift. All set to head out, Tony?" He stood and Tony got to his feet, scooping up Luvy on his way past Ella's desk.

"See ya later, girl. I mean it about helping with the case. I can keep Decker in line. Sidekick to the sidekick." Tony stopped at the doorway entrance. His expression turned serious. "Did you see Adele three days ago?"

"She's back?"

"I'm not certain but thought she was outside the house. She didn't come inside, as far as I could tell."

"That's strange. Does Finn know?"

"I haven't had a chance to ask him."

Ella sat staring out the window above her desk after Tony and Decker disappeared down her short hallway. Finn's wife Adele had been gone several months. She'd missed their baby Lena's first birthday two months earlier, not even making contact. Her return would send ripples through their lives like a stone tossed into a pool. The recent calm would dissipate. Ella hoped Adele's re-entry into Finn's life would be permanent, if she'd decided to come home. He didn't deserve any more heartbreak.

Tony reappeared a moment later and leaned against the doorjamb. "Say Ella, that woman's body … you don't think—"

"That it's Adele? No, that would be too cruel."

"But not impossible. We don't know where she's been or with whom since she left last summer."

"Finn kept in touch with her mom in Belleville. He sensed she was hedging around, not sharing everything she knew about Adele's state of mind or location." Ella hesitated. "Adele had an affair when they were together, before she was pregnant with Lena."

Tony and Ella stared at each other, neither voicing their deepest fear. Adele was in town and hadn't been seen for a few days. She'd left a trail of unhappy people in her wake. Ella decided nothing would be gained by idle speculation. "I'll get on the story and track down the facts. Let's not think the worst until we have more information."

"Tell me as soon as you've found out the name of the victim. I can't see myself relaxing until I know Adele is safe and sound."

"Nor I, but we shouldn't worry Finn about this until we're certain."

Tony made a heart with his hands before following Decker downstairs to his apartment.

———

HUNTER DIDN'T ANSWER her text, but Ella followed up her first message with an invitation to meet at Daisy's diner whenever he had time. He'd been at a dinner party in Tony's apartment once, the only occasion with Adele present that she knew of, but would he remember her? It was several months back, soon after Lena's birth. Adele had been in a manic kind of mood. She'd had her hair cut short and lost the pregnancy weight since then. If Hunter realized the dead woman was Adele, he wouldn't be allowed to reveal her identity yet, not before the official release to media. He'd be busy with the murder but might be able to nip out for a coffee at his break. He'd need to eat at some point, and the police station on Elgin didn't have a cafeteria. Ella put in a call to Sherry to catch up on what she knew, which turned out to be not much.

"No idea the vic's name yet. That new staff sergeant, Kurt Auger, announced a media briefing around two. You planning a podcast on this case, Tate?"

"Yeah. I'm interested in the name of the dead woman. Can you text it to me as soon as you know?"

"Of course. Canard spoke about getting you to write a profile on her once we get the name. You in?"

"I can make time."

After ending the call, Ella considered next steps. She'd already sent two messages to Sally, asking to reschedule their meeting, but so far, nothing back. The morning had become a string of loose ends, and hunger gnawed at her belly, despite the muffin. The fridge was sadly lacking in food, so the decision was easy. She'd drive to Daisy's for breakfast and stop at the grocery store on the way home. Hopefully by then somebody would have gotten back to her — Hunter, Sherry, or Sally — and her afternoon would find a focus and stop her from feeling like a sheet pegged onto a clothesline, flapping in the breeze.

CHAPTER 5

The night had been so cold that Nicola found shelter inside an apartment's downtown parking garage when the coffee shop where she'd hung out for a couple of hours closed at eleven. She'd been able to buy a hot drink because over the past few months, she'd collected change from the man's pockets when he'd been in the shower and had accumulated enough for a few cups of coffee. She'd been careful to tuck away some coins for the next day.

After leaving the coffee shop, she'd walked to this apartment building and waited huddled against the back wall until a tenant raised the garage door with a fob and drove inside. She'd made it through the door with inches to spare as it rolled back into place. Even though the garage was heated, the large underground lot was still cool. She'd wrapped her arms around herself and crouched in a corner behind an SUV, hopefully out of sight, leaning against the block concrete wall, trying to stay warm.

Her high-heeled boots and nylons under the short

skirt were not meant for such a night, and she cursed the men who'd literally stripped her of everything. They'd taken her from Thunder Bay to Windsor for a few months, then to Toronto where she'd been kept in a motel for a longer period of time, and finally to this city to be locked in the condo. The man had wanted her for himself, although that didn't mean he wouldn't share her if the price was right. If the pattern held, she'd be taken to Montreal before the calendar flipped to February. But she'd be long gone before that happened. Never to return.

She chided herself for not waiting until morning to get out of the apartment when the temperature would be higher. Then she remembered that night was better for making an escape because darkness was her friend. Once she left the parking garage at daybreak — impossible to determine in this dark dungeon — she'd need to stay away from places they'd expect her to go, like restaurants and bars in the ByWard Market. They wouldn't be searching for her yet, though. She had a day at least to get somewhere safe.

This morning, Veronica would meet her, like they talked about, and take her to a location where the men would never think to look. They'd still been in Toronto the last time they met at a party, knowing they were being shipped to Ottawa next. Veronica had assured her that she'd find a way to get out once they moved to the city she knew well. She'd whispered a place to make contact if Nicola got free too and promised to help her. Nicola hadn't any way of knowing if Veronica had received the message she'd left at the restaurant, but there was no choice except to carry on and hope she had.

As if on cue, the garage door lifted and a car crept through the lot, its engine as silent as a panther stalking its prey. She recognized an electric Tesla that she knew cost a small fortune. At first she thought they'd found her, but the car drove into an empty parking spot and the driver strode toward the elevator without looking around.

It was time to leave, before others began retrieving their cars to go to work or wherever they went on a Friday morning. Nicola walked as if she belonged to the exit and gave thanks when no alarm went off as she stepped outside. The sun was barely above the high rises, the sky streaked pink and orange, foretelling bad weather, if the old sailor's adage was anything to go by. Her breath hung a frosty plume in the frigid air that prickled her skin with icy shards. She pulled her toque lower down her forehead and looked both ways before turning right and walking to the corner, where she headed north toward Rideau Street. She'd figured out the evening before that this was a major road across the city because of the steady stream of buses going in both directions. She'd find a different coffee shop from yesterday's and get a cup to go. The busboy in that one had been eager to fill her in when she told him she was from out of town and needed help finding places. It had been near to closing, and the place was almost empty. After he'd written bus numbers and street names on a piece of paper, along with the sketch of a rough map, she'd gone to a bus shelter and studied the routes on a proper map posted on the glass until she was confident that she'd be able to get where she needed to go.

Veronica had said during their last hurried conversation in the Toronto restroom that she would make their captors pay if it was the last thing she ever did. At the time, a frightened shiver had travelled like an electric current up Nicola's back, but with her new life so close, she now thought that retribution would be a cold dish, more delicious than anything she'd ever tasted in her eighteen years on this earth.

———

WILMA ARRIVED at the house carrying full shopping bags as the detectives were leaving with Peter and Foster, who had agreed to accompany them to the General Hospital morgue to identify Marnie. Wilma stood in the foyer, clasping her purse and staring at the closed front door after they'd told her where they were going and departed. "So, this means the wedding is off?" she said to Cassie, waiting behind her. "I bought all this food for nothing?"

"Why don't we put the groceries away and have a cup of something hot?" Cassie asked, taking her gently by the arm. She was at a loss how to process what had just happened and could see that Wilma was struggling too, despite her insensitive statement.

They entered the kitchen, and Gordon rushed over to take the grocery bags from Wilma. Mick was standing at the counter making coffee and turned his head to look at her. "You've heard the news then. It's unbelievable."

"That girl had it made," Wilma said. She'd followed Gordon and took a jar of peanuts out of one of the bags after he set them down. She hesitated and opened a cupboard. "Why would she do something to get herself killed?"

Gordon and Cassie exchanged glances. "Maybe she

had no choice," Cassie said. "Come sit, Wilma, and Mick will serve some coffee. We've all had a terrible shock."

"I do feel a bit off." She walked to the table and dropped into the seat Cassie had pulled out for her. "I can't believe the police took your father to look at her body. They should have spared Peter that." Wilma shook her head and tsked before pursing her lips.

Mick set mugs of coffee in front of them and took his cup to a chair at the end of the table. Gordon remained leaning against the counter. His face glowed a sickly ashen shade in the overhead lighting. "The cops will be back shortly to question us. We should be prepared," he said.

"We have nothing to hide. Hell, we barely knew the woman." Cassie tried to lighten the moment, but her comment fell flat, and she regretted having spoken.

Wilma rested her elbows on the table. "Everyone has to be careful about what they say. Nothing you tell them will be forgotten, and they can twist our words, make us doubt each other. We all worried about your father's … infatuation with a woman out to get his money." She held up a hand to stop Cassie from what she was about to say. "I know you always want to believe the best of people, but she was an opportunist at the very least. Now we need to look at the situation from the police point of view. We're all suspects unless they come up with proof that we're not."

"I never met her, so I should be in the clear," Mick said, leaning back in his chair.

"Take nothing for granted." Gordon scrunched his face into a picture of sternness and deepened his voice. "So, what time did you leave Kingston, young man, and where were you between then and arriving at your brother's? How did you feel about your father marrying a woman close to your age? Did you resent her?"

"All right. All right. I get it." Mick sat forward, the tension in his body returning. "What about you, Gordon? Cassie? We're all in the same boat. None of us was keen on this marriage."

"All of us who cared about your father are passengers in that boat," Wilma said. "We need to negotiate the police together."

The four of them froze at the sound of the doorbell chiming through the house. Wilma recovered first and got to her feet. She spoke fast and forcefully. "Remember to keep your heads. Stay on message. We all wanted your father to be happy, and Marnie was doing just that. We were only concerned that the marriage was too quick — the police won't believe us if we paint too rosy a picture — but we were all prepared to give her a chance. Keep your answers short and believable."

"It's almost as if Wilma's done this before," Mick said after her footsteps tapped down the hallway to the front door.

"She's got a point, though," Gordon said. "We need to support each other."

Cassie nodded but was less certain about the direction Wilma was advising them to take. They had nothing to hide and shouldn't have a need to be so guarded. She kept this thought to herself when Wilma returned with two officers in tow.

"I'm Detective Bottes, and this is my partner, Detective Jorgenson with the Ottawa Police Service, Major Crimes Unit. Let me first say that we're sorry for your loss and apologize for this intrusion. We need to take your statements, however." His gaze swept over them and landed on Gordon. "Is there a den or somewhere private we can talk without interruption?"

"Of course, but is that necessary? None of us has anything to say that the others can't hear." Gordon held up the palms of both hands as if he was being completely open and transparent.

"I understand, but we have to do this by the book, seeing as how this is a murder investigation. Now, who would like to go first?" His gaze shifted to each of them in turn.

Cassie raised her hand. "I was the last one to see Marnie on Thursday afternoon, so perhaps you'd like to begin with me."

"Good enough."

She tried not to shiver under the scrutiny of his piercing stare. They left the kitchen, where the taller detective with the horsey face and thinning brown hair had made himself comfortable at the table. The plumper, bald one named Detective Bottes followed her into her father's den in the east wing of the house.

CHAPTER 6

Daisy limped across the floor to Ella's booth and set a hand on the back of the seat to steady herself. "All alone today, duckie?" she asked before pouring coffee into her mug.

"Looks that way. What happened to your leg, Daisy?"

"I fell on the ice yesterday. This weather will be the death of me. Another storm rages in tonight, if you believe the meteorologist's report."

"We're having a snowy, cold January without a doubt. You should rest up. Take a day off."

"Not folding my tent over a little pain, but thanks for the suggestion, I'm sure."

Ella ordered her usual breakfast of scrambled eggs and sausage before settling in with the newspaper. The body found on a trail at Shirley's Bay had made the front page. She skimmed the article before giving it a closer read. The woman's identity was unknown at the time Sherry Carpenter penned the story. *Could this mean the victim isn't Adele? Hunter certainly would have recognized her.*

Or maybe not. He'd only met her once, and that was months ago.

Ella ate slowly, checking the door and hoping to see Hunter stride into the foyer and look around for her with his intense, blue eyes that she liked to believe lit up when he saw her. Likely a stretch. By the time she'd drunk her third cup of java, she'd accepted that he wasn't coming. To be certain, she checked her messages again, but he hadn't responded, adding to her illogical anxiety about Adele. No word from Sally either.

"So, what's on tap for you today?" Daisy asked when Ella walked up to the cash to pay.

"I'm going to work out at my friend Finn's gym. I could use some exercise." It would give her a chance to find out what Finn knew. If the police had been to see him with devastating news about Adele, he'd need support. Ella prayed she was leaping to conclusions, overreacting without evidence. It wouldn't be the first time she'd gotten ahead of the facts, but Tony's worry about Adele and her erratic behaviour had ignited her own concern, even if the odds that the dead woman was Adele fell on the unlikely end of the spectrum.

———

FINN WAS ON THE FLOOR, spotting a woman who was lying on her back lifting weights when Ella arrived. He nodded at her but kept focused on his client while she crossed the floor and went into the locker room. She changed into her gym clothes, relieved to see that Finn was carrying on as if this was a normal day, something he wouldn't do if the police had been by to tell him Adele was dead.

She warmed up on the mats before a half hour on the treadmill and another on the stationary bike. Finn had been in his office when she started her exercises and hadn't emerged by the time she finished. She took a quick shower and stopped in to see him on her way out the front door. He looked up from his desk, where he sat with baby Lena on his lap. Lena squirmed and held out her arms to Ella. "Lala," she said. "Lala." She hadn't quite nailed "Ella," but at least she'd stopped calling her 'Mama'.

"Hey, Finn. I thought Piper was looking after Lena today."

"She's taking a couple of classes at university, so I'm setting up here for those mornings."

"You could have asked me to mind her. I'd make time."

"I know, but I hate to keep inconveniencing you and Tony; plus, I like having more dates with my best girl." He hugged Lena before handing her over to Ella.

"Have you considered daycare, Finn?"

"Considered and discarded. Adele and I agreed Lena should be in her own home the first three years, and I'm doing my utmost to honour that."

Ella set Lena on the floor, and the kid tottered over to a playpen filled with her toys. "In," she said, and Finn hoisted her high up in the air before placing her amongst the stuffed bears.

"She'll be happy in there playing by herself and will eventually fall asleep. She's amazingly self-reliant."

Ella was beginning to understand why Tony kept comparing her to the baby, not certain he was paying her a compliment. She hesitated, but her need to prepare Finn guided her next words. "Speaking of

Adele, Tony thought he saw her outside the house three or four days ago. Did she make contact?"

An annoyed then hopeful expression crossed Finn's face. "You're kidding. No. Last I spoke with her mother, Adele has been living somewhere in Ottawa but refused to say where or with whom. She's also refused to talk about me or Lena. Her mom's at a loss as to how to explain what's driving Adele to act this way, but she keeps telling me to hang in. If Adele came by Percy Street, maybe it means she's missing us." Finn ran a hand through his hair. "She's been gone nearly six months, and it's getting tougher to be patient, although I still worry about her."

"We all do. I'm sure she's missing you and Lena. How could she not?" Ella paused. What Finn had just revealed fuelled her anxiety. Adele was living in Ottawa? She needed to check in with her sources. "I'll be on my way then. See you at home later, Finn."

She hugged him and Lena before hurrying outside to drive to the media scrum about the dead woman to be held at police headquarters. Hopefully, Liam Hunter would be one of the cops on hand. She'd been avoiding contact since he began dating Georgina but couldn't ignore the gap his absence left in her life. Tony had said Georgina and Hunter were serious — he'd started cutting his sister Hannah's hair, and she was the source of all Tony's scuttlebutt. If another person could help ease Hunter's demons, she'd be the last one to deny him the opportunity. She'd decided to shut down her feelings and stay out of his orbit unless a murder case brought them together. So what if she let herself get a little excited at the thought of seeing him again? There was no harm in looking forward to catching up with a trusted friend.

———

THE MEDIA BRIEFING was a stand-up scrum that took place in the lobby of the Elgin Street police station. CBC French and English stations and CTV had arranged cameras to get footage for the TV news cycle. Ella recognized most of the reporters angling for the best spot, although everyone went about their set-up good-naturedly, having done this many times before. Sherry Carpenter broke away from a group to join Ella at the back of the throng.

"Not a whole-enchilada event," Sherry said. "I hear the new staff sergeant will be speaking alone. No family members or crime scene detectives."

"Kurt Auger."

"Yeah, have you met him?"

"Once. Let's say we aren't on friendly terms." She didn't want to go into it. The fact he'd so far gotten away with intimidating and sexually harassing three young female cops made her past crazy. Rosie Thorburn had been moved out of Major Crimes, convinced he was behind her transfer with nothing to refute the idea. Ella hadn't figured out a way to bring him down, but he was on her watch list. She might have made a tactical error by confronting him a few months back without evidence; luckily, she didn't have anything of value that he could take from her.

"Here he comes," Sherry said. "The guy exudes power, doesn't he? So much rizz."

"He exudes something," Ella muttered.

Sherry gave Ella a curious look before turning her stare on Auger at the microphone. Ella also zeroed in on his face and got a certain satisfaction when his eyes skimmed over her and returned to gaze coldly into her face before he began speaking. She stared back without blinking. *Yeah, that's right. I'm watching and waiting.*

"Good day, everyone. I am Staff Sergeant Kurt Auger. Thank you for coming. As most of you are aware, a woman's body was found on a trail at Shirley's Bay last evening. Cause of death is strangulation. We are in the process of notifying her family, and I'm not at liberty to give you her name at this time. I can say that she's in her late twenties, early thirties." He looked directly into the cameras. "We do not have a suspect yet, but I promise you that we will leave no stone unturned to track down her killer. If I could say one thing to whoever did this horrific crime, it would be we're coming for you. Turn yourself in now."

"Good sound bite," Sherry said.

"I'm surprised he didn't say 'make my day.'"

"Is that scorn I'm hearing in your voice?"

"Was it that obvious?"

Auger raised a hand to stop the buzz in the room. "I can take a couple of questions, although there isn't much more to tell you at this early stage in the investigation." He pointed at a reporter in the back row. "Yes?"

"Do you know when she was murdered, and was it in the location where she was found, or had she been moved?"

"These are good questions. Preliminary findings are that she was killed sometime within twenty-four hours before her body was discovered Thursday evening. I can't say yet if she was murdered in a different location.

Another question? Yes?" He pointed directly at one of several raised hands.

"Do you think there could be a serial killer on the loose in our community?"

"We have no evidence of a serial killer. In fact, it would be premature and reckless to speculate." He surveyed the crowd of reporters with a stern expression meant to end any further conjecture on that score. "I'll be sure to keep you informed when we have more. That's all for now." He nodded at the cameras and strode away from them into the building.

"Jeezus. For all the information he gave us, he could have sent it out in an email." Ella regretted wasting her time coming down here. Hunter's absence made her irritable. Then it hit her. Finn wouldn't have known if the victim was Adele when she visited the gym if the police were in the process of notifying her family. Hunter might be avoiding her because of her connection to Finn. She pulled out her phone and took a step back. "I have to get home. Let's keep in touch, Sherry."

"You got it. I'll let you know when I find out her name."

"Likewise." *And please don't let that name be Adele.*

CHAPTER 7

Sara McGowan finished ringing in a sale and glanced again at the young woman sitting alone at a table for two. She'd ordered a coffee with double cream and sugar and had somehow dragged out drinking it over the past three hours. Her clothes were not suitable for this kind of weather. To be honest, the way she was dressed in a low-cut top, short skirt, and high white boots not made for snow looked skanky, but Sara was reluctant to tell her to leave. She'd seemed so hopeful when she first sat down and had craned her neck to look at the door every time someone entered. When a mom with two little kids sat at the table next to her, she'd dragged over a high chair and helped the frazzled mother get the infant into it. Sara, a self-proclaimed student of human behaviour, found herself intrigued.

Lunch hour arrived with its usual surge of high school students and construction workers. Sara got busy at the cash and lost track of the young woman. An hour later, as the lunch crowd thinned, a couple of sketchy-looking men dripping in gold chains and decked out in black leather entered and scanned the coffee shop as if they were searching for someone. Sara's eyes automatically swept the room as they approached. The young woman in the mini skirt was nowhere to be seen.

"What would you like?" she asked.

"Two double doubles and a couple of Boston creams," the heftier of the two men said. He leaned on the counter. His eyes reminded Sara of a boxer dog: black and wide apart, with an unblinking focus that felt as if he could read her mind. Her gaze landed on the green cross tattooed on his left cheek for a moment. He might regret that someday. She got busy pouring the coffees and getting the doughnuts out of the case. She pulled up a cardboard carton and set everything inside before ringing up the sale.

Hefty guy paid with cash and picked up the cardboard container. "Say, you seen a girl about your age, straight black hair past her shoulders and brown eyes, skinny, about yay high? Likely was high, if you get my drift." He held a hand up to his chin. The boxer dog had become a Rottweiler.

Sara put on her thinking face before shaking her head. "Nobody like that's been in since I opened this morning. Why?"

"She's my sister. We were supposed to meet up, but I guess we missed each other."

Sara almost told him about the girl who'd spent the morning waiting for someone. She fit his description exactly. But something about the two men felt off. Why hadn't this guy simply texted his sister to make a different arrangement? She'd been here a long time. Come to think of it, Sara hadn't seen her use a phone, which was odd. Nobody her age went ten minutes without checking a screen. Sara shrugged. "Sorry."

She watched them leave and wished she could close up and follow them. She'd give her eye teeth to see what they were up to.

The last of the high school kids left, already late for class if it started at one. Sara checked her watch. Her replacement would be here within the hour, and then she'd drive to the university and work in the library for a few hours on the psych paper due next week. The topic — is gaslighting real? — interested her a great deal, since her own father could have taught lessons on the subject. He'd left a string of victims in his wake, but she wouldn't let herself be one of them any longer. Damned if she'd care about him that much.

There was a motion off to her left, and the girl she had thought was long gone came into view from the direction of the washrooms. She stood for a moment, looking around while buttoning up her far-from-warm coat.

"Would you like a coffee refill?" Sara called out even though they never gave them.

The girl turned. "I threw out my cup."

"No worries. You can have a fresh one."

"If you're sure."

"Take a seat, and I'll bring it over. I have to clean tables now that the crowd is gone."

"Thanks." The girl's smile made her look younger.

Sara pulled a doughnut out of the case and brought it over with a cup of coffee. She set both down. "Are you waiting for somebody?"

"Yeah, my friend who I thought would put me up for a few days. Guess she's not going to show."

"Did you text her?"

"No. I don't have a phone and haven't got her number anyway."

Sara returned to the counter and picked up a tray. She began loading it with wrappers and empty cups from tables near the window. The girl had followed her lead and was clearing tables at the opposite end of the room. They smiled at each other and met ten minutes later at the waste bins.

"I wanted to earn my refill," the girl said before returning to her table. She sat and took a bite out of the doughnut.

Sara got busy with customers, and the rest of the hour sped by. She was pleased to see the girl still sitting at the table when her replacement arrived and went over to say goodbye after cashing out. Sara hesitated when she realized the girl had been crying. "Do you have somewhere to go?" she asked.

"I'll be fine. Thanks for asking."

"I don't know your name. I'm Sara."

"Nicola, but my friends call me Nikki." She swiped at her cheek with the back of one hand. "My boyfriend was abusive, so I left him." She gave a trembling smile. "He didn't even let me own pants." Her voice caught.

Sara thought about the creepy man who'd been in at lunchtime looking for her. "Say, why don't you come with me? I can take you somewhere safe."

"I don't want—"

Sara cut her off. "It's no problem. Honestly. My car's in the back lot."

Nikki took a moment before nodding. "Okay, but on condition you let me know when you need to be somewhere. I can be dropped off at a mall or something. I don't want to be a burden."

"Deal. Let's go out the side exit." Sara was no stranger to sneaking around, since her goal in life was to open a PI agency. If Nikki's boyfriend wanted to find her, Sara would use everything in her toolbox to keep her safe. The very idea of hiding out and evading capture sent quivers of excitement up her spine. This was turning into one interesting day, and it was far from over.

CHAPTER 8

After Cassie gave her statement to Detective Bottes, she climbed the stairs to her bedroom at the back of the house overlooking the swimming pool and gardens, the entire vista covered in a thick coating of snow with more expected in the evening. This was her old room and still contained her childhood double bed, dresser, desk, and bookcases. Posters from Broadway plays filled the wall space. It felt odd to be sleeping here, as if she were stepping back in time. She'd lived in Vancouver for seven years, and her life was firmly established there, with three summers spent on stage in Stratford. Four years ago, she'd been hired as lead in a television drama, and filming took place in Vancouver, the fifth season still up in the air. Her acting career had taken off and kept her from visiting her family for the last two years.

Guilt filled her as she pulled *Anne of Green Gables* from the bookcase. At the very least, she could have made time to speak with her father by phone more than once a month. She should have taken some initiative and gotten a better sense of this woman he'd begun dating and sussed out her intentions. Perhaps she could have intervened before he asked Marnie to marry him. Cassie sighed and set the book back on the shelf. Who was she kidding? They weren't close enough any longer for her to have that kind of sway.

She pulled a laptop out of her luggage and sat cross-legged on the bed while she caught up on email. She reread Heath's message before closing the case.

I've found a place to stay for a couple of weeks while you decide if you can forgive. I hope you're enjoying family time. I miss you, Cass. xo

She stared out the window and wished back the numbness instead of this overwhelming pain. Four years living together: the length of time she'd loved him. Four words uttered: the length of time it had taken to blow her world apart.

I slept with Amy.

She lay back on the pillow and closed her eyes. Could trust ever really be reinstated once broken? Was she willing to give him another chance? She still didn't know the answer, but the ache in her chest every time she closed her eyes and envisioned him and Amy together made her think not.

There was a knock at the door, and she straightened. "Come in." She shut her laptop and set it on the bedside table.

Khloe poked her head around the door. "Up for some company?"

"Of course. Have you already been interviewed by the detective?"

"Yeah, right after Gordon, but I had nothing much to tell. After lunch with you and Marnie at Viv, I went to the hairdresser for a wash and blowout. I still had some time after that, so I went shopping for shoes and a wedding gift. Gordon took a leave day and waited at home for Mick to arrive from Kingston. The twins stayed late at school for volleyball practice. After they got home around six, we ordered Chinese food and spent the night in. None of us saw Marnie after lunch yesterday." Khloe kicked off her shoes and sat on the end of the bed. "How are you doing?"

"Not great. I hate seeing Dad so upset, and while I didn't know Marnie, this is still horrible. I hate to think of what she went through … at the end."

"I can't even go there." Khloe shivered noticeably. "I never trusted her, but this is beyond anything I could have imagined happening."

"Wait, you think because she was untrustworthy, someone killed her?"

"No, that's not what I meant. I just felt as if we were all holding our breath and waiting to see where your dad's infatuation with her ended up. Nobody believed she was good for him or the family."

"Perhaps we never gave her a chance."

"And maybe she didn't deserve one." Khloe stretched out her legs and wiggled her toes. "On the risk of sounding like a snob, Marnie was not from the same class as your father. I'd wager she grew up in city housing in Vanier or Lower Town. Every time we interacted, the words 'gold digger' would pop into my head."

Cassie studied her sister-in-law. Khloe had a fragile beauty: porcelain skin, raven-black hair styled in a pixie cut, wide hazel eyes, and the tall, slender shape of a runway model. She'd been born with the proverbial silver spoon in her mouth, her mother a lawyer and her father a dental surgeon. Cassie had often wondered how and why Gordon landed her. All the girls he dated growing up had been on the jock side, beer drinkers comfortable in a tavern, football lovers, and weekend campers. Khloe was their polar opposite. She'd no sooner be found in a tent than a cat in a roomful of dogs. "Some fine people have grown up in those neighbourhoods. Your elitist roots are showing."

"To quote Popeye, I y'am what I y'am." Khloe shrugged and grinned. "So, you and Heath — wedding bells ringing soon?"

"Not in the foreseeable future."

"Shame. You suit each other. Will he come to Ottawa if this drags out?"

"No."

"You're quite definitive."

"He's on deadline. Script for a pilot based on a book." Cassie imagined Amy splayed across Heath's desk, his buttocks pumping. She attempted to blink away the image and changed the subject. "Wilma's being a bit intense. What's that all about?"

"God knows. It's as if she's been through this before."

"Does make one wonder. Are the twins at home?"

"Yeah, and I'm not looking forward to telling them Marnie's dead. They both liked her for some reason. Maybe because they're close in age."

"Ha, not exactly. Your girls are fifteen, and Marnie had to be late twenties."

"They thought she was cool, unlike me, whom they regard as a stick in the mud. Being a mother of teenagers is not easy. They push every limit and act as if

I'm a barrier to their happiness. Gordon is useless when it comes to discipline."

"I suppose." Cassie had watched Khloe helicopter her daughters throughout their early years. She was the stay-at-home parent, and her life revolved around raising them. Gordon used to encourage Khloe to take up a sport or hobby out of the house, but she always said she'd get to it when the girls didn't need her anymore. Cassie was sure the twins would be happier if their mom became less focused on their every move. She knew Gordon would be.

Khloe turned an ear toward the door. "Your father's home. I hear Foster speaking to someone in the front hall. We should go downstairs and get an update."

Cassie nodded, although she'd have preferred to lie back on the down pillows and nap. The flight the day before from Vancouver and three-hour time change had her internal clock out of whack. She pushed herself sideways and swung her legs over the side of the bed. A wave of dizziness struck her, and she put a hand up to her forehead. "Go ahead, Khloe. I've got to use the washroom and will be right down."

"Don't be long. Wilma wants us to put up a united front with the detectives still here." Khloe jumped off the bed but stopped at the door. "This all seems surreal, doesn't it? We were supposed to be celebrating your dad's marriage, and now we're planning his fiancée's funeral. Life can be a bitch."

"It certainly isn't fair a lot of the time."

Cassie lowered herself onto the bed after she was certain Khloe was gone. She took deep breaths and waited until the lightheadedness had passed before standing again. This day was turning into a nightmare with hours yet to go. She crossed the hall to the bathroom and rested both hands on the sink while looking in the mirror. Her tired eyes and pale face were reflected back. She grabbed a blusher stick from the shelf and spread colour across her cheeks, rubbing it in with her fingertips. She was going to need to employ all her acting skills to make it through the rest of the day without breaking down. She'd thought her father's wedding and time with her family would help her to gain some perspective on Heath and give her a chance to get over him. Marnie's murder only magnified her loss, because Heath was the one she'd always confide in when life turned horrible. They'd talk through whatever was troubling her, and he had a way of making even the worst things better. *But not anymore, and the sooner I accept that I'm on my own again, the better*, she thought before walking out of the bathroom and down the stairs.

———

HER DAD LOOKED A WRECK, older than before he'd set out to identify Marnie. He was standing in the living room, speaking with Gordon and Mick when Cassie entered, and she crossed the floor to give him a hug. He held on to her as if he were drowning. "Sit down, Dad," she said. "I'll get you a drink." She grasped onto his arm and led him to the couch, settling him against the cushions before straightening.

"I'll get this round," Gordon said. "Scotch okay, Pop?" He poured a tumbler and added ice without waiting for an answer. "Get you something, Khloe? Cassie?"

"I'll join your dad," Khloe said. "Easy on the ice."

"I'll pass." Cassie sat down next to her father and looked around the room. "Foster with the detective?"

"They're in the den," Gordon said as he handed Khloe her drink. "Mick, you want anything? A beer?"

"I'll get my own, thanks."

Khloe motioned for Gordon and Mick to sit, and they took chairs across from the couch. "So, it was Marnie, Dad?" Cassie asked. "There's no doubt?"

"It was. I can't … what happens now?"

"Wilma is cancelling the caterer and flowers. I'll call Edward and Beatrice, if you like, to let them know?" Khloe said. They'd been the only couple outside the family invited, since they were her dad's oldest friends.

"That would be helpful." Peter slumped against the pillows while Khloe got to her feet and left the room to make the call. He stared after her. "Whatever was Marnie doing out there? It makes no sense."

"Did they find her car?" Mick asked.

Peter shook his head. "No sign of it. The odds of her driving that far out of the city to go for a tromp through the woods, meeting a killer, and having her car stolen … it strains credulity."

"Did she go walking on trails often?" Mick asked.

"I haven't heard of her doing it before."

Cassie swallowed the first thought that entered her head. *You didn't know much about her, though, did you? She was a stranger that you let into our world only four months ago.* She'd received increasingly worried updates from Deirdre and Foster whenever they texted. Gordon hadn't voiced his opinion one way or the other, and Mick had been away at university, not aware, it seemed, of Marnie worming her way into the family.

They all turned as footsteps sounded in the hallway.

Wilma entered a moment later with the detective who'd broken the news about Marnie earlier in tow. The Irish one who exuded sex appeal: curly black hair, thoughtful eyes, lean physique. Even his clothes — black jeans and cream-coloured cable knit sweater — made him appear like a lead actor in a crime fiction television series. The detective motioned for them all to remain seated. His eyes landed on Peter. "I'd like to speak with you now about Marnie."

Cassie met Khloe's wide-open eyes and appreciative smile. He must have entered the house when they were upstairs chatting in her bedroom. Her dad got up from the couch.

"If this is necessary, let's get it over with."

Detective Hunter's direct gaze landed on each of them in turn before he focused on her father. "I know this is a terrible shock, but time is of the essence, and your insights will help us to piece together what happened to Marnie. I know this is what everyone wants."

"Of course it is," Peter said. "But I've got little to tell you that will help find her killer. It had to be a random act of violence perpetrated by a stranger. There is no other explanation."

Cassie sensed a change in the room. Everyone avoided meeting anyone else's eyes as the uncomfortable truth hit them at the same time. The killer could very well be a stranger, but if not—? Nobody in the family had wanted Marnie to marry her dad ... and now she was dead. It didn't take a leap in logic to understand that they were the ones the police would place on the top of the suspect list. They'd each had a lot to lose by the nuptials, mainly financial, but also emotional. Wilma had been the canary in the coal mine earlier that day, warning them of what was at stake. And now this movie-star gorgeous detective with the intelligent blue eyes had each of them in his sights. For the first time, Cassie thought that Marnie could cause them more grief dead than alive.

CHAPTER 9

Ella was trudging through the snow on the shovelled pathway to her apartment when she heard her name called. She stopped and watched Liam Hunter striding toward her from across the street. She waited until he caught up, her stomach sinking in despair at what his visit could mean for Finn.

"You don't appear happy to see me," he said, giving her a lopsided grin.

"It's just that I'm worried." She pivoted toward the front door and motioned for him to follow her inside. "It's too cold to stand out here chatting."

They stomped the snow off their boots on the mat in the hallway. She half-turned to face him. "Do you want to come up, or is it Finn you're here to see?"

"I'm here for you. Lead on, MacDuff."

They passed the second-floor landing. A dance beat blasted from Tony's apartment and followed them to her garret on the third floor. "He's got company visiting," she said over her shoulder as she inserted the key into the lock.

Hunter removed his boots and unzipped his parka. He stood in the entrance to her small living room, gazing around the space. "Same Bart Simpson artwork above your desk. I'm waiting with interest to see your next purchase."

"I've yet to find something I want to look at for any length of time. Would you like a cup of coffee? I haven't anything stronger because I forgot to make a run to the liquor store."

"Coffee would be great."

She took her time making two cups in the machine Tony had bought her a few months earlier. It had taken that long for her to begin using it, but she had to admit it produced a much better brew than instant. While she added milk to both mugs, she thought about time and the final carefree seconds before receiving news that could change your life for better or worse. If Adele had been murdered and Hunter was here to tell Finn, she needed to know but feared finding out. Ever since her brother Danny's murder, she'd lost the feeling of safety. She'd mentally steel herself for the worst possible news, while hoping it wouldn't come to pass. Craziness, she knew. Maybe even a form of PTSD. She wondered if the feeling of dread that had made a home in her stomach would ever completely go away.

She found Hunter standing motionless in front of the window, staring out at the pale light filtering through the bare branches of the oak tree. The warmth in her chest at the sight of him after so long was both uncomfortable and exhilarating, a feeling she couldn't allow herself to dwell on. He'd found a relationship, and she wouldn't open herself to rejection. She frowned and padded across the room to stand next to him. He accepted the coffee before taking a seat on the couch while she settled in her desk chair, angling it to face him. "Are you here about the woman found murdered at Shirley's Bay?"

"I'm here because you left three messages on my phone. It seemed urgent that we connect."

"Then the woman isn't Adele? It's not Finn's wife?"

"No." His expression turned quizzical. "What made you think it was?"

She took a deep breath and let it out. "Thank God. It's just that Adele was spotted outside our house a few days ago, so she was in town. Her behaviour has been so erratic that I … well, I thought the worst. I can't tell you how relieved I am to be proven wrong."

"The victim's name is Marnie Vaughan. She was engaged to be married to Peter Grady this weekend, and I've just come from his house in Rockcliffe. We're piecing together her last hours."

"How tragic. He must be absolutely devastated. Do you have any suspects?"

"None yet. Canard hasn't got you on this story?"

"Not so far, but I'll be talking about it on my podcast, giving updates. Is any of what you told me being kept back?"

"Hopefully a media release will be out in the morning, so hang tight until I give the word. Her parents live in Europe, and we're still working to notify them."

"Well, thank you for trusting me enough to share her name ahead of everyone. I won't reveal her identity until after it's been made public."

"You've never let me down." He smiled. "The odd thing is I'm certain I've seen her before. I can't place where, and it's nagging at me."

"You meet a lot of people in your line of work."

"That I do." He took a sip of coffee and studied the contents of his cup. "This isn't your usual blend."

"Tony gifted me a machine. He was tired of my instant stuff."

"A self-serving present then." He grinned and ran a hand through his black hair, unruly and too long for a cop. She saw fatigue in the lines on his face. His eyes met hers. "You're looking well, Ella. Have you been doing okay?"

"I can't complain. And you? How're things going?"

"Work's busy. I promised my nephews, Jack and Hugh, a ski weekend at Tremblant, but this case … I hate to disappoint them."

"They'll understand and the trip will mean even more when you're free to spend time together. Learning patience is a good thing. Are you seeing—" She was about to ask about Georgina, but a pounding on her apartment door interrupted. "I wonder who that could that be," she said, deadpan, as she got to her feet. She tuned in to the music pulsing through the floor from Tony's apartment. Beyoncé was calling to all the single girls. "Sounds like party time," she said, reaching the doorway.

Luvy scampered past Ella to her place under the desk. "Yoo-hoo!" Tony called. "Shut off your computer, girl, and let's get this weekend started." He held a pitcher of drinks in one hand and a cheese plate in the other. "Decker is bringing the shrimp dip and martini glasses. Oh, hello, Detective. Good timing or what? I have a martini with your name on it."

"I wish I could stay, but I've got plans." Hunter's gaze slid past Tony and landed on Decker, who'd come up behind him. Decker, in a tight white T-shirt, torn jeans, and work boots, looking like a he-man in a truck commercial. Tony set the tray on Ella's desk and disappeared into the kitchen with the pitcher and glasses. "Meet Decker," he called. "Decker, meet Detective Liam Hunter."

Ella figured Hunter had jumped to the same conclusion as she had. "Decker is Tony's childhood friend," she said as Hunter stood and shook his hand.

"We grew up together," Decker added, "in the same house."

"Wouldn't that make you brothers?" Hunter asked.

"Not blood, but we're close."

"How long you visiting?"

"Who knows? I've taken leave from my business after I tie up a new venture in Montreal and am trying to convince Tony to join me on a trip somewhere tropical. Maybe you can come along too, Ella? We can watch sunsets on the beach, drink mai tais, dance the night away."

"Uh, probably not." She felt Hunter's eyes on them. "I have responsibilities."

"And I have all week to convince you." His smile spread like warm butter across his handsome face.

Hunter accepted a glass from the tray Tony offered without taking his eyes off Decker. "So, what is it you do exactly?"

"Decker doesn't like to talk about his business," Tony said. "Too much at stake."

Decker laughed. "Could you make it sound any more mysterious? I assure you, Detective, my business dealings are legal. So, I hear you've got a disturbing new case. A woman murdered?"

"And I also can't speak about my work." Hunter downed half his drink.

"Two men of mystery," Ella said. "Shrimp, anyone?" She passed around the plate before dipping a plump one in sauce and popping it into her mouth.

Hunter pulled a phone out of his jacket pocket and checked the screen. "I need to take care of this," he said, "so I'm on my way. Enjoy your evening, and I'll be in touch soon, Ella."

"I don't think I'm going to have a choice but to party." She smiled and walked him down the hallway to the door. "I'll wait for that news release, and if there's anything—"

"I'll update you on WhatsApp. Take care, Ella." He looked over her shoulder. "Tony never ceases to amaze. I'll be interested to hear about his friend's occupation. Did you catch his last name?"

"Kincaid, and he lives in Vancouver." She could see the wheels turning in Hunter's brain. "You're going to check him out, aren't you?"

"No, that would be considered invasive. Just ... be careful." He gave her a quick smile before stepping into the hall and closing the door behind him.

Ella stood for a moment, listening to his footsteps clump down the stairs. Was his worry well founded or simply an odd reaction? She wasn't certain but thought it might be a good idea to find out more about Tony's friend and the reason he'd suddenly appeared on their doorstep.

CHAPTER 10

Sara drove as if they were on the run in a Jason Bourne movie. Nicola had watched the series over and over when she had time alone, television being her only entertainment. Escaping into those shows had kept her from slowly going out of her mind.

"My dad's house is empty, but I stay there sometimes to make sure nothing needs fixing. He's asked me to look after things while he's … away. Actually, I've pretty much moved in since the school term started."

Nicola turned her face from staring out the side window to look at her. "Where is he?"

"On a state-paid holiday." Sara checked the rear-view and side mirrors. "It's starting to get dark. Your ex is definitely not following us."

Nicola turned to look out the back window. "He has a lot of friends." She didn't see anyone suspicious on their tail and settled back in the seat, facing front. "I guess your parents aren't together?"

"Mom lives with my brother in the east end. Dad knocked up his secretary. They had two kids and are separated. Ginger lives with her parents in Halifax for now."

"That must have been tough." Nicola watched Sara shrug off her comment and felt sympathy for the girl. She had a loneliness about her that Nicola understood. They were roughly the same age, and Nicola had lived a life the past few years that Sara could not imagine, but that didn't make her reality any less tragic.

Sara took a right turn off Carling Avenue, and the landscape changed from concrete to country. Conifers, their boughs sagging under the weight of snow and ice, towered over snow piles that bordered the narrow streets. Front porch lights were set well back on large lots, the houses increasing in size the deeper they went into the neighbourhood.

Sara turned left onto another street called Locke Isle Road. Fat flakes of wet snow landed on the windshield, and she turned on the wipers. "We're supposed to get ten centimetres overnight," she said. She pointed to their right. "The Ottawa River runs behind our property. This part of the city is called Rocky Point." She squinted through the falling precipitation and glanced over at Nicola. "You'll be safe here. Your boyfriend will never find us. Plus, my dad had a monitored security system installed, seeing as the place sits empty a lot of the time."

Nicola stared straight ahead. This girl was too trusting. She had no idea who she was bringing into her father's home. It was fortunate that Nicola wasn't up to anything nefarious, but the men searching for her were violent and evil. They would stop at nothing. She bit her bottom lip and thought about warning Sara, but self-preservation kept her silent. If Sara turned her away, she may as well give up. She had nowhere else to go where they wouldn't find her.

The house was set back from the road, and while not as large as many on the street, it was a fair size with a gate and fence to the right of the entrance, enclosing a side and back yard. Snow-capped trees swayed over the peak of the roof from behind the house. Sara backed into the driveway, and they trudged through the darkness and drifting snow to the front door. Nicola shivered in her short skirt and unsuitable boots that gave the sensation of walking barefoot, the cold numbing her toes through the thin leather. Sara punched in a code, and they entered a tiled entranceway.

"The outside light is on a timer but set for later," Sara said, hitting a switch that bathed the foyer in brightness. "The temperature is kept a bit low, but it won't take long for the house to get toasty. Come into the kitchen, and I'll find you something warmer to wear. I keep some clothes upstairs."

Nicola sat at the counter and looked around the spacious, modern room, wondering at the twist of fate that had brought her here. She could just as easily be huddled over a hot air vent downtown, alone and hopeless. Taking refuge in that coffee shop had been an unforeseen bit of luck. She felt nothing but gratitude for the series of events that had taken her to Sara.

Sara returned with a pair of grey sweatpants, a navy fleece pullover, thick wool socks, and slippers. "We're almost the same height, although I must be twenty pounds heavier. I hope these will do."

"They're perfect, and you're really kind."

She changed while Sara put the kettle on and took eggs and bread out of the fridge. It was a relief to be wearing normal clothes. For the first time in a long while she felt like herself. She returned to the kitchen and took over scrambling the eggs and stirring the hash browns while Sara toasted bread and made tea.

"So how long were you married?" Sara asked when they sat at the table to eat. "Was he always abusive, or did it happen gradually?" She blushed before adding, "I'm taking psychology and criminology at university, so I'm not simply being nosy."

"We weren't married. He came into my life almost two years ago."

"You were young."

"Sixteen. If I had to do it over again, I never would have started up with him. I never would have left my home town." *God, what an understatement. He owned me. Said he'd kill me if I ever left him.*

"Men can be such dicks. I gotta say, though, you look older than eighteen. We're the same age, but I only just turned. Well, you can stay here as long as you like. I have class in the morning and a late shift at the coffee shop, but I'll be back in the evening. Will you be okay on your own?"

"You don't need to worry about me."

Sara's pale blue eyes searched her face. "I know this is crazy … my taking you in, but I'm not stupid. Sometimes you have to trust your instincts, and if I get burned, well, it's not because I didn't try to do the right thing."

Nicola reached across the table and grabbed onto her hand. "You've saved me, Sara, and I won't ever forget it. No matter what happens next, I won't let you down."

"I've been let down before and survived." Sara gave

a sideways grin before standing and gathering up their dirty dishes. "I'll pick up a pizza on my way home tomorrow for supper. I work until six, so don't worry if I'm late. Help yourself to whatever's in the fridge or in the cupboards. It'll be nice to have some company for however long it takes you to figure out what to do next."

CHAPTER 11

Liam tramped behind Quade along the well-worn path to the location where Marnie Vaughan's body had been found near Shirley's Bay. If not for the murder, he'd have enjoyed the morning walk through the forest and found the sunlight sparkling off the winter wonderland snowscape invigorating. Icy shards of frigid air pricked the exposed skin on his face like needles, but otherwise, he was warm inside his down parka. Quade was similarly bundled, impossible to recognize with her hood up and a red scarf wrapped around the lower half of her face. They reached the opening in the woods where Marnie's body had lain in the snow, and Quade stopped to stare up at the cobalt sky visible through the treetops.

"Nice to see the sun for a change. The gloomy weather had me searching for an island getaway."

"It has been a depressing stretch."

"Months like the last one, and I wonder why we live in this godforsaken country. Then I remember all the blessings. All the good days."

Liam knew she wasn't only speaking about the weather. "I'm happy to have you as my partner again, although this isn't where you saw your career heading."

"No, it's not." She nudged him with her shoulder. "But you are one of my blessings."

"You've been handling Auger okay."

"It's all I can do to stop myself from punching his insipid, smug face. How that man weasled my promotion out from under me is a mystery I intend to unravel before I leave this earth." She exhaled a plume of frosty breath as she spoke and ended her proclamation with a laugh. "Listen to me wasting energy on that asshole. Just ignore me, Hunter."

"None of us is happy with how that went down."

"Well, let's set it aside and get on with our daylight tour of the crime scene."

They strolled around the perimeter of the small glade, stopping to inspect the location where Marnie's body was found.

Liam squatted and studied the ground before looking up at Quade. "Green believed she was killed elsewhere and carried here. Whoever did it was taking a chance, because cross-country skiers and dog walkers frequent these trails."

"Perhaps not as reckless as one would think. It was a bitter cold day, windy with snow falling off and on. The man whose dog found the body said he hadn't seen anybody else during his walk. The snowfall and wind helped to hide the killer's footprints into the woods while the dog and its owner made a bit of a mess of the crime scene."

"Which leads us to ask if it was a crime of opportunity or one of planning. Any word finding Marnie's car?"

"Not so far. A carjacking hasn't been ruled out. Apparently, she owned a brand, spanking-new BMW worth more than my house. My guess is that whoever killed her left it in a high-traffic location with the keys in the ignition and the doors unlocked."

"Entirely plausible. The car is likely on its way overseas as we speak."

"The car's registered in Peter Grady's name. He said Marnie preferred it that way."

"That's odd. Most people like items of value in their own name. Perhaps he wrote it off as a business expense?" Liam thought this might be significant without knowing why.

"No idea. We can ask him when we next meet up."

They finished their inspection and returned down the path to the road. Liam had parked in the empty lot, and they fought the wind and blowing snow to make their way back. It took several minutes for the car heater to blast enough hot air to take the chill off and to defrost the ice coating the windshield.

"How is the research going into Marnie and the Grady family?" Quade asked.

"Boots and Jingles should have something for us when we get back to HQ."

"Let's pick up some coffees and breakfast on our way. This is going to be another overtime kind of day." Quade loosened the scarf around her neck and pushed back her hood. "I swear if this frigid weather continues much longer I'll be booking a flight outta here. We could be laying on a Cuban beach by next weekend, Hunter."

He hunched forward and squinted through the

spreading clear spot on the windshield. "Maybe when this case is over. I keep promising myself a trip somewhere." He wasn't the lying-on-a-beach type, though. He'd narrowed down his choices to the British Isles or Western Europe. Georgina had talked about a holiday, but he thought time away on his own would give him a chance to clear his head. Too much murder and overtime was turning him morose, and the idea of a solo trip was a light at the end of this dark, winter tunnel. He wasn't convinced Georgina would understand his desire to be alone, but this was something he needed to do. He just didn't know if he could find the right words to make her understand.

———

THE STATION WAS a hum of activity when Liam and Quade arrived a half hour later. Auger's door was closed, and Liam relaxed. He believed Auger kept it open to maintain tabs on the team, knowing they sided with Quade for the most part. The tension magnified every time Auger was on site, but he was doing nothing to ease the conflict.

Boots motioned for Liam and Quade to cross to his desk. "Something peculiar going on," he said, rubbing his bald pate.

"A whole new can of worms," Jingles agreed.

"Well, don't keep us wriggling in suspense," Quade said.

"This woman, Marnie Vaughan. We can't find anything on her. No history or paper trail," Boots said.

Quade frowned. "She must have a birth certificate and driver's licence. She owned a car."

"You'd think. Her driver's licence isn't under this name, though. It's too bad her purse is missing with her phone and all her ID. We might have better luck figuring out her identity."

"And remember she didn't have the car registered in her name," Liam said. "She was getting married today. She'd need to use her real name on the marriage licence."

"Or would she?" Quade asked. "If she lied to Peter Grady about who she really was, she'd have to continue with the falsehood."

"Peter Grady appears to have considered their relationship the real thing. He planned to share his wealth with her."

"Look at the age difference, Hunter. She could very well have been conning him." Quade shook her head. "It's amazing how many older people fall for these Romeo scams."

"Fake name. Fake love. Real mid-life crisis," Jingles said. "Happens a lot, and not only to older victims."

"Well, this opens up an entirely new network of possibilities," Quade continued. "Time to pay another visit to the Grady house. Hopefully, Peter can tell us more about the woman he planned to wed."

"Gives him a reason to want her out of his life," Boots added, "if he found out she was using him to get at his money. Hell hath no wrath like a lover scorned."

"Tell me about it," Quade said. "I'm still dreaming about getting back at my ex, and we've been separated three years. My anger at the man got me through the first year, and then I realized he'd done me a favour leaving when he did. Still, it's hard to let go of the urge to bring him to his knees, but I've learned restraint." She gave a self-deprecating grin. "However, this isn't about me."

"Your ex should move over and make room for Auger," said Jingles. "I wouldn't mind if you brought him to his knees too."

They all glanced over at Auger's closed door before Liam and Quade returned to their desks. Nobody felt the need to comment further about the elephant in the room.

CHAPTER 12

Cassie found Wilma flipping pancakes in the kitchen when she made it downstairs at 8:00 a.m. Nobody else was up yet. She poured a cup of coffee and sat at the island, leaning her elbows on the counter and thinking about all the times she'd watched Wilma cooking throughout her teens. She'd been a source of comfort, a constant in those growing-up, confusing years.

"Dad still in bed?"

Wilma nodded. "I stayed over in the spare room. Your father was awake all night in the den and only fell asleep a short time ago. I met him on the stairs as he was heading up to his bedroom."

"I wish there was something I could do to make this better for him."

"You being here is enough. How long are you able to stay?"

"I rebooked my flight yesterday. I thought Dad would need me for a few more days until he gets on his feet."

"Well, I'm not going anywhere, so no need to sacrifice your holidays, but I know he always values time with you."

"And we thank you for all the care you take looking after him."

"Happy to do it."

"Are my brothers coming over this morning?"

"Foster is picking up Deidre at eleven, if her flight's on time. She decided to return early with all that's going on. Everyone plans to be here for lunch at one."

"Can I help get the food ready?"

"I've got quiches defrosting and baked a cake last night. All is in hand."

"Then I'm going for a walk after breakfast. I need some fresh air and exercise."

"It's another bitter cold day, so bundle up."

Wilma set a plate of pancakes in front of her along with the bottle of maple syrup. Neither had mentioned Marnie, as if pretending this was a normal Saturday and not one shrouded in grief and loss. Cassie couldn't get a read on Wilma's mood. She'd been acting oddly since Cassie arrived on Wednesday, before the murder. Marnie had usurped her position, the marriage effectively curtailing Wilma's free rein over the house, and Cassie had been sensitive to how difficult this must have been for her to accept. She'd have been superhuman not to be affected or resentful.

After finishing off two pancakes and another cup of coffee, Cassie bundled up in winter clothes she'd never bothered to pack up and bring to Vancouver: a powder blue parka, thick woollen toque and mitts, waterproof ski pants, and fur-lined boots. She put up the hood of her coat and wrapped a scarf around the bottom half of her face. Even at that, the strength of the wind when she stepped outside surprised but didn't deter her.

Her father's house on Blenheim Drive was one of the smaller ones in the Rockcliffe neighbourhood, but it was still a five-bedroom, red-brick Tudor gracing a fair-sized lot at the end of a street. A two-block trek on the ploughed street took her to a walking trail that wound around a large pond in a conservation area. The path entrance was nicely tamped down, and she decided to venture into the woods to get out of the bracing wind. A short distance in, she edged carefully across a narrow wooden bridge, alert to icy patches under a coating of snow. It was about a ten-foot drop to a sheet of ice covered in patchy snow. On the other side, the trail opened into a view of the pond, now iced over with layers of snow mounded in places near the shore. She stood and looked across to the slope thick with trees and bushes on the eastern perimeter, letting the wind's force buffet her and revelling in its raw strength. Startled by the sound of an animal crashing through the under-growth, she pivoted and waited. A black Labrador retriever leapt into view, followed seconds later by their neighbour, Wesley Saunders, who lived in the house across the street from her father's. He'd moved in when she was heading off to university but had always been friendly when their paths crossed. She'd heard his wife had run off with their accountant but couldn't remember the details. Had he watched her leave the house and followed her here? She took a step back and turned around to face him. His eyes behind black-rimmed glasses focused on her face.

"Hello, Cassie. Cold day for an amble. I understand your father's fiancée is the body found at Shirley's Bay?

The police were by my house yesterday asking questions."

"We're devastated, as you can imagine."

"Your dad more than anyone. Have the cops got a lead on who did it?"

"Not that they've told us."

"Well, it's a terrible thing." He whistled for the dog. It had galloped halfway across the icy pond and was rolling on its back in a pristine stretch of snow. "Your father might have lived to regret marrying her, but that's no comfort now."

"What do you mean?"

Wesley dropped his gaze from the dog to glance at her. "She was completely inappropriate." He raised his voice while scrambling down the bank to the pond. "Nova, get over here!"

"Why would you say that?" Her question was carried away by a gust of wind, and if he heard, there was no indication. He was striding toward his dog, and Cassie decided whatever he'd say would only upset her anyway. She entered the woods and headed back toward the road, less settled than when she'd set out. Had Marnie made a bad impression on everyone except her father? What was it about the woman that made someone angry enough to strangle the life out of her and dump her body where they probably hoped it wouldn't be found until spring? The questions troubled her all the way home.

As she rounded the corner and started down Blenheim, a charcoal-grey sedan eased past. She recognized the Irish detective in the passenger seat with the Black female detective at the wheel. They pulled into her father's driveway. Cassie slowed her steps as they got out of the car and began striding up the walkway. She'd enter by the back door and avoid them for the moment. She needed time to collect herself before round two of the inquisition got underway.

——

After Sara drove away in her little car, Nicola felt a strange longing for her company. While Sara was in the house, she hadn't been alone, but now the old fears resurfaced as she made herself a cup of coffee. What if the man or his associates found her in this isolated place? They could force their way into the house and overpower her without much effort. She'd been exercising and working to keep strong in the motel and then condo, but heroin had eaten away her resolve, made her weak. Her captor had acted as if she was the chosen one, the girl he'd selected over all the others, when he introduced her to the stuff. Lucky for her, she hadn't taken much of it. Enough for her body to get hooked, though. She knew he'd tire of her before much longer and put her back in circulation. Imagining what he'd do if he caught her now made her skin crawl and sent a violent shudder the length of her spine.

She took her coffee with her as she made a tour of the house, checking that every window and door was locked before she returned to the kitchen and stood in front of the sliding patio door. The place had the air of an empty shell without Sara to distract her, a space not filled with love or warmth. Perhaps she was being fanciful, but she didn't think this had been a happy home even when Sara's father and his second wife and their children had lived here.

Deep snow had piled up on the deck and drifted into uneven heaps, the hollows tinged blue in the weak sunlight. Beyond, a large fenced-in yard contained conifers and bushes laden with more snow. The leaden sky lent an air of gloom to the scene, but a sliver of joy rose up in her chest at the sight of the outdoors and freedom. It might be too cold and the snow too deep to go outside, but that meant nobody would easily make it inside either. For the first time, she actually believed she might be safe here. Perhaps by the time she made a plan to leave, the man would have given up searching for her. After all, he had other girls to fulfill his needs and bring in cash. Yet this thought brought her no comfort. She'd gotten away, but so many others were being held captive. How could she forget about them?

She turned from the window and made her way down the hall into the living room. Sara had showed her how to operate the television mounted in the wall, but she decided to choose a book from the shelf, curl up under a blanket, and put off thinking about reality for the morning.

CHAPTER 13

Sara chewed over the Nikki situation all the way to Carleton University. If either of her parents knew she'd brought this stranger into her dad's house, they'd have freaked and forced her to put Nikki back on the street. They'd believe that the stranger was conning her. Well, even if she was, Sara didn't give a flying fig for what happened to her father's house or anything in it. Nikki could back a moving truck up to the front door, steal all the contents, and burn the place to the ground for all she cared.

As for Nikki's situation, less and less was adding up the longer they spent time together. If a woman was in a relationship with a boyfriend so abusive he wouldn't let her own pants, wouldn't she reach out to her family or friends? They weren't married, and Nikki was only eighteen — sixteen when she started up with him, not even old enough to buy alcohol in this province. Surely, somebody in her orbit would have noticed what he was doing to her? Then there was the question of the abuser. Nikki was beyond scared of him and said he had friends everywhere who would bring her back to the guy. Surely, that wasn't normal? Sara didn't pretend to know everything about women in abusive relationships and thought she might need to start doing some research. A real-life case gave weight to her education and made it relevant.

She parked in the lot and walked across campus, arriving seconds before the psych class started. It was a first-year, introductory course with four hundred or so students, which suited her. This was a make-up class, scheduled on the Saturday morning with special permission. The prof had been ill for the entire month, and they needed to catch up on the course content before exams. She could slide unnoticed into a seat and concentrate without feeling out of place. Nobody would judge her for not having any friends. A seat was open next to a boy she'd sat beside a few times, and she hesitated before lowering herself into it. He glanced over and smiled at her. He had a nice smile and wide eyes the colour of nutmeg.

"You just made it," he said.

"No point coming early and wasting my time."

"I should take a page from your book."

The lecturer called for silence and the class got underway. Today's lesson centred on Freud's theory of psychoanalysis: id, ego, and super-ego. Sara half-tuned in while spending most of her time looking up articles on abusive relationships on her laptop. She didn't notice the boy watching her until his arm pressed against hers as he leaned closer.

"I hope this isn't anything you're experiencing," he said. His expression was serious.

She snapped the screen shut. "I'm working on a paper."

"That's all right then. You had me worried for a minute." He grinned.

She couldn't tell if he was joking until his smile got wider. "You can borrow my notes," he said. "You missed most of what he said, and it could be on the test next week."

She looked toward the front of the class and saw that the prof was shoving papers into his briefcase. Other students had started standing and chatting. "Thanks, but you'll need them so you can study."

He took three pages out of his binder and handed them to her. "Meet me tomorrow in the library. Second floor by the elevator at two o'clock."

"Deal … and thanks, I'll owe you one."

"My name's Jeremy, by the way. What should I call you?"

"Sara."

"Well, good to meet you, Sara. See you tomorrow." He got up, and she watched him chatting with a couple of friends as she trailed him down the hall. He didn't appear to be unpopular, like her. In fact, he seemed a normal, good-looking guy with buddies and self-confidence. She had no illusions about his offer to meet up, although it did make her wonder why he was being so nice to her. By the time she reached her car, her thoughts had shifted from him to her job and the fastest route to take into the east end so that she wouldn't be late. Sometimes she felt as if her day was spent running from one place to the next with no time for herself in between.

Olina was on the cash when she arrived at the coffee shop with five minutes to spare. Sara waved hello and rushed into the back to change into her beige uniform, including brown apron. The lunch crowd had begun drifting in, so she and Olina worked together until one o'clock, when Olina's shift ended. Sara poured a cup of coffee, snapped on a plastic lid, and handed it to her for the road. Their manager would blow a gasket if she knew, but Sara was willing to take the chance. Olina had three little kids at home and a husband working three part-time jobs. If anyone deserved a free coffee, it was her.

"I can stay longer if you need me," Olina said, looking around at the nearly full tables. "They don't mind if I'm a bit late picking up the kids at daycare."

"No, I'll be fine. You should go home and put your feet up."

"I wish. My work day is only getting started. The youngest has a doctor's appointment, and then we all go grocery-shopping. That's always an adventure. Oh, I almost forgot. Some guy was in and asked when your next shift was."

"My brother?"

"No, this fellow was in his twenties, but he didn't look like anybody you'd hang around with. Said his name was Marco."

"What did you tell him?"

"I said that the schedule changed all the time, so I wasn't sure. I wanted to check with you first to make sure you wanted him to know."

Sara's brain scrambled to understand what this could mean. Nikki had said her ex had friends everywhere, and he wouldn't let her get away easily. Somebody must have seen them together yesterday. "Thanks for letting me know, Olina. If anyone comes in again asking for me, don't tell them anything, especially not my last name."

Olina's eyes widened, and she slapped her forehead with the palm of her hand. "I'm so sorry. I told him by mistake. I asked if he meant Sara McGowan, and he said yes. I'm such an idiot."

Sara's stomach dropped. "You didn't know. It might be nothing anyway."

Or it might be something very, very bad.

CHAPTER 14

"This conversation is going to be awkward as hell," Quade said to Liam after ringing the doorbell and stepping back. "Excuse me, sir, but the woman you were going to marry today was not the person she claimed to be."

"There must have been signs," Liam said. "Peter Grady would have had to be wearing blinders not to notice something amiss."

The door opened, cutting off her reply. The housekeeper looked over her shoulder before staring back at them.

"Yes?"

"We're here to speak with Peter Grady," Quade said.

"He's sleeping. As you can imagine, he had a difficult night."

"It's all right, Wilma," a woman's voice called as she started toward them down the hallway. Liam refreshed his memory. Cassie Grady. Actress living in Vancouver but arrived Wednesday evening in advance of the wedding. He'd found the TV drama she starred in the night before on a streaming service and watched an episode. Her acting had stood out in an otherwise forgettable show. Wilma stepped back, a sour expression hardening her face. Liam nodded in her direction on the way past into the foyer.

"Wilma, please brew a fresh pot of coffee, and I'll get Dad up." Cassie looked at Liam. "Make yourselves comfortable. It could take a few minutes for my father to be ready."

Wilma led them into the same living room where they'd met the family the day before and made a hasty exit, Liam assumed into the kitchen.

Quade looked around and whistled. "I can't get over how much money was spent on this one room."

"And Marnie Vaughan, or whoever she was, snared the owner."

"Yeah, gives one pause."

Quade stood and made a circle of the space, running her fingertips across walnut tables and silk curtains. She paused in front of the watercolour painting of a woman who looked a lot like Cassie hanging next to the fireplace above a table holding a vase of roses, luminescent in the pool of light from a Tiffany lamp. The woman in the picture sat sideways on the same couch Liam was on now, her feet bare, long dark hair loose around her face, and silky green dress hugging her body. The book in her hands was open wide, and the artist had captured a dreaminess in her eyes and smile.

"My mother," Cassie said from behind them. "Dad had it painted after Foster was born. She was twenty-two." She moved across the room to stand next to Quade and stared at the painting.

"She was a lovely woman," Quade said. "You take after her."

"Thanks. We miss her a lot. My father will be down in a few minutes."

She took a seat in one of the plush chairs, and Quade joined Liam on the couch as Wilma entered with a tray. They'd each settled back with a mug of coffee when Peter walked in, looking as if he'd barely slept. Cassie fussed over him and made certain he had a coffee before they began their questions.

"I'm guessing you haven't any news about who did this to Marnie," Peter said. "I realize it's only been a day, but I want the person punished to the full extent of the law. Marnie didn't deserve to die, especially in such a cruel way. I can't stop thinking of how terrible it must have been for her alone in the woods with the killer."

"We will work diligently to bring the person to justice. You can be assured of that," Quade said. "Can you tell us how the two of you met, Mr. Grady?"

"Not sure that has any relevance, but it was at my gym. She arrived one day, and we got to talking. I invited her to share a cold drink after our workout, and we hit it off. Wasn't long before we began meeting at the gym and going for lunch or dinner."

"How long before your romantic relationship began?"

"Three weeks, I guess." He sent Cassie an apology with his eyes. "When you know, you know." He shrugged. "There was the age difference, of course, but she said that didn't matter to her. She convinced me." He smiled at whatever memory that brought to mind.

Liam signalled to Quade, and she nodded. His turn.

"What can you tell us about her life before the two of you met?"

"Well, let's see. She was born in Croatia but travelled the world. Her father was an American diplomat."

"And I understand her parents and family are still overseas."

"That's correct. She said they'd landed in Germany, but I never got their contact information. It's on her phone."

"We haven't located her purse, phone, or ID."

"Your people took her laptop yesterday and went through her things. Unfortunately, I still haven't been able to find her passwords."

"That is routine procedure when someone is murdered. We attempt to trace their last movements and interactions. Our tech team is working to gain access to her files. Have you met any of her family members or friends?"

"Marnie only arrived in Ottawa a month or so before we connected. She didn't have time to make friends. Her family is in Europe, as I mentioned. She'd invited her parents and brother to come in the summer and was planning some special activities. She'd started a temp job that she quit after a few weeks. I can't remember any of the details, since it didn't seem important."

"Do you have her previous address before she arrived in Ottawa?"

"No. When I met her, she was living downtown, but we always got together at the gym or restaurants later on. She had very few possessions because she travelled light."

Cassie was watching her father with a quizzical

expression. "Dad, how did you know she … what made you trust her?"

"Marnie had a kind, generous soul. You can't pretend these qualities. You either have them or you don't."

Quade's gaze met Liam's, and he nodded for her to take over. "The thing is, Mr. Grady, we cannot find any records that Marnie Vaughan existed. She could have been using a fake name. Did you ever see any ID or mail addressed to her?"

Anger flushed Peter's face a dull red. "I didn't need to see ID. There was no reason to distrust her. I cannot believe you people would enter my home with your half-baked accusation when Marnie's the victim and not here to defend herself. Of course her name was Marnie Vaughan. Why would I have had any reason to doubt her? She was the loveliest, the kindest, my most—" His voice trailed away, and he covered his face with both hands.

Cassie stood and put an arm around her father's shoulders. She looked across at Liam and Quade. "I believe we understand your point, and there's no further need to flog this horse. You have all of Marnie's personal possessions, so I'd suggest the police are better placed to figure this out than we are. My father is a good man, and I pray that she didn't take advantage of him, but we get it. She might have been lying or hiding her identity."

"If she did, then she had a good reason," Peter said, dropping his hands. "I still trust that the woman she showed me to be was who she was — a giving, kind person who'd had a tough life."

"Did she tell you she had a tough past?" Quade asked.

Peter's expression became guarded. "Not in so many words. I only surmised she'd had a difficult go."

"Then we will keep searching for answers," Liam said. "We also don't believe the worst until we have all the facts."

"I appreciate that," Peter said. "She deserves the truth to come out, because I know she genuinely wanted to marry me, and it wasn't for my money. We were in love, hard as that may be for some people to believe. I waited a long time after my first wife passed to enter another serious relationship. Marnie wasn't playing me, and I'll believe that until the day I die."

"One more question," Quade said. "Marnie wasn't wearing an engagement ring, or any jewellery for that matter, when she was found. Did she normally—"

"I can tell you that she turned down my offer of an engagement ring. She only wanted a wedding band, and I had one made with five diamonds inserted. I should have been putting it on her finger today." His voice shook, and he paused for a moment. "She didn't usually wear any jewellery that I saw. She was a simple woman at heart."

"What do you think of Peter's reaction, Hunter?" Quade asked as they walked toward their car.

"I believe the man honestly loved his fiancée, and all this has come as a terrible shock. Of course, that doesn't mean he's not complicit in her death. We can't be absolutely certain yet that he didn't discover she was lying to him or that he didn't confront her on Thursday and lose his temper."

"His daughter seems more on the ball. Did you see the look she gave her father when she realized where we were heading with our questions?"

"It's difficult to have a parent fall for a hoax, but as we know, it happens all the time. Cassie appears more aware, but she wasn't emotionally invested in this relationship like her father."

"Man, these con artists are a blight on society. It's like we're waging war against liars and fakers as they find new and better ways to catch people off-guard."

They reached the car. A thin layer of snow coated the roof and windows. "You can get the heater going while I brush this off," Hunter said, running a hand across the windshield. They both knew that elderly folks were more often than not the target of scammers who had no scruples or remorse. He wondered how these people rationalized their crimes to themselves. If stealing someone's life savings and destroying their retirement didn't faze them, then they appeared beyond redemption.

He finished wiping off the snow and climbed into the passenger seat. Quade sat huddled over the steering wheel, shivering. He couldn't yet see through the windshield as the heater valiantly worked to clear the frost.

"Marnie paid a terrible price if she was running a Romeo scam. She could have had a partner or even syndicate behind her. They often don't act alone," Quade said.

"We need to get into her laptop and files. Hopefully she didn't keep all her interactions on her missing phone."

"She'd be careful, though, wouldn't she? Maybe she corresponded by text or through an app, and that's why her phone was taken. I'm not convinced the laptop will generate our answers."

"Then we'll need to figure out other avenues to access her past. She didn't drop into the city out of the sky. Somebody knows something."

"Let's put out a public notice asking for people who recognize her to come forward. Shake the bushes and see what falls out." Quade's jaw tightened. "You get busy typing, and I'll run the draft past Auger. It'll give him something new to talk about in his next media scrum, and it'll get him off our backs for a bit."

CHAPTER 15

Auger gave his late approval at 7:00 p.m to Liam's draft request asking the public for information about Marnie Vaughan. Relieved, Liam forwarded the notice to Communications before packing up to go home. Their recently appointed staff sergeant had been off-site for most of the day, schmoozing with the mayor and other dignitaries and hadn't responded to texts. Liam had sent Quade home an hour earlier with her promise to take the next late night. While waiting, he spent the time researching Decker Kincaid. Something about the guy didn't sit right, even if he'd grown up with Tony. He was too smooth. Too slick. Liam convinced himself Decker's flirting with Ella hadn't gotten under his skin and wasn't the reason he was suspicious. No, it was his cop sixth sense that triggered this mistrust.

It didn't take long to bring up images. Decker had an Instagram account filled with photos of himself and two dogs in various country settings — dipping a hand into a lake, sitting on the porch at a rustic cottage, walking through the woods. His page linked to another site: Big Bear Winery and Bistro. It took more digging to realize that Decker owned this business in the heart of British Columbia wine country. Additional searches brought up stock actor photos of Decker and advertising campaigns with a younger Decker, promoting a clothing line, men's cologne, and tourism in the province. Newspaper articles about his modelling career, bistro, and winery touted his entrepreneurial spirit and well-deserved success. Liam sat back. This guy had lived a charmed life, it seemed. His cop sixth sense had let him down. He thought about Ella and all the reasons she could fall for Decker Kincaid. Hell, the man was a walking billboard for male perfection.

Liam stood and paced in front of his desk, stopping to answer his cell phone. Georgina was calling to see how his day had gone and to wish him goodnight. She hoped they could get together when his workload allowed. Liam signed off after assuring her he'd have a free evening soon. They were still in the information-collecting part of the investigation, and there was bound to be a lull. After he put the phone into his pocket, he resumed pacing. He'd keep what he learned about Decker to himself for now and not share the information with Ella. He'd only been looking out for her welfare, after all, and found nothing of concern. Knowing Ella, she wouldn't appreciate his efforts. She might take his interest the wrong way.

———

Wilma had called everyone to tell them not to come for lunch until one thirty. "No need to have them grilled again by those two cops," she'd said when Cassie asked. Cassie thought Wilma's antipathy to the police could be attributed to her being overly protective of the family. She'd always been a momma bear when it came to them.

Gordon and Khloe arrived first with their twin girls and Mick in tow. Trisha and Bobby at fifteen had grown into self-assured young women since Cassie last saw them. She hugged each in turn and promised to take them somewhere fun before she returned to Vancouver.

Deirdre and Foster were running late as usual and made a grand entrance, their voices loud and commanding as they entered the living room. In stature and temperament, Deirdre was the opposite of Khloe. A husky five-foot-ten, Deirdre enjoyed time outdoors and challenging herself. Marathons, triathlons, mountain-climbing. Even her career as a university recruiter involved surmounting obstacles and outmanoeuvring other schools to get the brightest prospects. Foster always spoke about his wife's accomplishments with admiration, downplaying his own high-flying career in their dad's architecture business. They'd remained childless by choice to focus on career, or so Deirdre had told Cassie and anyone else who would listen. She didn't appear to realize or to care that Khloe, who'd stayed home to raise the twins, might be offended.

Deirdre spent some time alone with Peter in the den before drawing Cassie aside in the hall. She dropped her voice. "Is it true Marnie Vaughan was a made-up name? She was running a scam on your dad?"

"We don't know for sure. The police are checking into it."

"What a mess. I probably spent more time with her

than anyone else in the family, with the exception of Peter, naturally."

"You'll need to speak with the detectives. They're keen for information about her."

"She was good at whatever game she was playing, I give her that. The stories she told about her family in Europe and her recent move to Ottawa sounded true enough."

"Did you like her? Trust her?"

"I never felt completely comfortable around her, but she didn't strike me as a bad person. It just seemed like there was a lot going on behind her big blue eyes that she didn't want to talk about." Deirdre barked out a short laugh. "I guess now we know why."

Cassie paused as she tried to phrase her next question. She felt terrible for even thinking it. "Dad seems not quite himself aside from the trauma of what happened. Do you wonder ... has he been..."

"Losing it?"

"Well, slipping, maybe?"

"We've all noticed for a while, but nobody wants to make a thing of it ... yet. Wilma keeps him steady."

"A doctor hasn't checked him over?"

"Not that I know of, but Foster recruited Gordon as backup when he broached the subject with your dad as delicately as one can a few months back. You know how Foster always takes on the darkest chores, being the eldest, while Gordon avoids confrontation?" Deirdre didn't stop for Cassie's response. "Anyhow, your father became irate at the mere suggestion his mental sharpness was on the decline. He called them a couple of fools and said they were trying to stop him dating, which wasn't the issue at all then. The next thing we know, like two weeks later, he's asked Marnie to marry him. It was almost as if he was raising his middle finger to his sons for meddling. I have to say, though, marrying a girl in her late twenties was a slap in all our faces, especially your mother's. We could have embraced an older woman, but someone your age, Cassie? Forget it."

"What do you believe happened to her?"

Deirdre bit her bottom lip while she thought. "She double-crossed someone from her past or one of her co-scammers. Sad to say whoever killed her did our family a favour, but that's how I see it after speaking with your father just now. I'm hoping he'll come around to the same opinion once all the facts come to light."

Cassie nodded but wasn't convinced her dad would ever get over Marnie's death. He wasn't a man who loved lightly. She also hated the idea of someone murdering the woman, no matter what awful things she'd done. Speaking with Deirdre hadn't tamped down any of the anxiety roiling around in her stomach. The dark foreboding continued to grow, and she felt helpless to stop whatever malevolent spirit had infiltrated her family.

Khloe called from the entrance to the kitchen that lunch was ready, and they broke apart from their huddle like guilty children. Their eyes met, and Cassie looked away first.

"Chin up and mask on," Deirdre said with a wry grin. She looped her arm through Cassie's. "We can and will survive this. Our family is stronger than any gold digger who tries to divide us. Remember, we can ride this out if we stick together."

Wilma and Gordon had said much the same thing. Cassie still wasn't convinced the family could withstand whatever trouble hovered on the horizon but would keep that thought to herself. She also wondered why everyone felt the need to close ranks when they'd done nothing wrong. Wouldn't it serve them better in the long run to say their truths and leave the rest to the police? The guiltless should have nothing to hide. If she'd learned anything from Heath's affair, it was that keeping secrets often equated to lying. Only after she'd pressed him about the time he'd been spending with Amy did he 'fess up. She'd have gone on blissfully unaware if her intuition hadn't detected something off and forced her to push the issue. Marnie's secrets might be innocent, but odds were she was a liar too. The question was whether whatever she was holding back had led to her death.

CHAPTER 16

Wilma served lunch at precisely two o'clock. Everyone was on their best behaviour with Peter at the head of the table overseeing the meal. He'd recovered somewhat, although the dark circles under his eyes and a pale complexion spoke of a sleepless night. He chatted with Cassie's brothers between forkfuls of quiche and salad, with long stretches of quiet in between. Foster and Gordon sat on either side of him, Mick to Gordon's right. Trisha and Bobby were next in line, across from each other and the three women at the far end of the table. Cassie would have preferred to eat alone in her room, but she put on her friendly face and joined in the discussion while keeping a watchful eye on her dad and brothers.

Gordon and Foster looked alike, blond and of similar build. They'd been inseparable growing up, Foster the natural leader, older by two years and on the gifted end of the spectrum, Gordon the amiable sidekick who preferred sports and the outdoors to school. Cassie had believed when they became teenagers that Gordon would leave Ottawa to get out from under Foster's shadow in order to find himself, but he'd never roamed far. He had, however, become a high school biology and chemistry teacher, much to the surprise of everyone, most of all Foster, who'd more than once attempted to pull Gordon into the family architecture business. Mick, being several years younger than the rest of them, had grown up like a single child, doted on by their mother when she was alive, replaced by an equally doting Wilma after her death. He was self-confident, verging on spoiled, expecting all good fortune to come his way. He was always trying to make his older brothers notice him while acting as if their attention didn't matter in the least.

They nearly made it through lunch without upset. Wilma served chocolate bundt cake and coffee after clearing away the main course, and Deirdre let Bobby and Trisha take their plates to the family room to watch a movie. Cassie skipped dessert because she had to stay in shape for the next shoot. It wouldn't do to put on weight between episodes. She sat back with her mug of coffee and sipped while staring at nothing and thinking about a nap. She wondered if this need to sleep was her body's way of dealing with the grief of losing Heath. Mick's question jolted her back to reality.

"Will we be holding a funeral for Marnie, or will her parents want to take her body overseas?"

"I have no idea." She hadn't thought that far ahead. If Marnie had lied about her identity and her family, where did that leave all the legalities? Surely, the Gradys wouldn't be responsible for her body? She realized that Mick hadn't been told what was going on behind the scenes. He couldn't know that Marnie had made up her name and likely fabricated her life story. Only she, Peter, and Deirdre were in on the detectives' allegations, as far as she was aware.

"They have been notified, though, right?" Mick's voice grew insistent.

"The police are trying to reach them." Cassie tuned in to the silence around the table. She looked up. Everyone was staring at her.

"Wilma said the police were back this morning. What did they want?" Foster asked.

Her dad signalled Cassie with his eyes to take this no further. "They just … they were going over some details about Marnie's past. We didn't have much to tell them."

"They must have notified her parents by now, though, right? It's been two days," Mick said. He was being annoyingly persistent about something that shouldn't concern him.

Cassie's mind scrambled. To continue this conversation would reveal how little her father had known about his bride-to-be, how easily he'd been fooled. She couldn't do that to him while he was in such a vulnerable state. "Yes, Mick. The police are in the process of contacting Marnie's family."

"Perhaps they'll come to Ottawa to retrieve her body or to have her cremated," Foster said. "In either case, we could hold a celebration of life with them present. It would be an intimate affair, but Marnie didn't appear to know many people here. Deirdre can book a chapel, and Wilma can fix sandwiches and bake some squares."

"We shouldn't make plans until the police track down her folks. After all, we have no legal obligation, since the marriage never happened," Deirdre said. Her gaze held Cassie's for a moment, her eyes signalling that the others didn't know about Marnie's made-up identity.

"Maybe not legally, but we have a moral reason to be involved in the arrangements. An engagement is a promise," Foster insisted.

"A promise isn't binding. Nobody could expect your dad to foot the bill for her funeral. They only dated a few months." Deirdre held up a hand as if to end the discussion.

"But they were hours away from being wed." Foster glared at her before he looked at Peter. It was as if he was letting their dad know that he was arguing on his behalf and seeking his approval.

Khloe and Gordon sat back and watched, not unusual when Foster and Deirdre began one of their tussles. The two continued debating the ins and outs of Peter's legal responsibility, ignoring his presence as their voices rose. Cassie exchanged glances with Mick, whose eyes widened and rolled back as if he found the entire conversation highly comical. Cassie glanced over at their father. His face had transformed from pale grey to mottled red. Before she could calm things down, he stood in one swift motion and pushed back the table, rattling the dishes and startling the two debaters into silence.

"Enough! I'll decide what happens to Marnie's remains, and none of you need be involved. Now, I'd appreciate if you all go home and leave me in peace to grieve the woman I loved. There'll be no more talk of funerals in this house. Have some respect." He tossed his napkin on the table and strode from the room.

"Well, you've been schooled," Mick said to Foster and Deirdre when the silence got uncomfortable. He waited a beat while they looked back at him with sheepish faces. "What say we three brothers take our sorry selves to a pub for a pint and hash out our sins?"

"And leave us women folk to clean up?" Deirdre asked grumpily. Cassie knew she hated to be chastised at the best of times.

"If you like," Foster said. "However, we all know Wilma's the one who does the work around here."

Gordon stood and looked across at his wife. "You okay to drive home with the girls, Khloe?"

"I'd prefer that you—" She bit off her words when she saw everyone staring at her. "I'll stop drinking wine and should be fine in an hour."

"Good, because I wouldn't mind some brother time." Gordon's shoulders relaxed, and he grinned at Foster.

"Just promise to bring Mick back in decent shape. No puking in the sink."

"One time," Mick said to his water glass. "You do it one time, and they never let you forget."

Cassie started to stand to go in search of her dad but thought better of it. This day had been exhausting, and he required alone time to absorb the troubling news from the police on top of Marnie's death. He needed his space. Instead, she helped Wilma clear the table before excusing herself for a nap. Deirdre, Khloe, and the twins had started putting on their winter clothes to go home when she finally climbed the stairs to her room.

CHAPTER 17

A nagging sense of dread stayed with Sara for her entire shift. Every time she had a moment, she checked out the customers to see if anybody was watching her. Wiping down tables, she'd scan outside the windows, trying to spot someone loitering on the sidewalk or in the parking lot. When Enrico arrived at five, their shifts overlapped for an hour, and together they handled the supper-hour rush. She didn't have time to worry about somebody waiting to waylay her. At six o'clock, she hung up her apron and left by the back exit, checking over her shoulder to make certain no one was following her down the hallway.

The early winter darkness greeted her as she stepped outside and hurried toward her car parked in front of the fence and the uneven piles of snow that edged along the back of the lot. Enrico's truck was next to her car, and she thought the other vehicles belonged to the two women who worked in the back kitchen preparing food. Nothing appeared out of order.

She started the car and waited a minute for the

heater to kick in before circling the building and merging into traffic. At the last moment, she turned her head to the right, and her brain registered a black car idling in the laneway next to the coffee shop exit. Out of the corner of her eye, she caught its lights snapping on as she passed by. Glancing forward and checking her mirrors, she sped up and cut off a van to merge into the far-left lane. The black car had wormed its way into traffic in the right lane, but a truck and another car had it boxed in as Sara turned left on a yellow light at the last moment. Heart pounding, she made another left turn and zipped down a couple of blocks before another left that took her back onto St. Laurent Boulevard. She stepped on the gas and zipped through green and yellow lights toward the Queensway on-ramp that would take her into the west end.

Fifteen minutes later, she exited the highway a few stops early and zipped onto Carling heading toward Rocky Point, stopping at a strip mall to pick up a pizza as she neared her father's neighbourhood. Nobody followed her into the parking lot. She placed her order and watched out the window while she waited. Nikki could be gone when she got home, and while this might be for the best, she didn't like to think of her roaming around the city with no money or place to go. Her ex and his creepy friends were obviously looking for her. The hold that man had on Nikki made Sara's blood boil. It also confused the hell out of her.

Back in her car, the radio disc jockey began speaking as Rihanna finished singing about an umbrella ... ella. "Weather alert. A winter storm is expected to dump close to a foot of the white stuff beginning tomorrow afternoon. Plan to stay off the roads if you're able. A street parking ban will be in effect, and school buses could be cancelled Monday morning if the storm intensifies Sunday night. Going to be a bad one, folks, so be prepared and remain vigilant."

"Great," Sara muttered as she turned onto Locke Isle Road. She wouldn't have the luxury of staying indoors tomorrow. She had to meet Jeremy in the library to return his notes, and she had a reference book to consult for an essay that was due early next week. She'd also promised her mom she'd show up for dinner. A blizzard, however, might give her an excuse to skip the meal. One small silver lining.

The outdoor light was on, and Nikki appeared back lit in the living room window as Sara pulled into the driveway. She stepped out of the car and waved, then started toward the front door, which Nikki opened before she had a chance to punch in the code.

"I got a little worried," Nikki said as she took the pizza box from Sara. "Thought maybe you'd gone to your mother's and forgotten about me." She added, "Not that I couldn't have gotten by on my own."

"I wouldn't have done that."

Sara followed her into the kitchen after taking off her boots and hanging up her coat. Nikki already had served up pizza slices and poured glasses of juice and was sitting at the island. Sara settled on the stool across from her, and they dug in.

"I couldn't find much to drink in the fridge or under the counter," Nikki said after swallowing. "Your dad has lots of wine, but I wasn't sure if you were into that."

"I try to abstain. My mother and uncle drink way too much, and it's turned me off alcohol, to be honest."

Not really, but she liked sounding badass. She hadn't ever tried much beyond a beer or two.

"I get it. I've had some issues myself."

Sara thought about that. Nikki was only eighteen and seemed too young to have had a drinking problem and to have lived in an abusive relationship. Still, it didn't feel right probing. Nikki would tell her when she was ready to share. In the meantime, Sara'd use her detective skills to figure out what was really going on. "So, how'd it go today?"

"Read until eleven or so. Then I found the vacuum, dust rag, and cleaning products and went through the downstairs. Tomorrow I'll start on the bedrooms."

"You don't need to do that," Sara looked around, "but the place looks and smells great. Thanks."

"It gives me something to do. I hope you don't mind, I took a shower and used your shampoo and soap."

"Use whatever you need, and no need to ask." Sara reached for another piece of pizza from the box. Nikki was staring at her when she looked up. "What, do I have tomato sauce on my face?" She self-consciously rubbed a hand across her mouth.

Nikki laughed. "No, nothing like that. It's just I can't believe how kind you are. You have no idea who I even am."

"I know a good person when I see one."

Nikki turned her face away. "Sara, it might be better if I—"

"Your ex is still searching for you."

Nikki swung her head around to stare at her. "What do you mean?"

"A guy was in the coffee shop earlier today, asking about me and trying to find out when I'd be in for my next shift. Luckily, my coworker didn't say anything." Sara thought about Olina telling the guy her name but decided not to worry Nikki. He'd still have a hard time finding her at her dad's house. "I left work at six o'clock. A car was waiting in the laneway and tried to follow me. I lost him right quick, though." She smiled at the memory.

"Shit, Sara." Nikki rubbed her forehead.

"Don't worry. They didn't follow me here, and nobody at work knows about this place."

"My ex isn't a nice man. He associates with lots of nasty people."

"Then you're better off away from him. We only have to wait him out, right?"

"Maybe." Nikki opened her mouth as if to say more and then clamped it shut.

"Well, big snowstorm hitting the city tomorrow afternoon, so we might be stuck here for a day or two. I've got research to do in the university library in the morning, and I'll pick up groceries on my way back. I'll show you where the flashlights, candles, and matches are in case the power goes off while I'm out."

"As if things aren't tough enough."

"I like to think life is an adventure. The obstacles are what make it interesting." Sara decided to forego her mother's dinner plans the next day and would text her later. Her mom wouldn't get upset if she cancelled because of the weather. Luckily, she didn't have to go into work, so less distance to travel and no chance Nikki's ex would be able to follow her home. *Control what you can control and all should work out fine*, she thought. *Words to live by, even if they turn out to be a crock in the end.*

ALONE IN HER BEDROOM, Nicola gazed out the window at the night sky. Thick grey clouds scudded in from the east, blocking out the moon and stars. The room was at the back end of the house on the second floor and faced north toward the Ottawa River. Sara was staying down the hall overlooking the street. They'd both decided to call it a night, but Nicola wasn't tired enough to sleep yet. She couldn't stop thinking about the men looking for her.

She should tell Sara more about the impending danger and give her a choice. She knew it would be better for Sara if she simply walked out the door and saved her from whatever was coming, because now the man had the girl on his radar. As it stood, both were defenseless against the evil closing in on them. Guilt gnawed at Nicola. She was responsible for drawing Sara into her nightmare. She turned away from the window, crossed the bedroom floor, and creaked the door open. She padded down the hallway in the dark, and when she reached Sara's door, she leaned an ear against the wood. No movement, but Sara might be reading in bed. Nicola raised a hand to knock before thinking better of it. Sara had appeared exhausted at dinner and was likely already sound asleep. No, it would be kinder to wait until morning to share her story. That would give her one more night of warmth and safety before Sara wisely told her to move along. Nobody in their right mind would harbour her once they knew what they were up against.

Back in her room, Nicola took off her clothes and put on the pajamas Sara had lent her. Soft flannel covered in teddy bears — such a far cry from the skimpy lingerie the man had forced her to wear that tears filled her eyes and she had to swallow back a scream, the memories raw and humiliating. She climbed under the covers and stared up at the shadows criss-crossing the ceiling. Her mother would be devastated to learn what had happened to her. She'd believed, as had Nicola, that the promised summer job on the other side of the country in a resort would be a great opportunity. It would help her to recover from her dad's death the year before. "You'll get to see a bit of the world and save money for university. You deserve to have an adventure, Nicola. You'll meet other girls your own age, work, and have fun in a beautiful setting."

Little did they know that she'd be stepping from one painful situation into a nightmare. She hadn't contacted her mother in two years and knew she must be heartbroken, but the man had said he could find her mom easily and had promised to kill her if Nicola ever left him. Was he capable of carrying out this threat, or was he playing mind games? Nicola prayed her mom would stay safe if she didn't make contact. She needed to believe that the man really didn't know where her mother lived, and that even if he did, his reach didn't extend that far. He had to know that killing her parent would only make her disappear deeper into places unknown. It would also be incentive to go to the police. She'd have nothing else of value to lose.

Nicola shook out the pillow and tried to get comfortable. Tomorrow she'd rise early and catch Sara before she left for school. She'd explain as much as Sara needed to know to keep her safe. If that meant finding a new place to stay, then she'd do that, no matter how limited her options. Maybe Sara would lend her some bus money to travel to another town. Taking a handout felt wrong, but her choices were almost zero, and she'd promise to pay it back.

For now, this moment, she was safe and warm, her belly full. She'd been free an entire day, and that had to count for something. She snuggled under the covers and pictured her mother's face the last time they'd been together. As usual, the image comforted her enough that she relaxed and fell into a deep sleep.

CHAPTER 18

Ella emailed her elusive contact Sally at 3:00 a.m. and again when she woke up at seven, but her inbox remained stubbornly empty. *Where are you, and why aren't you responding?* she asked her computer screen before closing the app. The murky light coming through the window barely brightened the room. She hurried into the shower before Tony or Decker drained the hot water tank and then dressed in black leggings and an oversized grey sweater. Her hair had grown shaggy but was long enough not to stick out all over her head. Tony had given her a trim two months ago when she dropped downstairs with a bottle of red wine, so at least the shape had held.

A knock at her door, and Tony called for her to come to his place for coffee and muffins, if she had time. Ella slipped on her shoes and made her way to the second floor. Lena toddled toward her, dragging a stuffed teddy bear with Luvy following behind. "Lala," she squealed and reached out her arms to be lifted up.

Ella scooped her into a hug and buried her face in

Lena's soft, downy hair that smelled of baby shampoo and sunshine. "My gorgeous girl," she said before setting her down. Tony appeared in the doorway with mugs of coffee.

"Come sit and we can catch up on your latest case. I have the day off."

"Where's Decker?"

"Montreal on business. He left last evening and is due back later today."

"You never did say what he does." She made herself comfortable on the couch, and Lena came over to pound blocks on the cushion next to her. Tony picked her up and strapped her into the high chair that he'd pulled closer to his seat. He put a cup and blueberry muffin on the tray, and Lena got busy making a mess.

"Decker is a bit embarrassed about his past profession. He currently owns some properties, including a winery. He's making a deal to expand distribution."

"You've piqued my curiosity. This embarrassing previous career choice, did it involve taking off his clothes?"

"Close but no cigar. So, tell me what you've been up to. New podcast in the works?"

"I had a lead on a scandal, but my contact didn't show up for our rendezvous and has gone silent. I'm at loose ends."

"Scandal? Sounds delish."

"It could have been political… She said it involved someone in a place of power."

"What about the woman found dead on that trail at Shirley's Bay? You on that one?"

"Sherry Carpenter is lead on the story for the paper, but I plan to give updates on my weekly podcast." Their earlier fear that the woman was Adele seemed unhinged in hindsight. "Any further word on Adele?" she asked.

"No more sightings. I worry, though."

"About what? We know she's not the murder victim."

"Finn hasn't spoken with the family lawyer I recommended, and Adele could ask for full custody."

"She doesn't seem to be interested." They both looked at Lena smearing muffin into her hair. Luvy was licking the floor as crumbs sprayed down. "Such a terrible shame she's not involved in Lena's life."

"I'll be devastated if Adele takes her away from us."

"Finn won't let that happen. I know mothers have had an advantage when it comes to custody in the past, but Adele hasn't proven to be reliable. Not to mention the courts now favour having both parents involved in child-rearing when the family breaks up."

"She can claim temporary mental illness, postpartum depression, something…"

"And whatever is going on with her is likely valid, but even the courts can see how wonderful Finn is as a dad. You should have a child, Tony. You'd make a wonderful father too."

"Down," Lena said, reaching out both arms. Tony stood and lifted her from the chair, shaking crumbs from her shirt and kissing the top of her head before setting her amongst her toys. "That had been the plan when I was with Sander." Tony sat and began twirling the coffee mug.

"Finn is essentially a single parent. It's doable."

"I can't see it working for me."

"We could make a pact. If neither of us is in a relationship three years from now, we have a child together."

Tony stared at her; his fingers stilled. "You shouldn't suggest something you have no intention of doing."

"I'm serious, Tony. Since Lena has come into our lives, I know I'd like a child. After taking care of my brother Danny, I felt helpless to make him happy, but I've learned not to shoulder all the blame. Life … relationships aren't that simple. When Danny died, all the love I felt for him had no place to land — until Lena. But she's not my child, and as you say, Adele could come back into her life, and our role would end. That would be best for Lena, but not for you and me."

"Let me think about your offer before I sign on. Three years is a long time, and anything could happen."

"Agreed. If you end up having a child with someone else, I would be beyond thrilled. What I'm suggesting is only a back-pocket option." She grinned. "I might have gotten the idea from a rom-com."

Tony stood and crossed the floor to pull her up into a hug. "You're my girl, you know that, Ella? Others might find you reclusive and prickly, but I see through your defences. Your heart is as soft as an overripe cantaloupe, and you've got a squishy marshmallow core."

"Gee, thanks, Tony … I think."

"Lala," Lena said, grabbing on to Ella's leg. "Me wuv lala."

Tony laughed in her ear. "And me wuv lala too."

CHAPTER 19

Sara parked her car in the university lot and crossed the grounds to the library as the first flakes of snow began falling from a threatening sky. The wind stung her face with pinpricks of ice. The storm was on its way, at least five hours earlier than predicted. It would be wiser to head home now, but she had to transcribe Jeremy's notes and meet him near the elevators at two o'clock to return his papers. She had no way to contact him to change the time and didn't want to stand him up. He'd need the notes to study for the upcoming quiz in any case.

As usual, once she became immersed in the subject matter, time slipped past without her noticing. She'd always had the capacity to focus and tune out the world around her. "Single-minded," her mom used to call her, as if Sara's concentration trait was a negative. Sara preferred to see herself as tenacious. She'd learned that this ability served her well in school. It also helped when she was following her dad or undertaking surveillance, because her goal in life to become a PI required this skill in spades.

At ten to two, she packed up her bag, holding Jeremy's notes in her hand as she exited the cubicle. Hunger rumbled in her stomach. She hoped he wouldn't be late so she could get to the grocery store and home before others got on the road too, trying to beat the impending bad weather to wherever they needed to go. The storm would be awful enough on its own.

At ten after two, the fire escape door opened and Jeremy strode toward her. He was wearing a parka, and his hair was wet. "Sorry I'm late. I worked out in the gym and spent too much time talking to the trainer. I can't believe you waited. It's so stormy out there, I figured you'd be long gone."

"I keep my promises, but if I'd had some way to contact you, I would have left already. I was giving you five more minutes."

"You should have taken off." He accepted the papers and stuffed them into the bag slung over his shoulder. "Let me walk you to your car or bus stop, at least. I'm guessing you're a townie and drove here or took transit?"

"What makes you think I don't live on campus?"

"I never see you around the residences or dining hall."

"Well, you're right. I drove."

She followed him into the stairwell, and they descended to the main floor. "You don't need to come with me," she said, zipping up her coat. She pulled a toque down over her ears and yanked up her hood, tying it under her chin. Falling snow obscured her view when she looked outside the window. Heavy cloud cover filtered the light so that it appeared more like dusk than midafternoon. The sun would begin setting close to four thirty, but that was two hours away.

"I could use the walk, and it'll make me feel better for keeping you waiting."

She shrugged. "Suit yourself."

The wind battered them as soon as they stepped outside, making conversation difficult. Jeremy said something to her, but his words evaporated into the air, blown away in a swirling gust. The ten-minute walk took closer to twenty as they struggled through the snowdrifts, careful not to slip on the patches of black ice. Jeremy grabbed her by the arm as her boot slid awkwardly sideways and she nearly lost her footing. He kept a firm hold the rest of the way as they pushed against the wind and forged slow but steady headway.

The parking lot was almost empty. Sara pointed out her little car nearly hidden under a thick layer of snow.

"Get inside and start it while I brush off the windows," Jeremy yelled near her ear.

"Sounds good." She nodded in case he hadn't heard her. She eased the door open so as not to fill the driver's seat with snow and reached for the scraper, which she handed to him before climbing in. The key made clicking noises, and the engine sputtered once, twice, then nothing. She tried a few more times, the sinking feeling in her stomach magnifying with each attempt. She opened the door and set a foot on the ground. "It won't start," she shouted as Jeremy rounded the hood.

"Mind if I try?"

"Go ahead." They changed places, but he had no luck either.

"You might need a boost. Is it a new battery?"

"No, but there's never been a problem before."

"My car isn't far. I can drive you home."

"It's okay. I'll catch the bus." She had no idea where the stop was or which one to take, but she'd figure it out. She locked her car and turned to walk into the wind toward Bronson Avenue.

Jeremy grabbed her arm and spun her toward him. He leaned in closer. "I insist. This is no weather to be wandering around searching for a bus."

Ordinarily, she would have put up a fight, but common sense told her this was not the time. She met his eyes and nodded her assent. They hurried along University Drive to the parking garage, the going easier with the wind pushing them from behind, although the snow was deep in places and tough to wade through. Sara kept her gaze fixed on Jeremy's back as he led the way and broke trail. He had broad shoulders, like a football or rugby player. He turned once to make certain she was following. She saw no chinks in his nice-guy persona and wondered again why he was giving her the time of day.

It was a relief to step inside the garage. They shook off their clothes and stomped on the concrete floor, knocking snow off their boots. "It's a hell of a mess out there," he said and led her to the back of the parking area. He clicked a fob and opened the passenger door of a new silver Mazda. "You need to tell me your address," he said, starting the engine.

"Far west end, I'm afraid." She told him the house number on Locke Isle Road, and he punched it into his GPS.

"Might be best to avoid the highway and take Carling if that's okay with you?"

She nodded. "I was hoping to stop at a grocery store, if it's not too much trouble. I need to pick up some supplies, especially with my car out of commission."

"Sounds good. I could pick up a few things too." He drove to the ramp leading out of the garage, and they emerged into the blizzard. He grinned at her. "Some white-knuckle driving coming up. Tighten your seat belt and give thanks for my winter tires and new wiper blades."

The only thing that saved them from a fender bender or worse was that few other vehicles were on the road. At times, visibility dropped to zero as snow pelted the windshield and congealed in an icy film. Jeremy cranked the heat to high and gripped the steering wheel with both hands, peering through a circle of foggy glass. The wipers worked at max speed to clear the windshield but with mixed success. Sara kept her eyes on the road, warning him whenever she saw another car swerving toward them, wheels losing traction on patches of black ice. They passed two accidents at different intersections, and Sara thanked whatever god of traffic that kept them from a similar fate. At long last, Jeremy pulled into the Fresh Mart halfway through their journey and parked in the nearly empty lot.

"This is the biggest blizzard I've ever driven in," he said, the tension in his shoulders relaxing as he took a deep breath.

"You should take a break at my place until it lets up a bit. I have a friend staying with me too." She added the "friend" bit so he wouldn't think she was putting the moves on him. *As if.*

He nodded and looked sideways at her. "I'll take you

up on that. The whiteouts are downright dangerous. Let's hope this is the worst of it and eases up soon."

They ran inside the store and separated. Sara tossed food into the basket as she hurried down the aisles. Luckily, a paycheque had landed in her bank account the day before, so she threw in enough to make a couple of meals and feed three people. Jeremy was waiting for her at the checkout with his own bag already packed and paid for. He helped her carry the groceries to his car, and after another round of cleaning snow off the windows, they merged back onto Carling Avenue as Sara's phone rang in her pocket. The noise was startling in the enclosed space. She had felt as though they were alone in their own small world, travelling through a muffled snow globe. Her mom's number came up, and she hit receive.

"I'm guessing you won't make it home for dinner?"

"Sorry, Mom. I meant to call. I've been researching in the university library this morning, and I'm almost at Dad's. The roads aren't great. We can reschedule in a day or two if that's okay with you."

"You could have come here and stayed the night, but no choice now. I hope you intend to stay put until this storm ends."

"That's the plan."

"Oh, I almost forgot. Your friend was by, asking when you'd be home. I told him you were staying at your father's."

"You told him that? What did this person look like?"

"He was bundled up, and I didn't get a good look. He told me his name so fast, I didn't catch it, but he said he knew you from work. Mark, Markus, Marco, something like that."

"You didn't give him Dad's address?"

"No, dear. I'm sure he'll catch up with you on your next shift."

"I gotta go, Mom. See you in a few days."

"Okay. Until then, stay off the roads and call if you get lonely."

Sara put her phone away and rubbed her forehead. Whoever was after Nikki was going to great lengths to find her. They must have somehow found out she'd lied about Nikki being in the coffee shop Friday afternoon while she was on shift.

"Something wrong?" Jeremy asked without taking his eyes off the road.

"There could be." She owed him an explanation so that he had an idea what he was walking into if he stayed for supper. "I kinda brought a homeless woman … girl my age to my father's house a couple of days ago. She was living with an abusive boyfriend and made a run for it. He's somehow figured out we were together, and he's tracking me down. That was my mom. She said a guy was by the house asking for me."

"How do you know it was him?"

"Believe me, random men do not come asking for me at my house. I think the guy was in a car outside my work yesterday too. I managed to lose him in traffic."

"Do you do this often?"

"Do what?"

"Take a random stranger home. It's a big leap of faith."

"The boyfriend was so controlling, he wouldn't let her wear pants. What kind of asshole does that? She had no cell phone, no money, and the person who was supposed to help her never showed. She didn't want a handout and cleared tables when I gave her a free coffee."

"I get it. Sounds like her situation was desperate. Still, not everyone would take a chance to help a stranger like you did."

She pointed out the side window. "Turn right at the next street. I couldn't leave her without trying to help."

"I guess you did the right thing then."

His smile warmed her, and she didn't know how to respond. Was he actually proud of her for what she'd done?

This neighbourhood always made her breathe easier. It was calmness personified with a canopy of evergreen and deciduous trees, large, widely spaced lots, showing off colourful gardens and flowering bushes when not covered in a blanket of snow. The streets hadn't been ploughed since the blizzard began, but Jeremy's car made it through without problem. However, drifts made her dad's driveway a challenge that he wasn't willing to tackle. The city had banned street parking during a snowstorm, so Sara considered options. Two doors down, Molly Unger's driveway had been ploughed recently. Sara suggested Jeremy back in while she went to ring her doorbell. She knew Molly didn't drive anymore and might not mind a car in her laneway. Sure enough, Molly said no problem, they could park there as long as needed, although Sara would have to move her car if the snow removal company she'd hired came by again. Problem solved, Jeremy and Sara loaded up with bags of food and waded through the snow to her dad's house. Nikki met them at the front door and carried the groceries into the kitchen while they took off their jackets and boots.

"I was worried you wouldn't make it back," Nikki said when they'd gathered around the island. "The radio announcer called this snow Armageddon. Apparently, it's the worst snowstorm in fifty years." She darted worried looks at Jeremy until Sara introduced him and explained how he'd helped her out.

"I told Jeremy that you'd left an abusive situation." Sara thought hiding stuff wouldn't help Nikki to trust her, and she was rewarded by Nikki's nod and smile. She added, "He's going to ride out the worst of the storm and stay for dinner."

Jeremy had moved over to the patio doors and was looking outside. "If you have a shovel, Sara, I can clear off the deck and make a path. You really should have two ways to get out of a building if there's ever an emergency."

"I've left a couple of shovels by the side of the house near the driveway."

"I'll help if you can lend me some clothes, Sara," Nikki said.

"And I'll make dinner while you're both outside. If it's too awful, though, come back in and we can shovel later."

She'd popped a macaroni and cheese casserole into the oven and had started on a salad when Jeremy and Nikki came laughing through the back door, faces flushed and clothing soaked. Sara put the kettle on to make tea while they dried off.

"We managed to clear the deck and make a path to the side gate, but that's it till the storm lets up. Too bad your dad doesn't own a snow blower," Jeremy said.

"The neighbour across the street has one and will be by after the snow stops to clear our driveway. He checks in on me now and then." She'd stayed here enough that she'd gotten to know everyone nearby. They'd rallied around her after her father went to jail. She guessed she'd miss this house when her dad finally sold it. He had another eighteen months on his sentence and then would likely need the cash. She imagined he'd move out of Ottawa, where his reputation in the financial world had hit rock bottom.

They gathered around the island, and she served up plates of food and mugs of tea. A few bites in, the lights flickered and the entire house heaved an exhausted sigh as the power went off and all the appliances shut down.

Nikki let out a shriek. "He's found me."

"I think the storm took down a power line. Stay seated and I'll check outside." Sara jumped up and moved carefully into the living room in the dark. She stared through the window at the houses across the road. "It looks like the entire street is out," she called. She felt along the wall and checked that the front door was locked before returning to the kitchen. Jeremy and Nikki had lit candles with matches she'd left on the counter. Sara took the flashlight that Jeremy handed her.

"You were prepared," he said.

"Girl Guide training 101. Let's finish eating, and maybe the power will come back on."

"It felt like a horror movie there for a minute," Nikki said, laughing at herself. "Thanks for keeping me from panicking, Sara." Her wide eyes glowed in the flickering candlelight.

"I'd have been scared in your place too."

"If it's okay and you have a spare couch, I'll spend the night," Jeremy said. "It's safer here than out on the roads, and I can drive you back to your car in the morning if the streets are passable. I'll borrow jumper cables from one of my buddies and give your car a boost."

"We can get the gas fireplace going in the family room and sleep in there. It'll be a pajama party." Sara wasn't entirely certain why Jeremy wanted to stay. Was it only the poor driving conditions, or had he and Nikki made a connection? Nikki was attractive and had way more experience with guys than she had, that was for sure. It never crossed Sara's mind that he was hanging around because of her. That was an idea so far-fetched, it wasn't even worth considering.

CHAPTER 20

Cassie paced the downstairs of the house, stopping at different windows to watch the storm raging outside. The building was a solid Victorian brick, but the strength of the wind rattled the glass and buffeted the walls. Listening to the soughing and creaking, she imagined the house was a ship in the middle of a raging sea. Humankind believed it was in control of everything, but Mother Nature would never be tamed. Cassie thought it was a good thing to be reminded of their smallness in the universe now and then.

She hadn't spent much time in Ottawa over the last ten years. The close connection she'd had with her father and brothers was weakened but not broken, for which she was thankful. She was more to blame for their separation, having gone in search of work and fame. Gordon was the one she'd kept in touch with the most, the brother she had the most in common with even if they'd chosen different careers and family situations. They were both introverts, living inside their heads, although she came out of her shell when playing other people in front of a camera. Acting made her feel whole. She imagined teaching did the same for him. *You're both too weak for your own good.* Her exasperated father had said the words more than once when she and Gordon failed to stand up for themselves. *People are going to walk all over you if you don't grow a backbone.* Is that why Heath thought he could cheat on her and she'd let him back in? Someone cleared their throat, and Cassie spun around.

"Can I get you anything before I take my afternoon break?" Wilma asked, standing in the doorway.

"No, go have your rest. I'm fine." She wondered how long Wilma had stood there silently watching her.

"I heard on the radio that parts of the city have lost power. Luckily, your father had that generator installed two years ago, so no need to worry."

"Good to know. I'd forgotten how brutal the weather can be in this city. Where is Dad?"

"In the den with the door closed. He asked not to be disturbed."

Wilma crossed to the couch and fluffed the pillows. She appeared reluctant to leave. Cassie asked, "Is there something else?"

"Your father tells me he doesn't have an alibi for the afternoon Marnie died. He went out around four and arrived home after seven. I was running errands as well. There were final details to manage before the wedding."

"So, you don't have an alibi either?"

"I suppose not. The police didn't appear overly concerned when I told them, but they never show their hand early on."

Cassie could have added that she was alone most of that afternoon too, but she needed to speak with Khloe first to find out what she'd told the police. They'd met for lunch and left the bistro around one o'clock. Surely, Khloe had told the truth, but she might not have noticed the time when they parted. Then there was the matter of Deirdre not showing up at the restaurant after promising to join them. She'd sent a late text to Cassie that morning, explaining that she had too much to do before catching the plane to Toronto. Cassie hadn't told the detective that detail, not certain what Deirdre would say when questioned. She hadn't thought to compare stories with either of them but now wondered if she should have. It was awful to think how the most inno-cent movements could look guilty under the murder-suspect microscope. "We have nothing to hide," she said firmly to Wilma. "Marnie's killer must have been someone from her past or a stranger who chose her at random, maybe to steal her car."

"The police have our stories, and there's no way to know who's under suspicion. I warned everyone, but you thought I was being foolish. Well, the police are good at the divide-and-conquer game, so we'll wait and see how this plays out." Wilma pursed her lips and left the room, leaving Cassie to wonder why she was so worried. Surely, none of them had committed murder. With the knowledge that Marnie had made up an identity, Cassie figured she had a past she was trying to hide. The answers to her killing lay there, not with the Grady family.

Wilma had no sooner climbed the stairs to her room than Peter came out of the den. His rumpled appear-ance and unkempt hair signalled his despair, and Cassie closed the space between them to give him a hug. "Are you holding up okay, Dad?"

"Do I have a choice?" He squeezed her shoulders before releasing her. "How about some tea? It might help settle my stomach, which has been acting up lately. We haven't had a chance to chat, and I know you'll be leaving in a few days."

"I'd like that."

"Let's see if we can make the tea without Wilma hearing us."

She linked her arm through his, and they walked into the kitchen, dreary in the greyish gloom filtering through the windows. Cassie flicked on the overhead lights and settled her dad at the island before boiling the kettle and filling the teapot. Wilma had left a carrot cake on the counter, and Cassie cut large pieces. She didn't think her father had eaten all day, and she'd barely nibbled at anything herself. His face had a pale, feverish sheen that worried her.

"You're the only one who didn't tell me I was a fool to marry Marnie," he said after she sat down across from him. "I appreciate that."

"Everyone was just concerned about you, Dad. She was much younger, and you'd only met a few months ago." She wanted to add his wealth making him a target of scammers but held back. Slinging mud at Marnie's character and motives might be a step too far at this point in his grieving.

"I got earfuls from each of your brothers over the past month. Marnie laughed off their animosity, which they didn't hide from her all that well. The more they carried on, the more determined I was to marry her."

"I thought Mick hadn't met her before this week?"

"Oh, he was home for a few days over the Christmas holidays, enough time to voice his opinion. He had to tell me that she wasn't much older than he was — as if I hadn't noticed — and called our relationship indecent. He texted an apology to me after he returned to university, but it's hard to erase that kind of vitriol."

"I'm sure Mick told me he'd never met her before."

"I don't believe he did. She wasn't living here until after Boxing Day. Gordon had filled him in, and the idea of her was enough. I hate to say it, but I believe the knowledge they might need to share their inheritance drove the hostility."

"Oh, Dad, surely not."

They were quiet for a moment as they sipped tea and ate cake, giving Cassie some time to think how best to ask about what lay at the heart of the detective's stunning revelation concerning Marnie's identity. She set down her fork. "If Detective Hunter believes Marnie Vaughan wasn't her real name, who was she really? Do you remember anything more about her, Dad? Can you prove him wrong?"

"If I say no, you'll think me a fool like your brothers."

"Not a fool. A kind man who perhaps trusts too easily. These qualities make me proud to be your daughter."

He dropped his head and took a moment to control his emotions. "I've been racking my brain, trying to think if there were any signs that she was lying. It's just with all this upset, my thoughts are confused, as if I'm seeing images through water." He rubbed his forehead. "There's no question it was odd that none of her family could make the wedding. I offered to pay their airfare and put them up in a hotel. As for Marnie not introducing me to any friends, she said Ottawa was only going to be a stopover, and she hadn't had a chance to meet anyone of consequence. She'd taken a temp filing job for a few weeks that honestly was a waste of her skills, and I urged her to quit once we started getting serious. She had resumes out in Toronto and thought she'd move there until we began dating. I had to convince her not to leave."

"What kind of work did she do?"

"Marketing and communications." He paused. "But there was one other peculiar thing."

"Tell me."

"I wanted to take her to Europe for a honeymoon and suggested we could visit her family before going to a resort or wherever she liked, but she insisted we stay in Canada. When I countered with a Las Vegas spa getaway, she vetoed that idea too."

"You think she didn't have a passport?"

"Looking back, what other reason could there be? For a woman who claimed to be a world traveller, she was mighty reluctant to get on an international flight."

"Oh, Dad, I'm so sorry it all blew up this way."

He stared Cassie dead in the eyes. "I know none of this looks promising for Marnie's reputation, but the woman I knew was good deep down where it counts. I wanted to give her a secure, happy life with the time I have left, and if that's a crime, then I guess I'm guilty."

"Wilma worries you don't have an alibi for that afternoon. Did the detective seem concerned by that?"

"I never gave it much thought."

"Well, we won't worry about it then."

He reached over and patted the back of her hand resting on the counter. "How about you, Cass? Your young man, oh, what was his name again—"

"Heath."

"Of course. Is Heath still in the picture?"

"For the moment." She tried to smile and thought the effort produced more of a grimace than anything resembling happy. "We're not in a good place, so time apart gives me a chance to decide whether to stay with him or not."

"I'm sorry to hear that. You deserve the best, my girl. Don't sell yourself short in whatever decision you make."

As usual, he'd cut to the pith of the matter without knowing any of the details. Her father was not a foolish man, making his attachment to Marnie even more of an enigma. She must have been a brilliant con artist to gain his trust and affection so quickly and so deeply. Cassie wondered what he'd have done when he discovered Marnie's treachery, if they'd had the chance to wed. Even more disturbing, what would he have done if he found out before the marriage? He was a man of immense passion with impulsive gestures, and when ignited, his temper flared red-hot and violent. He wouldn't have cared about an alibi or anything else if he'd driven off to confront her. Cassie prayed she was overthinking things; she blamed the storm, a lack of sleep, and the detective's visit for her jumbled thoughts. Her dad was no more a killer than she was.

CHAPTER 21

Gordon, Mick, and Foster arrived midafternoon, somehow driving through the storm without incident in Gordon's SUV. Foster and Deirdre owned a newly renovated Ottawa South home, while Gordon and Khloe and the girls rented an affordable townhouse farther south on Cahill Drive in the Hunt Club neighbourhood. It was easiest for Gordon to swing by and pick up Foster on his way to Rockcliffe. After they'd shaken off the snow and hung up their coats, Cassie joined her brothers for a drink in the family room, where they got comfortable around a crackling fire. Their father was upstairs taking a nap, and Wilma was in the basement ironing and doing laundry while watching "her show."

"What a mess out there," Gordon said. "Khloe refused to leave the comfort of the couch. She and the kids are watching a movie. Then they plan to paint each other's nails. Another girl day."

"Deirdre's spending the afternoon at her computer. She has a presentation coming up in a few days," Foster said. "It's almost like she's using her work to block out all the ugliness since the murder. Anyway, this gives us a chance to talk about Dad and what needs to be done."

"What do you mean?" Cassie asked.

"You must have noticed that he's getting mixed up more, forgetting names and appointments. If it wasn't for Wilma keeping track of things, we'd be in trouble."

"I don't think it's anything unusual for his age." Cassie could hardly believe the turn this conversation had taken. Gordon and Mick didn't question Foster's assertion, and she realized they'd discussed their father's health on the way over. "Could you be making more of this than it is?"

Foster and Mick exchanged pointed glances. "One reason we objected to Dad marrying Marnie was that we weren't convinced he was as sharp as even a year ago. We believed he got into a relationship with her because he'd become vulnerable."

"You agree with that, Gordon?" Cassie waited for him to meet her eyes. Gordon was the more measured one whose opinion she valued the most. He kept looking at his brothers.

"I'm afraid so, Cass. Mick also observed changes when he was home at Christmas. Tell her what you shared with us, Mick."

"Twice Dad called me by the wrong name. I caught him talking to himself a couple of times too. I noticed a change in his attention span, probably because I'd been away and was seeing him through more objective eyes."

Gordon finally held her gaze. "Marnie seemed to be controlling their relationship, Cass. Let's say her new car wasn't his idea. I've never known a woman to take so many spa days either. She was using him as her meal ticket, and he never objected. Not once. I spoke with Foster about it. Bottom line, Dad wasn't himself, and the marriage was a terrible idea. She wasn't … suitable."

"Would you ever in a million years have imagined Dad asking a twenty-something to marry him? Like how crazy is that?" Foster added. "Even now Dad can't get his head around the fact she was using him, despite all the evidence to the contrary."

"We had a conversation earlier today, and I didn't see any signs of dementia, which I believe is what you're alleging." Cassie was desperate for this not to be true. Their dad had always been a rock, the solid presence in the background of her world, even if he spent most of his time working. "What has Wilma said about his state of mind?"

Foster shook his head. "She's so loyal to the man that you'd need to torture her in a windowless cell for a couple of days before she'd break his confidence, and even then I have my doubts. When she let her displeasure with Marnie be known, it was subtle. An eye roll when she thought nobody was watching or that steely glare behind Marnie's back. Never overstepping. However, her move to an apartment said everything. Wilma's been a part of our lives for so long we forget she's the hired help."

"Ouch," Gordon said. "Don't let her hear you say that."

"Do you not think she's always thought herself lady of the manor?" Mick asked. "She pretty much raised me while Dad buried himself in the business."

"Well, Dad never saw her that way," Foster said. He paused and grinned. "Good God, the man's not blind."

"Be kind," Cassie snapped. She'd forgotten how

nasty her brothers could become once they got rolling. Usually, Foster or Mick would throw in a sarcastic comment to get the other two laughing. She hated to have Wilma be the target.

"Yeah, that was uncalled for. Sorry," Foster said, looking anything but. "We should say where we all were Thursday afternoon. I think Wilma is worrying needlessly, but perhaps it would be prudent to share what each of us told the police."

"I'll go first," Gordon said. "I took the day off teaching and was waiting for Mick to arrive from Kingston. The twins were at school and had extracurricular stuff going on afterwards. Khloe met Cassie, Marnie, and Deirdre for lunch at a bistro on Preston Street—"

"But Deirdre never arrived. She sent a text that she had too much to do before her evening flight to Toronto," Cassie said.

"Did you tell the detective that?" Foster asked.

"No, but I'm sure Deirdre must have. Khloe, Marnie, and I separated at one o'clock. I assumed Khloe was going home, and Marnie drove off to run errands. She never shared what they were or where. I drove directly to Dad's — he'd lent me one of his cars because Marnie left earlier in the morning to get her nails done — but he and Wilma were both out when I got home. I preferred driving myself instead of waiting around for Marnie or depending on her to get me back here. I wonder now if I might have kept her from being murdered if I'd gone with her."

They were silent for a moment as this idea settled in.

"You might have been harmed too," Foster said. "Don't beat yourself up over a what-if."

"After Khloe left, having had lunch with you, she drove into the Glebe for a hair appointment. I'm surprised she didn't tell you. She got home around four after picking up a few groceries. Mick showed around five, much later than anticipated." Gordon looked at Mick. "Did I get the timing right?"

"Yup. My class ran long. Then I rushed home and packed, grabbed a bite at a drive-through, and hit the road. It was a slow ride in because of the weather, so five is accurate. What about you, Foster?"

"I worked Thursday until three, maybe three thirty, and drove Deirdre to the airport, but I didn't interact with anyone in particular. Only a few of us were in the office, and I had my door closed."

"So, none of us has an airtight alibi," Cassie said. Perhaps that made them appear more innocent to the police. Didn't those planning a murder make sure to cover themselves?

"We're all in the soup together then," Mick said with a laugh. "And maybe that's the perfect cover. One for all and all for one."

"Marnie was killed by somebody she knew from her past, or it was a stranger who stole her car and she was collateral damage," Foster said.

All three brothers nodded in agreement. Cassie could see the family putting on a united front as Wilma had advised them to do. Marnie's murder was somebody else's doing and not their problem. She could only hope that the police saw it the same way, but she remembered the intelligence in Detective Hunter's keen gaze and knew they were far from out of the woods yet. He was the one they needed to convince, and he struck her as far from a fool.

CHAPTER 22

Liam took a break early afternoon and fought his way through the sleet and snow up Elgin Street to the Happy Goat coffee shop. The wind took his breath away, so he turned and walked backward into the gusts. The physical exertion felt good after hours spent in meetings or at his desk. Working weekends when a murder case was in its early stages meant no time for self-care. He ordered coffees and fresh baking for the team and then watched the storm raging outside the plate glass window while he waited for his order.

"Not at its peak yet," the guy behind the counter said as he rang in the sale. "We're shutting down in a few minutes so staff can make it home before dark."

"Good idea. Glad I came when I did."

The wind was at his back, making the return walk to HQ less difficult and much quicker. There was little traffic on the roads and even fewer people on the side-walks. He thought closing early made good sense but couldn't imagine leaving the station before evening. He had phone calls to return and was waiting on Forensics to report back on Marnie's electronics. Auger had scheduled an update meeting at five o'clock, in any case. There'd be a lot of fender benders today if drivers weren't smart enough to stay off the roads. He thought of his ex-partner, Rosie Thorburn, working patrol. She would have her hands full tonight. Of course, there were people like the Happy Goat server who didn't have a choice but to venture out. Liam had all the sympathy in the world for the minimum-wage workers in the service industry, trying to make a decent living.

Boots, Jingles, and Quade gratefully accepted the coffees and Danishes and pulled their chairs around Liam's desk while they took a break. Other teams in Major Crimes were gone from the office, along with the normal hum of activity.

"The last suckers on Survivor Island," Boots said. "Might have been prudent to send us home along with our saner colleagues."

"The fearless leader wants his update. The least Auger could do is move up the timing," Jingles said. "Why did he pick so late in the day anyway?"

"You want reasons. Let's see." Boots began counting on his fingers. "Charity breakfast this morning. Lunch with some police board members early afternoon. God knows where and with whom between then and now. Oh yeah, let's not forget number four. He doesn't care about anyone but himself." He glanced toward Auger's closed door. "The man arrived while you were getting coffee, Hunter, and retreated to his office without looking our way. We don't dare disturb him because he's been known to loudly vocalize his displeasure when interrupted."

"It's so hard to bite my tongue and stay professional

sometimes." Quade sighed. "I'm not saintly, like Hunter."

"Complaining never solved anything," Liam said, sending her a quick smile.

Boots high-fived Jingles. "But damn, brother, it sho' do feel good."

"To change the subject, no progress tracking down Marnie Vaughan's family?" Quade asked.

"Nada. The woman is a mystery," Jingles said. "She appeared on the scene out of nowhere. It's hard to believe Peter Grady knows zilch about her past and connections."

"I guess being forty years younger and gorgeous is enough to warrant marrying a complete stranger," Quade said. "Grady makes my ex look downright prudent, having tossed me aside for a woman only fifteen years his junior with deep roots in the city."

"Doesn't make him any less of an idiot," Boots said.

"We haven't tracked down her movements that afternoon or found her car," Liam said before opening a message on his computer. He looked around the group. "Looks like Auger cancelled the meeting."

"Hallelu—"

They all turned as Auger's door opened and he stepped into the main office. He strode across the room until he stood next to Liam's desk. His eyes skimmed over each of them in turn and landed on the empty food container. Quade's eyes narrowed, and Liam prayed Auger didn't make a crack about them slacking off. Quade was itching for a fight, but no good would come from an outburst.

"I got word from above to let nonessential staff go

home. Do you have any new developments to report in the Vaughan case before we shut down?"

"We're still trying to locate her family and track her movements," Liam said.

"Forensics?"

"Nothing yet."

"All right. Be available on your phones, and see you tomorrow bright and early. I'm on my way." He zipped up his coat and continued on out the door before any of them made a move.

"Isn't there an unwritten rule about the captain being the last one to leave the ship?" Boots asked.

"Not our captain. He'd knock us down and stomp on our backs to get into the lifeboat ahead of the women and children," Jingles said.

"So hard to stay professional." Quade got up from her chair and stretched. "So hard. Well, my kids are home alone freaking out, so I'm out of here. I'll continue following up on the Grady family's alibis tomorrow. Kind of odd none of them has a solid one. So far, I have confirmation the daughter Cassie and her sister-in-law Khloe and Marnie had lunch at a restaurant called Viv on Preston Street on Thursday and left around one o'clock."

"Never heard of it," Jingles said.

"A French, posh-style kind of bistro, a few cuts above your preferred draft beer tavern. Khloe's hair appointment afterward checks out, but she finished up around two thirty and was a few hours getting home. The youngest son, Mick, was in class at Queen's until one. He arrived at his brother Gordon's at five; the drive is two and a half hours, so that leaves an hour and a half unaccounted for."

"Good," Liam said. "We may as well keep digging to cross each of them off the list while we work on figuring out Marnie's real identity."

"Far as I can tell, I haven't crossed any of them off," Quade said. "None of them has an alibi for Thursday afternoon."

"I'm still leaning toward a car-jacking," Jingles said as he pushed himself up from his chair. "*À demain, mes amis.*"

Quade looked over at Liam as she was putting on her coat. "You coming with us?"

"I've something to finish up. I'll be right behind you."

"Don't be too long. The storm's getting nasty."

It only took one ring before Georgina picked up. He'd put off answering her phone message until he was done for the day. "We got off early. I should be home in half an hour," he said. "Coming over?"

"No, the roads are too dicey. Let's plan something tomorrow night if you're free."

"I'll let you know."

He was putting on his jacket when a message pinged. He almost ignored it but stepped back to his desk. His contact in Forensics had sent a quick update. "We got into Marnie Vaughan's laptop and took an overview of her email. She must have used her phone and texted most of her contacts, but one interesting message chain with reporter Ella Tate that I've attached in a screen shot. More tomorrow when we have a chance to delve deeper."

Liam stood for a moment, trying to absorb what this could mean. Ella had said she wasn't working this story for *The Capital* but hadn't mentioned that she knew

Marnie personally. It wasn't like Ella to hold back such important information. He needed to find out what connection she had to the dead woman before Auger became involved. He'd pay her a visit on his way home to Kanata, even if it meant a detour and a less-than-pleasant longer drive through the storm. Some questions were better asked in person without an electronic record. Plus, it didn't hurt to check in with her.

SHANIA BEGAN BELTING out a song at quarter after four. Something didn't impress her much. Ella listened for a moment before pushing the chair back from her computer desk and ending work for the day. Tony was holding a storm dinner party, and it seemed like the music was his not-so-subtle hint that it was time for her to get down there.

Her apartment in the eaves of the three-storey house in the Glebe was the coldest spot in the building when the winds blew and the temperature dropped. Alex, her landlord, had given her a couple of space heaters, but they barely threw enough warmth to take off the chill. She changed from her sweatpants into jeans and took off the fleece pullover, opting for a black turtleneck under a grey cardigan. Tony wouldn't be impressed, but he never was with her style choices. As long as she let him cut her hair from time to time and dressed up in the clothes he sent her way for special occasions, he tolerated her lack of fashion sense without comment ... usually.

Decker and Finn greeted her in the living room with a glass of red wine. Lena crawled into her lap for a cuddle as soon as she sat down and then asked to get down to play with her toys on the floor. Tony danced into the room, carrying a charcuterie board and a bowl of sliced French bread and crackers that he set on the coffee table. He'd lowered the volume on the stereo, Shania now replaced by Dan and Shay singing about remembering some girl over a bottle of tequila. The music wasn't enough to cancel out the thrum of the storm, humming like an idling engine outside the window.

"Decker made it back here in the nick of time, because this storm's a lulu. I'm hoping our power stays on," Tony said. "Or at least until the chicken cacciatore finishes cooking."

"How was your trip to Montreal, Decker?" Ella asked, cutting a piece of brie and sliding it onto a slice of bread with a sliver of green apple.

"Productive. I'll be returning in a few days to finalize a contract."

Ella decided Decker was being deliberately evasive, and she wasn't going to play. She looked at Finn. "Gym closed up early?"

"No choice. I wanted to be home with Lena in case the power actually does go off. I was also worried the storm might scare her." They all looked at Lena playing happily on the carpet. "I might have been confusing her with a dog. Animals get more upset by storms than babies, it seems."

"I'm guessing no more Adele sightings," Tony said.

"Funny you should ask. She phoned the gym this morning. We're meeting for coffee in two days."

"That's promising," Ella said after taking a moment to absorb Finn's words. She knew he was hopeful that

Adele would come home, or at the very least start taking part in Lena's life.

"Adele is your wife?" Decker asked.

"Yeah, but she left me and Lena last year. It's possible postpartum depression played a factor, because Adele had a hard time when she was pregnant accepting the idea of being a mother. Anyhow, I don't know whether to be hopeful or anxious that she finally wants to meet."

"We're all wishing for the best, Finn, and are here to support you and Adele any way we can." Ella smiled at him.

"Hear, hear." Tony gave a thumbs-up.

"I appreciate that." Finn inhaled and let his breath out slowly. "So, Decker was telling me before you arrived, Ella, that he and Tony grew up together. What was that like?"

"Tony was the perfect adopted big brother. I looked up to him," Decker said.

"I didn't know you were adopted, Tony," Ella said.

"Not legally. They took me in when my mother disappeared." Tony looked at Finn. "In my case, my mother never made contact again. My father was a regular at the local jail, and I guess she'd had enough. Lucky for me, Decker's family lived on the same block and took pity on me."

"We were the fortunate ones." Decker raised his glass to Tony, and they grinned at each other.

"Is that the doorbell?" Finn asked, tilting his head to listen.

"Who would be crazy enough to be out in this weather? I'd better check." Tony stood and hurried from the room.

"I'll go with him." Ella got up and followed him onto the landing. The day had made her uneasy, and while perhaps silly, she thought Tony might need backup. She watched him push the front door open and Liam Hunter step into the hallway, shaking snow off his coat. Tony said something, and Hunter laughed. They started up the steps together, giving her time to scoot back to her chair in the living room before they made it to the second floor and caught her spying.

"Look who the blizzard blew in," Tony said. "Here on official police business, no less."

"Unofficial might be a better way to put it." Hunter directed his gaze at Ella. "Could I have a word … in private?"

"You have us intrigued, Detective. Why don't you use my kitchen?" Tony stood aside to let them pass.

"Maybe we can go upstairs. Will this take long?" Ella could picture Tony lurking outside the kitchen door if they stayed in his apartment. He had no scruples when it came to her and Hunter.

"Sounds good." Hunter turned and started toward the door.

She almost laughed at the crestfallen look Tony gave her as she passed by him. "We won't be long."

"The good detective is welcome to stay for dinner. I made lots."

"I'll let him know."

As usual, Hunter took up the air in her apartment, and she had trouble breathing properly, or that's what she put it down to. She thought about him so often that when he was actually with her, she became ultra-aware of his presence, like a tingling sensation on her skin. The disruption to her inner calm made her grumpy. "So what's this about?" she asked when they stood together in the hallway inside her apartment. "It must be urgent to bring you here in this storm."

"Our tech people broke into Marnie Vaughan's laptop today."

"The woman who was murdered."

"Yes. This is the first thing they found of interest in her email." Hunter clicked his phone and held up the screen for her to see.

Ella took the phone from him and read the messages in the screen capture, scrolling down with more and more confusion. She handed the cell back to Hunter. "I've never met her or even knew her real name. She called herself Sally, as you can see in the messages. We were to meet Thursday night, and she never showed. This is unbelievable."

"How did you link up with her?"

"She found me through my podcast website. She wrote that she had information about an illegal activity that needed to be exposed. She said it implicated people in power. My thought was a political scandal, since Ottawa is the seat of the government, but I honestly had no proof of that." Ella's brain slotted the horrifying pieces into place. "She didn't meet me because somebody killed her. Oh my God."

"It's a safe assumption. She made up the name Sally so you wouldn't find out her true identity. We have no idea what scandal she planned to tell you about. It's too bad she wasn't more forthcoming when she emailed you."

"Maybe somebody found out she'd contacted the news media and killed her to keep her from talking."

"Perhaps. Did you communicate with her by phone or any other means?"

"No. You have all the email exchanges."

They were standing less than an arm's length apart. Hunter's blue eyes studied her like a laser cutting into her core. She needed to shut this down before she said something that would make her look foolish. "Is there anything else?" Her voice came across harsher than she intended.

A change in his expression, and whatever message he'd been telegraphing disappeared. "I wanted to check with you before Auger hears about the emails."

"Auger." She said his name aloud and inwardly recoiled. She'd confronted him once about allegations of abuse made by two female employees in Toronto that both women had dropped. He had no love for her. "Thanks for the heads-up." Nothing would be gained telling Hunter her worst fears. "Tony invited you for dinner, by the way. He's hosting a storm party."

"I'll stop in for a minute but should be back on the road soon if I'm going to make it home to Kanata."

"We can always find a couch for you to sleep on."

"Now, why does that not seem appealing?" He grinned.

"I did have mine cleaned last month. Tony thought it a waste of money, but the couch is comfortable enough, albeit somewhat worn."

"I'll come with you for a drink and see about dinner. Might be good to eat. I don't think I've managed much food the last few days."

"Then you have to stay."

The lights flickered for a moment but remained on,

and Ella breathed a sigh of relief. "Let's get downstairs before we have to feel our way in the dark."

CHAPTER 23

Liam opened one eye and tried to place where he was. The events of the evening before started to come back to him, along with an ache in his head. He and Ella had joined the others in Tony's living room, and he'd been talked into one of Tony's martinis. That led to a second, a third, and dinner and cognac with dessert, all of which grew fuzzier as the hours passed. The power had shuddered off after the meal, and he had a distinct memory of walking upstairs guided by the beam of a flashlight to Ella's apartment to crash on her couch.

He turned his head on the pillow and blinked. Ella lay next to him, resting on her side with her naked back toward him. "We can keep each other warm," she'd said before they took off their clothes in the dark and climbed under the covers.

He lifted the sheet and saw he'd wisely left on his socks … but nothing else. He put a hand over his eyes. *They hadn't … no, he'd remember that.* He was about to ease himself onto the floor when Ella rolled toward him and put a hand on the blanket covering his hip. She snuggled closer, and then her body went still. Her eyes snapped open.

"Liam?" Her voice sounded puzzled. She sat up, clutching the blanket to her chest, and stared at him staring at her. She moaned softly. "It's coming back to me."

"Should I make us some coffee?" he asked, wanting to give her time to process the two of them spending the night in her bed. He nearly blushed as the memory of their long goodnight kiss filtered back. Her fingers in his hair, his hands on her body. "Power appears to be back, by the looks of your flashing clock."

"Coffee would be good." She flopped against the pillow and closed her eyes. "We can't let Tony know about this."

"Agreed."

"My head is pounding. Damn that man and his martinis."

Liam dressed in the semi-dark and escaped into her galley kitchen. A moment later, he heard the shower start. By the time she emerged from the bedroom ten minutes later, dressed in jeans and an oversized sweater, the coffee had brewed and he'd filled two mugs. She gratefully accepted the cup he handed her, and they settled in the living room, him on the couch and her in the desk chair. She looked slightly more awake but no less hungover. He hadn't any idea what to say to her and was relieved when she spoke first.

"I can't pretend that wasn't pleasant last night." She stared at him with an open expression, her usual prickly guard gone.

"It was that." He took a gulp of coffee and rested the mug on his thigh. "The thing is, Georgina—"

"Of course." She looked away, and when her eyes returned to his face, the wall was back in place, any trace of intimacy gone. "We'll say no more about last night. It never happened as far as anybody else has to know."

"Ella, if I could—"

"But you can't, so let's stop talking about it." She rotated to look out the window. "You'll need to dig out your car. I hear the snowplough coming this way."

"I should be on my way then." He swallowed the last of the coffee and stood. The awkwardness that had sprung up between them made his voice come out too formal, as if they'd just completed a business meeting. "Thanks for clearing up those emails about your correspondence with Marnie. I'll be in touch when we find out more."

"I'd appreciate that."

She didn't walk him to the door. He hesitated on the landing outside her apartment. If he returned to her now, what would he say? The urge to make things right fought with his natural reticence to ride out uncomfortable situations. He'd have liked to grab Ella out of her chair and finish what they started last night, but the moment for such action had passed. She'd made that clear. He pulled the phone out of his jacket pocket and checked messages. Two from Georgina asking where he was. He clicked on her number and said hello as he started down the stairs.

———

Sara woke from a deep dream. A cobra had wrapped itself around the length of her body, and she was frantically trying to kick her way free. It took a moment for her to realize she was twisted up in a blanket, lying in a recliner in front of the gas fireplace in the den. Nikki was on the couch, and Jeremy lay stretched out on the floor, both swaddled in blankets and sound asleep. Sara listened to the soft in and out of their breathing while she attuned herself to other noises. Something had woken her, and every one of her senses was on alert. The wind had eased, no longer battering against the window pane, but the power was still off. She'd left a lamp turned on in the far corner as a touchstone for when the power was restored, but the space remained in darkness. The room had chilled, even with the fireplace emitting heat that made the air dry and stifling. She reached for her cell phone on the table next to her. Two a.m. Monday morning. Still six hours until daylight.

She closed her eyes, but her initial unease kept her from falling back to sleep. After trying for ten minutes more, she moved the chair back into the upright position and tossed aside the blankets. Careful not to waken the others, she skirted around them and into the hall. She stood for a moment, letting her eyes adjust to the darkness and shadows. She'd forgotten to pick up a flashlight on her way out of the room but could make her way around the house without it. A car door slammed, and she strained to listen for other noises. Had she heard properly, or was her nervous mind playing tricks? She scooted toward the front of the house, silent as a cat in her sock feet. Greyish light streaming through the windows guided her to the living room, where she angled herself behind a curtain to look outside.

The snow had stopped falling, and the treetops swayed less vigorously in the dying wind. She glimpsed pockets of sky glowing silvery white through wispy tendrils of the thinning cloud cover. Gazing past the snowdrifts to the street, she saw a black car with lights off but engine running at the end of her dad's laneway, pointing in the wrong direction, as if ready to make a quick getaway. The exhaust from its tailpipe rose in a plume and hung in the frosty air. Sara moved farther back to get a wider view of the car. Caught in the streetlight, two men stood behind the trunk, talking. One of them partially turned, and she recognized the guy who'd approached the counter at work and asked about Nikki. She moved closer to the glass and cupped her hands around her eyes. Her heart pounded double time as the significance of his presence outside her father's house at 2:00 a.m. sank in. She crouched and backed away from the window, turned and raced down the hallway to the den. Both Nikki and Jeremy slumbered, unaware of the danger. Sara knelt by the couch.

"Nikki," she whispered, shaking her shoulder. "Nikki, wake up."

"Mmm. What's going on?" Nikki uncurled herself and stretched like a cat, arms above her head.

"Two men are outside, and I recognized one of them. He was at the coffee shop asking about you. He tracked me to my mother's house, and she told him I was staying here, at Dad's."

"Holy shit." Nikki sprang to a sitting position and set her feet on the floor. Like Sara, she was dressed in a couple of layers, a sweatshirt and pants over flannel pajamas and wool socks. Her eyes frantically searched the room. "Can they get in? Is the power on?"

"The power's still off. I guess they could smash their way through a window, but the alarm is on because it works off a battery. It'll take the alarm company a long time to get here, though, with all the snow on the roads."

Their voices woke Jeremy, and he propped himself up on the floor. "What's going on?"

"Nikki's ex has buddies trying to find her, and two of them are standing next to a car on the street in front of our driveway."

"They're violent people." Nikki said. "Maybe … maybe I should just go outside so they don't hurt anybody or damage the house."

"No way," Sara said. "You're not going back with that guy. And I could care less about this house."

"I'll check it out. Maybe get your boots and coats on in case we have to leave in a hurry." Jeremy grabbed his jacket from where he'd tossed it on a table and was zipping it up as he stepped into the hall.

"I'm so, so sorry," Nikki said. "I should never have come here. I should have explained—"

"I know you're in bigger trouble than you let on, but let's not worry about that now. I'll go get our boots by the back door, and I'll meet you in the living room."

Sara grabbed two flashlights and tossed one to Nikki before turning off the gas fireplace. "Don't let them see your light through the window." She kept her beam pointed at the floor, and they separated at the entrance to the den. The darkness gave them an advantage if the men got into the house. She knew her way around, and they'd need time to orient themselves. She ran down the hall into the kitchen.

Their three sets of boots were drying on the mat in

front of the sliding patio doors. She turned off the flashlight and sidled closer, checking that nobody was outside. She stopped moving when she heard a bang and scraping noises coming from the direction of the front door. A few seconds later, Jeremy and Nikki joined her in the kitchen.

"They've got a crowbar or something and are breaking in the front. I'm pretty sure I saw one of them holding a knife when they walked up the steps." Jeremy's voice was low and controlled, but Sara heard the urgency they all were feeling.

"Everyone put your boots on. We'll go out the back while they're busy breaking in the front." Sara slipped into her own boots. "Once they trigger the alarm, we'll get out though this door, run to the side gate, and then to Jeremy's car." Her voice was way more confident than she felt.

"My car will be covered in snow. Could take a while to get it going and on the road." Jeremy's slow, measured voice helped to calm her even if his words didn't.

"You both get to the car as fast as you can and work on that. I'll see about slowing them down."

"No," Nikki said. "It's too dangerous. Come with us."

"I won't be far behind." Sara hoped she wasn't making a false promise.

"This is all my fault," Nikki wailed. "I should have known he wouldn't let me go."

"Well, he's going to have to learn he can't always get what he wants."

Sara straightened and stepped away from the door into the kitchen. She pulled the sharpest serrated knife from the butcher block and held it loosely at her side as she moved to open the door once the alarm went off and masked the noise of their escape. Jeremy caught her eye and nodded. He was ready to get Nikki out of there and had given silent agreement for Sara to have their backs. She'd only use the knife to scare them off, with no intention of stabbing anybody. She'd need to make certain they didn't take it off her, because she had a feeling they'd turn the weapon on her without hesitation if given half the chance. Then she thought of a better idea.

CHAPTER 24

The security alarm blasted throughout the house. Sara raised her arm and signalled for Jeremy that it was time to get moving. He slid the patio door open, and the three of them filed outside into the bitterly cold night air, the girls stepping ahead of Jeremy to the edge of the deck. He eased the door back into place and followed Sara and Nikki down the steps, wading through the foot of fresh snow, guided by the beam of their flashlights aimed at the ground. The two men had already entered the house by the front door, and Sara imagined them going room to room, searching for Nikki, knife at the ready. The snow was uncomfortably deep, but Sara broke ground, and Jeremy and Nikki trod closely behind in her footsteps. She'd chosen a path along the outer edge of the deck and steps, hoping to escape detection if the men looked outside. Again, the darkness would work in their favour.

The going was tougher as they neared the gate, but since Jeremy and Nikki had shovelled out a path before the last round of snowfall, Sara was able to wedge the gate open enough to pass through. Jeremy picked up one of the shovels that he'd left leaning against the garage.

"Don't take too long," he said to her.

"I won't."

He patted her shoulder on the way past. She waited until they'd gotten to the other side of the driveway and checked the windows of the house to make certain nobody was watching. Then she hurried up the laneway to the road and crouched behind the black car, the engine turned off now. The security alarm was barely audible from this distance, not strident enough to wake the neighbours, but she knew it had triggered a signal to the monitoring company. She raised the knife and jammed it into the centre of the sidewall in one quick thrust and made an incision across its width, keeping her face averted to avoid the escaping air. Hoping she'd done enough damage, she crab-walked to the front of the car and repeated the process. She'd read up on how to slash a tire as part of her PI studies, never believing the information would come in handy. She'd be exposed in a sightline from her dad's house if she cut the other two tires, so this would have to do.

Keeping in a crouch, she began running toward Jeremy's car as she heard the front door of the house opening. She glanced back. One of the men was standing on the top front step and was yelling into the house. Her foot slipped on a piece of ice, and she tumbled, landing heavily on her side. She rolled and scrambled forward on her hands and knees and pushed herself up into standing position. Adrenaline pumped through her, overriding the pain in her ankle as she limped and hopped toward Jeremy as fast as she could go. He was shovelling a path in front of his car, the engine running and headlights cutting through the darkness. Behind him, Nikki was frantically clearing snow from the windows, the roof still covered in a foot-high layer.

"They've seen me," Sara yelled. "We've got to get out of here."

Nikki took one last swipe at the back window, and Jeremy continued shovelling while the girls got into the car. Once Sara slammed her door, he ran back and tossed the shovel into the open trunk, rammed it shut, and climbed into the front seat. The tires whirred and caught, and they lurched forward. Sara stared out the side window. One of the men was running toward them, a dark shape with arms and legs pumping. The tires spun on a drift of snow and ice, stopping their forward momentum. Snow from the roof slid onto the trunk with a loud thud.

"Go, go." Nikki pounded on the back seat.

Jeremy shifted the car into reverse, then second gear, repeated, and the car rocked as the tires gained traction. The man loomed to Sara's right and thumped on the window at the same time as the car revved and swerved onto the road. He continued running alongside, his hand grasping at the door handle until they pulled away and left him chasing their exhaust.

"Turn right here," Sara said, "and right again at the corner."

Jeremy navigated the snowy streets through the sleeping residential neighbourhood. He pulled onto Carling Avenue on his way to the Queensway that would take them downtown. Sara looked behind them. A police car was turning onto the street they'd just left.

"Those two thugs should get caught in the act. I think we can relax a bit, Nikki."

"Thank God." Nikki slumped back in the seat, and Sara righted herself to face out the front window.

Jeremy glanced at her. "Where to now?"

"Not sure anybody wants to see us at this hour. Those guys know about my mother's house, so not a great choice." She tried to think. It wasn't as if she had many friends.

"My dorm room has two beds, and my roommate went home for the week because his dad's in the hospital. You both can sleep there, and I'll crash in the lounge," Jeremy said.

"Are you sure? Can you even bring strangers into your residence?"

"Shouldn't be a problem. Nikki will be safe until we figure out what to do next."

"I really appreciate your help, but why are you doing this?" Sara stared at his profile. He glanced over.

"Why are you?"

Sara turned sideways and checked that Nikki wasn't listening. She kept her voice low. "Nikki seemed so lost and desperate when she sat all day in the coffee shop where I work. I couldn't just leave her, especially when she told me about escaping an abusive situation." Sara shrugged. "Plus, I like a challenge that involves outsmarting bad people. Your turn. Why are you helping us?"

"You're interesting. Then I find out you're a one-woman crusader. How could I not play backup?"

"How in the world could I possibly interest you?" She honestly didn't see it.

"The way you concentrate on the lecture and tune

out everybody and thing around you. Your questions
that are never predictable but always insightful. The way
you smile when you think something's funny. Yeah, I'd
be stupid not to find you intriguing."

"I'm … surprised, to put it mildly."

"You underestimate yourself, McGowan."

She shook her head. "I don't think so. I've always
been an outsider." He'd learned her last name without
her telling him. She was oddly flattered.

"I make my own decisions about the people I want
in my life."

She didn't know how to reply to that. Was he
implying that he wanted her to be his friend? She
tamped down the hope fluttering in her chest. Being a
loner was something she understood. The unseen one in
a room full of people. In a way, this was her superpower.
She wasn't ready to open herself up to more pain,
because in her experience that was what came whenever
she let anybody in. It wasn't a lesson she wanted to
repeat. Even if the person appeared as good and kind as
Jeremy.

———

CASSIE ROSE before her dad and was surprised not to
find Wilma in the kitchen. The storm had ended in the
wee hours, and she could hear a city snowplough
clearing the street as she returned to the living room to
look outside. Wesley Saunders was across the road,
using a snow blower to clear his driveway while his dog
Nova watched through the living room window. Cassie's
dad had hired a company to do the clearing of his
property, and their truck pulled up before she turned

away. A massive amount of snow blanketed the streets and lawns, sparkling in the unfiltered morning sunshine, the sky a brilliant blue dome above the houses. Cassie thought about taking a walk after breakfast so as not to miss the beauty of the day. Even in heartache, there was much to appreciate. The constants that kept one going.

She started back to the kitchen. Heath would still be sleeping and wouldn't have opened her text yet. He'd need to read it twice through before his brain would accept that she'd ended their relationship. The anger would come later once the truth sank in. He'd been so certain she'd relent and give him another chance. For a while, she'd leaned that way, but this time away from her life in Vancouver had given her new perspective and a backbone. She wouldn't allow herself to become the suspicious partner, always watching to see if he was going to stray again — and that's what would happen if they stayed together. Trust had been the bedrock, and hers now rested on quicksand. She deserved better.

"There you are." Cassie spun around. Wilma stood in the doorway watching her. "I've slept in but will have breakfast on the table in a few minutes. French toast okay?"

"Lovely. I was about to put on the coffee."

"No need. I'll have it ready in a few minutes."

"Perfect. Thanks, Wilma." Cassie wanted to ask if there was something else on her mind, but Wilma left before she had the chance. Wilma and her family had been so odd since she arrived, even odder after Marnie's death. Their behaviour was understandable but still unsettling.

Cassie followed her into the kitchen a few minutes

later and sat on a stool at the island, leaning both elbows on the counter.

"I've set you a place in the dining room," Wilma said without turning around. "Go take a seat and I'll bring your coffee."

"Of course." Cassie got up and moved into the adjoining room. The space was too formal for her liking, especially for breakfast alone, but Wilma obviously wanted her gone from the kitchen. Coffee, French toast, bacon and a bowl of fresh fruit — Wilma served up the meal and lingered after fetching Cassie a napkin from the hutch.

"Is there something you'd like to talk about, Wilma?"

"Not particularly. Have you decided when you'll be returning to Vancouver?"

"I'll have to check with the police, but I'm booked three days from now. Would you like me to stay longer?"

"I believe the sooner we get back to normal, the better for your father."

"Has he been … forgetful lately?"

"Your father is fine. He's no more forgetful than I am. Have your brothers been putting that idea in your head?"

"They're concerned."

"Nonsense. They thought he'd lost his senses by bringing Marnie into his life and had no use for her. Your dad's declining mental state would have been too easy an explanation."

"You haven't said how you felt about Dad remarrying."

"Not my place, is it? Especially with what happened to her." Wilma smoothed the edge of the tablecloth.

"Marnie was pleasant to me. Sometimes she sat in the kitchen and drank tea while I prepared lunch. She seemed to like having company. I had no cause to dislike her, although I have to admit I didn't approve of the idea of her. She'd inserted herself into our family and was creating dissension."

"Did she reveal anything about her past to you?"

"Not that I remember. She was a private one, that's for sure, but she wasn't snooty or unkind. Just young. Too young for your father."

"Why do you think—"

"He took up with her? She brought out his protective side. There was something lost about the woman. Didn't hurt that she made him feel young again. Foolish man." Wilma pursed her lips and shook her head. "No need to rehash it anymore. I'll leave you to enjoy your breakfast."

Cassie sat with her elbow on the table and hand cupping her chin after Wilma returned to the kitchen, thinking over recent conversations. Wilma's take on Marnie and her dad contradicted everyone else's. Based on the rest of her family's opinions, she'd been picturing Marnie as a money-grabbing, conniving woman who'd scammed her father. Which version was the truth?

The front doorbell rang, and Cassie heard Wilma greet Khloe and Mick in the foyer. They joined her in the dining room a minute later while Wilma bustled about pouring coffee and setting out more fruit and croissants.

"Dad still sleeping?" Mick asked before biting into an apple.

"He hasn't come downstairs yet." Cassie added

cream to her second cup of coffee. "Is Gordon teaching today?"

"Yup." Khloe gave a sideways grimace. "He's what you call a workaholic, always the first one in and last out of the school. It was tough for him to book time away from his class for your dad's wedding. He's been taking courses and plans to apply for a vice principal position at the end of this term."

"Why that's wonderful. And you, Mick. When do you need to be back at school?"

"I should be there now, but I have to check in with the police to see if it's okay if I leave Ottawa. I don't want them wondering if I'm fleeing the scene of the crime or something."

"I doubt they'd think that. You drove up from Kingston after Marnie was dead."

Mick met her eyes and quickly looked away. "Let's hope they see it that way."

Khloe glanced toward the door and back at Cassie. Her voice dropped. "Did you know Wilma was planning to retire after the marriage?"

"You're kidding." Cassie couldn't imagine this was true. Wilma had no other family or interests that she knew of. She'd dedicated her life to them.

"Her nose was out of joint when Marnie moved in. I think the inappropriateness of your dad's choice was a step too far."

"When I spoke with Wilma earlier, she didn't seem that opposed to Marnie."

"Hah. Then she's putting a new spin on reality."

They stopped talking as Wilma glided into the room, carrying a bowl of strawberries. She didn't look at any of them as she set it in the middle of the table. Khloe's face turned a rosy shade as a blush reached her cheeks. Cassie could not be certain Wilma hadn't overheard their conversation. Wilma straightened and took a step back. "Will Foster and Deirdre be here for lunch or dinner?" She directed her question to Cassie, but Khloe answered.

"Deirdre plans to be over late afternoon. Foster is in the office today, but I expect we'll all be here for dinner, if that doesn't mean too much work for you, Wilma. We can always order in or go to a restaurant. Mick and Cassie will be leaving soon, so we want to spend as much time as we can together before then."

"I'd prepared chicken cordon bleu for the wedding. Will that do?"

"That would be wonderful. Thanks, Wilma."

"Then I'll see to it." Wilma nodded and left them alone. Cassie heard her footsteps recede down the hallway into the kitchen.

"Yikes, that was awkward," Khloe said. "I hope she wasn't listening."

"And what if she was?" Mick said. "It's not as if she's part of our family. Dad pays her well to look after him and the house."

"She *is* a big part of our family. She pretty much raised you after Mom died, for God's sake." *And let you get away with just about everything,* Cassie thought but didn't say aloud. Mick never liked being criticized.

"Whatever. She's still an employee. Speaking of workaholics, Deirdre said Foster has been putting in a lot of overtime. I gotta say, my brothers are way more ambitious than I am."

"You're still young and footloose. Once you have a

family and responsibilities, you'll be the same." Khloe smiled fondly at him.

"I'm not convinced. As long as I have enough money to live well, why waste my life chained to a nine-to-five? You have the right idea, Khloe. Staying home, raising two kids. Genius once they get old enough to look after themselves, and you have all day to eat chocolates and read books. However, I'm not even sure about being tied down to one person long enough to have a family."

"You need to find something you enjoy doing that's meaningful. Then it doesn't feel like work," Cassie said.

"Like your acting? Not sure how meaningful it is to pretend to be someone else in front of a camera all day, but okay."

"You can be a real prick sometimes, you know that?" Cassie wanted to say more, but the distress on Khloe's face and Mick's big grin stopped her. She took a deep breath and calmed herself down. "Thanks for pulling my leg, but I'm not in the mood this morning."

"There's still a lot to do taking care of two teenagers and a house. It's not like I sit around all day. Gordon is always at school or prepping lessons. Somebody has to keep our lives running." Khloe's face was troubled, her voice defensive. Gordon had told Cassie a few times that he needed Khloe to get a job and help with expenses, but she'd refused.

Mick grinned at her. "Sure, Khloe," he said. "Bobby, Trisha, and Gordon would be lost without you."

Cassie pushed up from the table. Khloe hadn't caught the note of sarcasm and appeared placated. It was time to leave before she lost it on Mick. "I'm going to check in with Dad and freshen up. I'll be down in a bit."

Mick and Khloe were both engrossed in scrolling through their phone screens when she stopped in the doorway and looked back. If Heath were here, they'd go for a walk and dissect what was going on with her family, perhaps even laugh at the absurdities. He had a way of making terrible situations seem less awful. She was going to need to stop saving up things to tell him. She had to accept the loss of her best friend and get on with forging a new life on her own.

CHAPTER 25

Liam put on sunglasses and left Ella's building, a headache throbbing dully in his temples. He walked around the corner to his car parked on Third Avenue and cleared off the windows while the engine warmed the interior. He was fortunate not to have been towed or given a ticket with a citywide ban on street parking enforced during snowfalls. He loved mornings like this, even with a martini hangover: crisp and clear, the sky satin-blue and cloudless. The aftermath of the storm still clogged the side streets even as snowploughs continued their work. The hydro crews had also toiled through the night. The radio newscast reported several areas of the city still in the dark. He climbed into the driver's seat and thought about waking up next to Ella. His skin burned at the remembrance of her touch.

He stopped at Daisy's café on Bronson and ordered a couple of breakfast sandwiches and a large coffee to go. Daisy appeared to have the day off, replaced by a lad who looked young enough to be in high school. Liam glanced over at the booth where he and Ella usually sat whenever they met for breakfast. He'd feed her information to point her in the right direction on cases, and she'd share whatever she uncovered. He wondered if last night would put an end to their collaboration. The idea of not having her in his life darkened the day.

Quade was at her desk when he arrived at HQ. She glanced up at him over the top of her computer. "Rough night, mate? Jeezus, you look as if you drank a bottle of screech."

"Tony. Martinis. Late night."

"Say no more, although I appreciate that you had a chance to unwind for a few hours. Roads still atrocious?"

"Main roads are clear, but not the side streets."

Quade leaned back in her chair. "The report on Marnie Vaughan arrived early this morning. Green must have been burning the midnight oil, since she only finished the autopsy yesterday. Jingles sat in. She texted me that her report was uploaded into the system around 5:00 a.m., so I got here an hour later to check it out."

"Thanks for taking that on."

"You're welcome, and I'll be thanking you next time."

"So, anything interesting?"

"Died by strangulation, as we already knew. Throttled with a pair of strong hands, likely wearing gloves. She was moved from wherever she was murdered to the location off the trail. No discernible forensic evidence left by the killer on her body or clothes. Marnie was also wearing gloves, so nothing under her fingernails."

"Almost sounds planned."

"Strangulation is usually an up-close and personal kind of crime. I was disappointed by the lack of new leads in Green's report."

Liam thought for a moment. "The family members said Marnie didn't know anybody in Ottawa. She'd only just moved here when she met Peter Grady four months ago. That puts each of them in the spotlight, especially since their alibis are nonexistent."

"Yet we still haven't figured out her true identity, so who knows what people were in her past? It's amazing really, how she pulled it off. Peter didn't appear to question her story very closely. Nor did his kids. You'd think the oldest two sons would have checked her out on the sly at the very least."

"An interesting idea and one worth pursuing with Foster and Gordon. There was a lot of money at stake. She could have had accomplices and other victims. Scammers can be convincing. How often have we seen a senior victimized? It's only in hindsight that people see the warning signs. Although getting married four months after meeting a woman half their father's age is a big red flag." Liam opened another report on his screen. "No match for her fingerprints on the system, and no family member has come forward. The parents and brother she spoke about living in Europe have been impossible to locate, if they even exist."

"We're going to have to post her photo and ask for the public's help again. I'll run the idea by Auger when he gets in."

"I'll work on the notice in the meantime."

"And I'll check in with the tech team to see what they've found on her laptop."

Liam opened a new file and began typing. He was interrupted periodically by phone calls as he drafted the text and each time had to refocus. At nine ten, Auger called him and Quade into his office for an update before the entire team met in the boardroom at ten thirty. Auger agreed to another public notice and said to get the Communications team involved. "You've made little progress, and the clock is ticking. Leave no stone unturned," he said as they were leaving.

"Leave no stone unturned," Quade muttered under her breath. "What does he think we've been doing? What kind of damn pep talk was that?"

Liam dropped into his seat and picked up a pen. "Ignore him, Quade. He's trying to get under your skin."

"He does have that uncanny ability."

"We need to go through the process and continue being methodical. Isn't that what you always say?"

"It is. Thanks, Hunter." She sat and began working on her computer. After a moment, her hands stilled. "I've got a message from Mick Grady asking if he can go back to Kingston. He's been missing classes at university."

"I don't see why not. We have his statement and know how to reach him."

"I agree. I'll reply." She began typing and stopped a second time. "Like we said yesterday, we should take a closer look at each of the Grady family members beyond simply checking out their alibis while we wait to learn more about Marnie."

"Let's bring in Boots and Jingles. They've been handling the alibis and might have some information. No point going over the same ground."

"I got a note that they'll be in the office around ten. I'll talk to them about it then."

"And I'll give Media Relations a heads up about the public notice. Turning over one stone at a time." He grinned at her before swinging back around to his computer.

———

BY EARLY AFTERNOON, the hangover and lack of sleep caught up and steamrollered over Liam. He managed to keep working until three thirty before sending a message to the team and Auger that he was leaving for the day.

"Call if you need me," he told Quade as he put on his parka and boots.

"I'll manage. You get some sleep … and whatever you do, don't stop by to see Tony on your way home."

"Wild horses couldn't drag me up to that man's apartment."

He received a call as he was taking the stairs to his car in the underground parking lot. He almost ignored it, but a sense of responsibility won out, and he pulled the phone from his pocket. *Rosie Thorburn*. He clicked to answer. "Hey, Rosie, how are you?"

"Good. I'm good. Settling into my new job."

"We miss you in Major Crimes."

"And I miss you. Is now a good time to talk?"

He'd reached the bottom step and pulled the door open, moving into the hall. "Sure. What's up, Rosie?"

"A weird incident that I thought might interest you. Remember Sara McGowan?"

"How could I forget? Has something happened to her?"

"I don't think so. Her father's house on Locke Isle Road was broken into last night. Sara had been staying there, according to the neighbour across the street, but she and her car are nowhere to be seen. We contacted her mother, and she had no idea where Sara was, but she managed to reach her daughter by phone while I waited on hold. Sara said she couldn't get her car started after class at Carleton, and she's bunking with a friend in one of the residences."

"So, she wasn't at her father's house when it got broken into?"

"Apparently not although another neighbour said Sara had parked her car in her driveway for a while. She never saw Sara leave. There was a power failure in the neighbourhood most of the night, but the alarm system is on a battery, and the security service contacted the police when it was triggered. We arrived ten to fifteen minutes after we received notification. The snowed-in roads and storm held us up."

"You were on the call?"

"Yes, I'm on the Crystal Bay, Britannia beat for the next month."

"Catch anybody?"

"No, but we found a car with two tires slashed in front of the McGowan house. It had stolen plates."

"That's odd." He thought for a moment, picturing the quiet dead-end street, lined in trees and shrubbery on both sides with houses widely spaced. The homes on the north side backed onto the Ottawa River. A wealthy neighbourhood. Not a reach to believe random break-ins a possibility. "The car had to belong to whoever broke into the house, because there'd be no other reason for a car with stolen plates and flat tires to be there. I wonder how the tires got slashed."

"It's a mystery. The vehicle hadn't been parked long enough to be covered in much snow. Nothing was stolen from the house as far as we could determine, but snow and mud had been tracked in on their boots, and two sets of footprints were visible all over the downstairs. They were men's boots by the size of the treads."

"David McGowan made enemies, although it's been nearly half a year since his arrest. This feels like something unrelated, although who knows at this point. It would be good to talk with Sara."

"I'm heading off shift. The file has been turned over to the B & E division. Unlikely they'll follow up with her, since she wasn't home and nothing was taken. Anyhow, thought you might find it interesting."

"I do. Thanks, Rosie. It's been good to hear from you. Let's keep in touch."

"Sure, partner. Say hi to the team."

He walked toward his car while pondering the strangeness of Rosie's call. If he hadn't been so exhausted, he'd take a run out to see Sara's mother in the east end. Someone else could do that. He pulled the phone back out of his pocket and opened the message app. Ella and Sara had formed a bond, and he knew she'd follow up if he asked. He typed an overview with the highlights and sent it to her, stopping himself from saying anything personal. They needed to talk about what had happened face-to-face, when both were rested and had time to think about what the night together meant. His relationship with Ella had always been complicated, but their friendship predated Georgina, and he didn't want to give her up. He had no idea what that meant long-term, but until he'd worked through his feelings, he wouldn't say anything to Georgina. He wasn't certain how long he could put off her suggestion that they move their relationship to the next level, but for tonight, all he could focus on was making it home to Kanata without falling asleep at the wheel.

CHAPTER 26

"Who were you talking to just now?" Nikki asked as she plopped down on the single bed across from Sara.

"My mom. The cops phoned her about the break-in." Sara's cell had rung while Nikki was in the washroom down the hall, and she'd returned as Sara was signing off.

"Does she know about me?"

"Nope. I said my car conked out and I was staying with a friend in residence. That will likely surprise her, since I haven't got any friends."

"I hope I'm your friend, and sure looks like Jeremy wants to be." Nikki smiled. "Don't sell yourself short."

"Jeremy? I think he's more interested in you. He'd be stupid not to be." Sara squirmed inside at Nikki's assessment but liked that she'd called her a friend. Jeremy had also said she was selling herself short. Had they been discussing her?

"I never got that impression. Besides, I'm honestly not interested in a relationship with anybody. It's going to take a while, I guess. Maybe never." Nikki studied her. "What went down with your father? Is he in jail?"

"My dad let down a lot of people, and one of them ended up dead, although I'm happy to say he wasn't the killer. He owned a financial investment company and was ripping people off. Lying's his chosen lifestyle."

"Sounds like he let you down too."

"And I'm sorry your ex put you through what he did." She paused, hoping Nikki would fill in some of the blanks, but she remained silent.

There was a light rap on the door, and Sara got up from the bed to let Jeremy in. They were in his room, but he was being careful not to crowd them — or so Sara thought. He was carrying a cardboard carton with three coffees and a bag of sandwiches. He handed everything around before sitting in his desk chair and turning it to face them.

Sara took a bite of the tuna sandwich and set it down on the wrapper. She tried not to sound demanding, but things had escalated, and there was no time to wait for Nikki to reveal the truth of what was going on, if she even planned to do so. She leaned forward on her knees and waited for Nikki to look at her. "If we're going to figure out the best way to help you, we need to know the full story."

"I've told you, my boyfriend—"

"Is abusive, but this effort to track you down goes beyond possessive. He and his friend are willing to risk jail time to find you. They've been to both of my parents' houses, broken in, threatened us. What's really going on, Nikki?"

Nikki looked from Sara to Jeremy. He'd stopped with the coffee cup halfway to his mouth while Sara spoke.

He lowered the cup and said, "I can leave the room if you'd rather talk to Sara alone."

"No, we all seem to be in this together. I'm just worried that you won't want anything more to do with me once I tell you. I never should have gotten either of you involved." Nikki frowned and looked down at the sandwich in her hands.

"It looked to me like you had no choice. Besides, I offered," Sara said. "It's getting important that we have the entire picture. We won't stop helping, Nikki, no matter what."

"All right." Nikki took a moment before she looked up at them. "I'll give you some context first, though, so you know how it happened. My parents raised me in a small town out west. We didn't have much money, but they tried to give me every advantage. I was fifteen when my dad died, and money got even tighter, not to mention Mom and I were devastated by his loss. When I turned sixteen, my girlfriend Lorna and I saw an ad for counsellors at a summer camp in Ontario. We both liked the outdoors, and the pay was decent. They even paid our way to Thunder Bay. A few days before we were set to get on the plane, Lorna backed out. The reason isn't important. Mom and I decided that I'd go anyway. I needed to make money, and there weren't many opportunities in my town. So, I showed up alone in Thunder Bay." She trailed off, and Sara encouraged her with her eyes to continue, even though she had a good idea what was coming. Jeremy shifted positions in his chair, but otherwise the room was silent.

"Yeah, so it went okay at first. A woman and man met my plane. They seemed so nice. Kind, you know, and—" Her voice broke.

Sara had never seen anyone come apart so fast and so completely. She moved across the space and wrapped an arm around Nikki's shaking shoulders until their heads were touching. "You don't need to explain. It must have been horrific." She felt Nikki's forehead rub up and down against her in a nod.

Nikki pulled away. Her cheeks glistened with tears. "I had nobody to help me. They took away my phone and wouldn't let me go anywhere."

"How did you end up in Ottawa?"

"They moved us around to motels in different cities. First Windsor and then Toronto. A few months ago, they shipped me here, and Montreal was probably next. There were several of us. One of the men running the operation liked me and put me up in a condo when I came to Ottawa. He started getting me hooked on heroin when we were in Toronto."

"Monsters."

"He locked me in, and there was a camera in the hall in case I tried to break out. It took a while, but I watched and learned the alarm code and the best way to evade the camera. He could have seen me those times I left the condo if he looked at the footage really close, but he figured I was high all the time. I visited a free clinic a few times and got help detoxing. Every time I went out, I thought he'd see on the video and hurt me when I got back. Those were scary days."

"Without judgement, why didn't you tell someone when you were at the clinic?" Sara asked.

"He said he'd find me if I ever left and make me pay. He threatened to kill my mother and post videos of me doing sex acts. I needed to get clean, and that took a few months, but lately I felt like time was running out. I overheard him telling one of his people that I was becoming a drain. He was going to put me back in circulation. I'd made friends with another girl I met at one of their parties in Toronto, and she said if we ever got out from these guys, we should leave our names and a way to make contact with a restaurant server in the ByWard Market that she knew from before, because we were being shipped here. I left my name and where I'd be waiting the last time I got out of the apartment — before I left for good — but she never responded. I'm beginning to think she never got away. Maybe she didn't get my message."

"You had to escape that guy. Are you still worried about your mom?"

"Always. I'm hoping they've forgotten where she lives, if they even knew. I've convinced myself they were bluffing to keep me in line, but I'm afraid to contact her. She's going to be so disappointed in me."

"None of what happened is your fault."

"Knowing and believing are two different things." Nikki swiped at her eyes with the back of both hands. "Somebody must have gone to the condo to check up on me, because they began looking for me the next day, that afternoon I met you, Sara."

Jeremy had been sitting silently. Sara caught his eye. "So, what do we do next?" he asked.

"If you could lend me a bit of money, I can go somewhere like a hostel or motel," Nikki said. "They'll leave you alone once I'm gone."

"Another option is a shelter, but none of those places beat staying with us."

"Yeah, we can do better than that," Jeremy said. "You're safe here for now."

"Agreed. What about contacting your mom, for starters? She must be worried sick." Sara was pleased Jeremy had stepped up. He was becoming more interesting the longer this went on.

"I'm scared they'll be watching her, even if that's irrational."

"Is there a family member or friend that you could contact to reach out and warn her?" Jeremy asked.

"Mom has a best friend, but I don't have her phone number."

"We can find it." Jeremy opened his laptop.

"I think we should go to the police," Sara said.

"Definitely not." Nikki shook her head. "The one thing I do believe from all the threats is that they'll find my family and kill them if I go to the police. They'll also post videos to ruin my life and to undermine whatever I say. Plus I don't trust the cops either."

"Do you have names?" Jeremy reached for a pen and paper.

"Some. I listened in on conversations when the man thought I was high and out of it. Once, when he was asleep, I went through his wallet."

"Who are they?"

"It's better for you if I keep that to myself."

Sara held up a hand. "We need to slow down for a minute and take time to organize a plan. As Jeremy said, Nikki, you're not in danger here. Let's contact your mom through her friend and then think about the best way to proceed after that." She wanted to bring in the police but needed to convince Nikki. This was bigger than anything they could handle. Human trafficking involved organized crime, not a group they were equipped to take on and win.

"I want so bad to go home and see my mom and have things go back to the way they were, but I'm not the same innocent, bright-eyed girl that left almost two years ago. I've done and seen things that are … horrible. Those videos—"

"You're still you, Nikki, and your mom will be so happy to have you back. I believe that with all my heart. We have to figure out the best way to make that happen so nobody gets hurt and those scumbags don't ruin your future."

Jeremy nodded. "You're not alone. Sara and I are going to do whatever it takes to get you home safe and make those criminals pay. Group hug."

They stood and wrapped their arms around each other. Sara liked the warmth of Jeremy's arm across her back, which seemed like a frivolous thing to focus on with the trouble Nikki was facing. Sara was the first to pull away. This wasn't a Nancy Drew mystery, and they weren't best friends. She needed time to think things through.

"Jeremy and I have class in twenty minutes and should carry on like normal. Let's wait to call your mom's friend until we get back."

"That'll give me time to figure out what to tell her," Nikki said. "Waiting a few more hours after all this time won't matter."

CHAPTER 27

Ella redialled Sara's number and scowled when the line went directly to voice mail. "Pick up, pick up." Saying the words aloud did no good.

She set the cell phone on her desk and returned to editing the latest podcast for her show, *Crime in the Rear View*. In the final segment, she'd given an update on the Marnie Vaughan murder, along with her impressions of the case. The police were being closed-mouthed, and there were many unanswered questions. She promised her followers to keep digging and would report developments as they happened. After adding the musical score produced by her late brother Danny that ended every edition, Ella published the podcast to her channel and sat back, pleased with her efforts. She didn't allow herself to wallow in self-satisfaction for long, however, before the familiar doubt returned. Had she done enough research? Was she producing these podcasts with sufficient depth? Her audience had grown to nearly two hundred thousand. She'd been called the voice for victims and the wrongfully accused. *The only honest one.* Some days, the responsibility weighed heavily.

She remembered Sara with deep fondness. There'd been a gawky loneliness about her, offset by intelligence and kindness that the girl had held close like unopened treasures. Hunter's message sharing his concern for Sara and the break-in at the Locke Isle Road house triggered her own unease. Sara had been reckless in many ways when their paths crossed during the past summer. Secretive to a fault. It couldn't hurt to check in on her.

Ella rose from her desk and pulled on her boots and outdoor clothes. Action was better than sitting and stewing. She tromped downstairs and outside into the crisp winter day. Half an hour later, after cleaning off her car and shovelling out the end of the driveway, she was on her way to see Sara's mother, Claudette McGowan, in the east end. The Queensway had been cleared of snow, and the drive went smoothly enough. When she pulled onto Claudette's street, only one car sat parked halfway up the driveway, which it turned out belonged to Claudette. Sara hadn't returned home, but she invited Ella in for a chat. They took seats at the kitchen table, and Claudette poured them each a glass of white wine.

"Lucky you caught me home today. I'm working offsite because of the weather yesterday. So, how've you been? Podcast business going well?"

"It's had its moments." Ella grinned. "Keeping me out of the food banks."

"I check your show once a week. It's something to tell people that I know you. Sara follows you religiously."

"Good to hear. Do you know where she is, exactly?"

"With some friend at university. She often stays at

her dad's, especially since this school term started, so I don't see her that often. She's becoming independent, as they say. Breaks my heart a bit, but give them space and they will come back, with any luck."

"Do you know the name of this friend?"

"No. In fact, I'm surprised she's made one." Claudette laughed, but not unkindly. "Sara is something of a loner. I was shocked to get a call about a break-in at her dad's. Good thing she wasn't there."

"You know that for certain?"

Claudette lowered her glass. "Why, is she in some kind of trouble?"

"Not that I know of, but I'd like to speak with her, and she's not answering her cell."

"I spoke with her after the break-in, and she said she hadn't been in the house when it happened. She's become so grown up." Claudette laughed again before her expression turned serious. "Ever since her father's troubles, she's been hard to understand. It's like she's turned inward and doesn't want to get close to anybody except her brother ... and even then..." Claudette sighed. "I'm happy if she's made a friend at university."

"Is she still working at the Dairy Queen on Bank?"

"No, she quit and took a job closer to our house at a Tim Hortons on St. Laurent. I'm not sure of her schedule."

Ella tried to hide her frustration by lifting the wine glass to her lips. Claudette had given nothing helpful, only seeming to know the shape but not the details of her daughter's life. Ella wasn't a parent, but she'd want to be more involved. Yet it might not be that simple. This was a family surviving trauma on a few fronts, and Sara was no longer a child. Ella pulled back on the judgement and softened her tone. "Would you like to give her a call now? I'd love to speak with her."

Claudette checked her watch. "I believe she's in class and won't answer. She shared her school timetable, and I remember that much at least. She has late afternoon lectures every weekday except Friday. Try her after six and she should be available."

"Will do."

Ella finished her wine and left shortly before five o'clock. On the way to her car, a message arrived from Sherry Carpenter.

R u close to the ByWard Market?

Not far. Why?

Am at Gleason's on Cumberland. Up for a drink?

On my way. 20 min

See u then

Ella waited for the car heater to defog the windshield and backed out of the driveway. She hadn't been getting much intel on the Marnie Vaughan murder and hoped Sherry had uncovered some information. It also didn't hurt to keep her mind occupied and off Liam Hunter. How in God's name had she let last night happen? Damn Tony and his martinis. It was bad enough she couldn't concentrate when Hunter was around without welcoming him into her bed. She pounded the steering wheel with the palm of her gloved hand. The man kept her off-balance with his annoyingly vivid eyes that crinkled when he laughed, and his too-long black hair and his lean, muscular body. She stopped at a red light and glared at the car in front of her. She'd let her guard down, pretended amnesia about Georgina, and been a fool. She would be certain never to let that happen again.

SHERRY GOT up from the bar stool and hugged Ella. "I snagged us a table. Follow me."

The restaurant had dimly lit nooks and corners, allowing patrons to spread out and have some privacy. Crystal chandeliers and green, velvet-covered seats added elegance to the dark wood wainscoting and abstract paintings. "Bernard says hi. He's in the kitchen getting a start on some orders."

"It's a lot, running the restaurant and being head chef."

"But he loves owning his own business. Preparing food is like breathing for him. His family fled poverty and war, and he's never taken this life for granted."

"Why, Sherry, if I didn't know you better, I'd say you were smitten."

Sherry smiled. "Yeah, I'm surprised too. Cynical, show-off, ladder-climbing little me. Who knew?"

"Well, I for one love this softer side."

They ordered glasses of wine, and plates of calamari and zucchini arrived soon afterwards.

"I took the liberty of ordering a few nibblies before you got here," Sherry said. "Time to relax and catch up."

"So why exactly did you want to meet?"

"I'm not sure how up to date you are on the woman found dead at Shirley's Bay."

"Marnie Vaughan. I only know what's available to the public." She wouldn't reveal anything Hunter had told her in confidence.

Sherry leaned closer and dropped her voice. "I have a contact on the police force who told me that Marnie

Vaughan wasn't her real name. They have no idea who she is."

"You're kidding."

"Nope. She was about to marry a wealthy architect named Peter Grady with a house in Rockcliffe, and he was completely taken in. Apparently, he and his family know as much about her as the police, which isn't much."

"A scam?"

"That's the theory. It opens a plethora of new avenues for who could have killed her."

"Wow." Ella rolled a piece of zucchini around in the garlic dip and took a bite. She chewed while she thought. "Have you interviewed Peter Grady?"

"I tried, but he hasn't responded to my calls. You have that special thing going with one of the detectives. Any chance you can get him talking?"

"I haven't really been working this case."

"But you could, and I need help. My cop contact doesn't have any more dirt, and my male colleagues are lining up to take the crime beat away from me. There's no way in hell I'm letting that happen. I need a scoop in a bad way."

"Canard won't screw you over."

"He may not have a choice. Believe me, misogyny is alive and well at *The Capital* and banding together like wild dogs ready to take down a deer."

Hunter was the last person Ella wanted to contact at this moment. The night before was too fresh. Yet she'd had a hand in getting Sherry this job and knew she was a good reporter. She could guess which of her past colleagues was behind the coup. "Let me see what I can find out. Give me a day."

Sherry grinned. "You're the best, and I won't forget it."

"Well, I haven't got anything for you yet, so hold your thanks until I do. There are no guarantees."

"Yeah, but you're the miracle worker." Sherry raised her glass and clinked Ella's. "Cheers to us and to not going down without a fight. The sisterhood rules."

CHAPTER 28

After Sara and Jeremy left for class, Nicola began pacing. She was used to being in a small space with nowhere to go, but she'd never accepted it like some of the girls. At least here the door was unlocked, and she was free to leave. She'd even opened and shut it twice to be sure. She wondered how long it would take for her to feel safe again. How long for the nightmares to stop waking her at 3:00 a.m., thrashing at imagined terrors, her body breaking out in a cold sweat?

She began reading the spines of Jeremy's books, neatly lined up on one side of the desk. Psychology, kinesiology, and biology textbooks took up most of the space. He also appeared to like murder mysteries. She picked one up and flipped through the pages. She couldn't remember the last book she'd read. The man hadn't kept any in his condo. There'd been a television but not cable. No wonder she'd numbed herself with heroin. It took all her strength not to go in search of some now. She'd been feverish with a sick stomach all day.

She lay down on the bed and read the first chapter, not taking in the details but managing to concentrate enough to still the drug craving. She rested the open book on her chest and stared at the ceiling. Before long, her eyes closed and she began to drift, fighting to push away images from the past year that floated to the surface like pieces of pasta in a boiling pot of water. Sleep had mercifully nearly claimed her when voices in the hall snapped her awake and ruined her moment of peace. The clock on Jeremy's dresser said five thirty. She was going crazy all alone in this little room. The bad memories kept coming. Surely, Sara and Jeremy would be returning soon?

She got to her feet and resumed pacing. The voices receded down the hall, and she pulled the door ajar, watching two boys leave through the far exit. Her skin was crawling and itchy. She had to get out of this room, if only for a moment. The door would lock behind her, so she went back inside and took a pencil from Jeremy's desk that she wedged inside the door. It was enough to keep the lock from catching and was hardly noticeable. Satisfied, she walked down the passageway into a common room. Light poured through the floor-to-ceiling windows, and she took a seat on one of the couches that faced a television tuned to the CBC all-day news station. Another boy who looked about her age sat in a chair by the window, reading. He glanced at her and then back at his book.

The volume on the television was off, but text scrolled across the bottom of the screen, matching what the news anchor was reading. She was surprised that the war in Ukraine was still going on. It had started before she left home, and the prediction had been that it would be over quickly. The bombed-out buildings and traumatized people wandering the streets filled with rubble were difficult to watch. The video flipped to a smiling couple standing in front of a giant cheque. They'd won three million dollars in a local lottery that benefitted charity. The contrast with the previous story struck her as ludicrous. She started to look away when the screen filled with the face of a woman. Nicola got off the couch and moved closer to the screen. The woman's hair was short and blonde, not waist-length and sandy brown as she remembered, but the eyes and mouth were unmistakable. A man was standing in front of a crowd of reporters, reading from a paper. The woman's face stared from a poster behind him. Nicola read the words on the screen, transfixed, absorbing the information with growing horror. Staff Sergeant Kurt Auger — his name appeared above the scrolling text — was asking for the public's help. The woman, identified as Marnie Vaughan, had been found murdered on Thursday afternoon on a walking trail at Shirley's Bay, several miles west of the city. The police had learned she was using an alias but had not been able to identify her. Anyone who knew her was asked to come forward. A phone number filled the screen. They were invited to place the call anonymously if they so chose.

Nicola covered her mouth with a fist and backed away from the screen. "No, no, no," she said.

The boy looked up from his book. "Is something wrong?"

She dropped her hand and forced herself to control her breathing. "It's nothing. Sorry for disturbing you."

"No problem."

He resumed reading, and Nicola stumbled backward. She reached the doorway and ran down the hall to Jeremy's room. Thankfully, the pencil had remained in place, and the door opened easily. Frantic, she put on the winter parka Sara had lent her before pulling on the borrowed boots. She yanked a woollen hat over her ears and took one last look around the room. She had no idea where to go but knew she couldn't stay here. It was too dangerous. She wouldn't risk Jeremy and Sara being harmed, because now she knew these people would stop at nothing. But where would she be safe? She couldn't afford a hostel or motel. Then she remembered Sara mentioning shelters but without giving any details. If she could find her way to one, they'd have to take her in. Maybe they'd give her bus fare to make it to her mother's house, as far away from this city as she could get.

Reluctantly, she moved over to the desk and opened the drawers until she found where Jeremy tossed his spare change. She scooped up the loonies and toonies before counting the coins. Twenty-two dollars. It would be enough to get her on a city bus if she could figure out a destination. She scribbled an IOU note and a thank-you. He'd left his laptop open, and she began a search for women's shelters in the downtown. A query brought up Cornerstone, and she jotted down the address and took a moment to study the map before deleting her search. She hurried out of the room and down the hall to the exit. If nothing else, being outdoors and on the move would keep her sane. She could shut down the demons for a while as she worked on finding a secure place to land.

———

SARA CHECKED messages on her cell phone as she walked alongside Jeremy back to his room in residence. The lecture had run overtime, and she'd barely been able to sit through the question-and-answer period. Three texts from Ella Tate, asking her to call right away, which was odd. They hadn't spoken in months. Ella probably wanted to talk about her dad, so no rush. He wasn't going anywhere for a while. Another from her mom, checking in. Sara shoved the phone back into her jacket pocket. She'd deal with the calls when they were in the dorm room again. She stole a sideways glance at Jeremy. "You never told me your major," she said.

"Kinesiology for the moment. I'm thinking about applying to be a cop."

"No way."

"Yes way. My mom's not keen on the idea because of the risk, but she'll come around if I get accepted."

"You'll be great at it."

"Thanks. What about you? What's your game plan, Sara?"

"You'll laugh."

"Try me."

"I'm majoring in criminology and plan to become a PI. It's about the only thing that interests me."

"Tailing people and finding out their secrets?"

"Yeah. Sounds kind of shady when you say it, though."

"A female dick. I can see the appeal." He grinned and ducked his head. "We're on a similar path."

They reached the main door to the residence, and he used a card to enter. His room was on the first floor at the end of a long hall. He used the card a second time, stepped inside, and stopped, looking back at her. "Where's Nikki?"

"Washroom?" Sara moved past him, scanned the space, and pointed at the desk. "Is that a note?"

Jeremy walked over and picked up the piece of paper. He skimmed the words and looked across at Sara with puzzled eyes. "She's taken off. Says thanks for everything."

She returned his stare. "She has no money or place to go."

"She borrowed my loose change. I keep it in this drawer." He opened and looked. "There was probably twenty bucks or so in there."

"That'll take her far," Sara said deadpan. "I think we should go after her."

"We can take my car."

"Let's get moving."

Early winter darkness had sifted around the buildings, creating long shadows in the glowing streetlights as they hurried to the parking garage. The temperature was dropping with the waning day as they hustled across the wind-swept walkways and entered the building. Sara climbed into the front passenger seat and huddled into herself for warmth as Jeremy started the car and eased onto University Drive. "She'll likely be catching a bus on Bronson to go downtown. Maybe we'll find her waiting at the stop. The buses aren't always on time."

He pulled up at a red light at the Bronson intersection, and Sara squinted toward the bus shelter across the road. "I don't see her. Maybe she started walking to save money or to stay warm. She'll freeze standing in one spot for long."

"I'll drive toward downtown. You keep an eye out for her."

Sara scanned both sides of the street, squinting through the darkness. "Why did she leave? Something must have spooked her."

Jeremy glanced over in the glare of passing head-lights. "I'm amazed she was holding up as well as she was. We should have gotten her to somebody who knows how to deal with trauma."

"I agree. We shouldn't have waited, but there's no way we could force her either. She had to trust us first." Sara slumped back while continuing to look out the window. "Second-guessing isn't going to help her now."

"No, and it's not as if you didn't do everything you could."

They drove the length of Bronson, and Jeremy cut through downtown to the ByWard Market. If Nikki had taken the bus, she might have made it this far. Jeremy slowly cruised each street while Sara studied every woman and girl, but there was no sign of her.

"What now?" Jeremy asked as they idled at a red light in front of the art gallery.

"I guess we go home. She could be anywhere."

Jeremy rested his arms on the steering wheel and looked across at her. "Why don't you come back to resi-dence? I don't think it's safe for you to be staying in your dad's house yet. You can sleep in the same bed, and I'll take the other one. In the morning, I'll come with you to check out your dad's. You'll need to get the lock changed."

Sara considered his suggestion. It made sense, and the idea of sharing a room wasn't awful. In fact, it might be kind of nice. She wondered what Jeremy's friends would think, but she'd begun to realize that he didn't really care if he was seen with her. It didn't matter to him that she was a geeky outcast. She gave him a quick smile. "Okay. Thanks."

He nodded and put the car into gear as the traffic light turned green.

CHAPTER 29

Liam dreamt he was mowing the lawn on a sunny, summer morning. The heat on his head and the noise of the motor drew him into wakefulness. He opened his eyes and turned his face into Lucky's soft fur. She'd wrapped herself around him and was purring like a small engine in his ear. The dream receded with the realization that it was actually a chilly winter day, and the lawn wouldn't need mowing for another few months at least. He reached over and pulled the cat to his chest, giving her belly a rub while he thought about leaving the warmth of his bed for a shower.

The memory of Ella lying next to him the night before was fading, but the feel of her mouth on his and her body pressed against him had come back at odd moments throughout yesterday. He had a decision to make, because he had to be fair to Georgina and their new relationship. She'd spoken about staying over on weekends and perhaps moving in together if things went well. Although, in all honesty, Ella might not give him a choice. He had no idea if she would even consider starting something up with him — in seeing how they fit together.

He grabbed his cell from the bedside table and checked messages. The first, surprisingly, was from Ella, asking to meet at Daisy's for coffee or breakfast if he had time. No worries if he couldn't fit it in. He looked at the clock. If he rushed, he could make the café within the hour. He sent a text saying he'd be there for eight if that worked. She replied immediately with a thumbs-up. Energized, he hopped out of bed and into the shower, leaving behind a disgruntled cat, meowing her displeasure.

Ella was sitting in their usual booth when he stepped through the restaurant entrance forty minutes later. Daisy waved from the counter and followed Liam over to the table with the coffee pot.

"Nice to have you two darlins back. What can I getcha?"

"The usual," Ella and Liam said in unison.

Daisy laughed and sauntered away, calling, "Coming right up," over her shoulder.

Liam shrugged out of his parka while looking at Ella. She appeared to have just woken up, slumped back in the seat, her green eyes bleary. She'd once told him that she often had difficulty sleeping, and he wondered if last night had been one of those times. She sipped from her coffee mug while waiting for him to get settled. "So why did you want to meet?" he asked.

"I'm on a mission of mercy. Sherry Carpenter is on the Marnie Vaughan murder for *The Capital* and says she needs a scoop. Ordinarily I wouldn't ask you, but her male colleagues are uniting to get her ousted. They've never taken to a young, ambitious, not-male on the crime beat."

"You handled that job well, as I recall."

"Weird how these same men didn't find me a threat. I never flaunted my femininity the way Sherry does — and that's not a judgement. We're just different. The male dinosaurs who work on the paper can't see past her looks, believing incorrectly that they're what got her the assignment. I'd also had a lot more experience on the paper before Canard bequeathed that plum to me, which hasn't gone unnoticed." She tilted her head to the side and grinned.

"Your ability to seek out stories and get people to confide in you is a talent, Tate." Liam felt mild disappointment that Sherry was the reason for their meeting. "I can't tell you much that isn't already in the media."

"Sherry knows Marnie Vaughan isn't the vic's real name, and you have no idea who she is."

"Ahh. She must have another contact on the force. We've put out a public request for information. It was posted late yesterday."

"Anything come in?"

"Nope, unless overnight. I haven't any intel to give you. I'm sorry."

"It's odd that you haven't been able to figure out her real identity."

"Her phone and purse are missing."

"Still. No ID in her personal possessions at home?"

"Not even on her laptop. The messages from you are the only item of interest so far."

Ella thanked Daisy as she set down their meals and

refilled coffee cups. Liam waited until Daisy crossed the floor to greet two men in work clothes standing in the foyer. She sat them in seats near the window, not close enough to overhear their conversation.

"I wouldn't have any idea where to point you to find out about her," he said, ignoring the interruption.

"Surely Peter Grady must know something more. They were about to tie the knot."

"If he does, he's keeping it to himself. He honestly appeared as shocked as anybody when we told him that Marnie Vaughan wasn't her real name."

Ella's brow furrowed as she pondered what he'd shared. "So, this woman with the made-up name suddenly appears in Peter Grady's life, apparently by chance, although more likely by design. Within four months, she's moved into his mansion and he's set to marry her, much to the horror of his family — I'm guessing. A week before she's killed, she reaches out to me through my podcast website and says she knows something that will cause a huge scandal and bring down some important people. We arrange a meeting, and she doesn't show, because as we now know, she'd been murdered that same day, approximately forty-eight hours before her wedding. Whoever killed her takes her ID and phone, presumably to keep her true identity secret." Ella picked up a piece of bacon and began chewing on the end. "Could this involve a syndicate or crime gang?"

"Sure. It could also have been her working a con alone. Grady is wealthy enough to make him a target. He'd already bought her a BMW that we still haven't recovered. That car might have been why she was killed, if she interrupted a car-jacking."

"I don't know. Seems too convenient if she was running a scam and into something shady. Let's not forget that she reached out to me about a big story. People could have wanted her dead for either scenario. The missing car might be a decoy."

"Your deduction skills are suited to police work, if you're ever wanting a career change."

"Hah, not likely, but thanks for the compliment." Their eyes met, and hers slid away first. She toyed with the handle of her mug. "About the other night. Don't worry about Georgina finding out you slept in my bed. I won't be telling anybody, especially *not* Tony."

"I wondered—"

She held up a hand, palm facing him. "That evening was a drunken mistake that we can put behind us. I don't want what happened to be a problem in our friendship or whatever you call our alliance."

"Of course not. We'll always remain friends."

She smiled for the first time, and her shoulders relaxed. "Good, then we won't talk any more about the overnight, and we'll pretend it never happened."

But it did happen, and it's left me incredibly unsettled. He wanted to say the words aloud, but his phone picked that moment to ring. He checked the screen. "One sec. I have to take this."

"Okay, I'll be right there. Ten minutes, yeah." He slipped the phone into his pocket, took one last gulp of coffee, and reached for his parka. "Gotta go. I'll be in touch if I can help the Sherry situation." He paused. "Say, did you ever reach Sara McGowan?"

"No, but I left a few messages on her phone and dropped by to see her mom. Claudette didn't appear concerned. Are you really worried about her?"

"No identified reason to be. It simply felt strange to have a break-in at their house during one of the worst winter storms of the decade after all that went on last summer. If her mom is okay with it, then Sara must be all right." He stood and looked down at her. "Stay well, Ella."

"And you."

She had her head bowed, eating the last of her meal as he looked back before stepping outside into the frigid morning. Their exchange had been far from satisfying, but at least they'd cleared the air. The disappointment he felt was on him. Ella continued to be as elusive as the morning mist and as maddeningly difficult to pin down.

———

LIAM FOUND a spot in the station's underground parking and took the stairs to his office on the second floor. Auger had already started the meeting in the boardroom, and Liam found a space to lean against the wall, since all the seats were taken.

"You missed the updates," Carmen Abela said. He recognized her as the recently appointed manager of the helpline. She turned sideways so that Auger couldn't see her talking. "Nobody's made any breakthroughs."

"No leads from the public?"

"It's been a bust." Carmen frowned. "Hopefully, someone will call in today."

"Keep me updated."

"Of course." She gave him a quick smile and turned back to face Auger at the front of the room.

Lisa Flint from Communications was giving her update on media efforts to gain information on Marnie

Vaughan's movements before her murder and to have someone come forward who knew her. She took her time outlining what had been done without focusing on how little had been achieved. Auger cut her off mid-sentence.

"So, basically you're telling me you've got diddly squat, like the rest of your colleagues."

"Well, no. We've put out a lot of feelers and need to be patient while we wait for someone to come forward."

"Does this seem like a sound strategy to everyone? Passively waiting and hoping?" Auger stared at faces around the room. "Anybody? What are your thoughts, Abela?"

A rosy blush suffused Carmen's face as she shifted uncomfortably next to Liam. She kept her tone reasonable. "It seems like a part of our strategy ... at least, it always has been when we call on the public for assistance."

"Good for you," Liam said under his breath. He raised his voice to carry around the room. "We're all frustrated by the lack of progress, but this happens in almost all our murder cases. It doesn't stop us from pursuing every lead and methodically reviewing evidence."

Auger's face turned a brighter shade of red than Carmen's. He didn't speak for a moment, staring down Liam and waiting until the silence became uncomfortable. "Let me put it this way, Detective Hunter. It's time this team begins thinking outside the box and takes some initiative. It's unconscionable that I stand in front of the media day after day with nothing to tell them. It's unfair to the Grady family, and it's unfair to the public, who have to be wondering why a killer is running free while we're being called incompetent. So, Detective, I'm putting you in charge of coming up with a plan to get this investigation on track. I'll expect your report by end of day. Now, everybody, get back to work."

Quade caught up with Carmen and Lisa in the hallway and spoke to both of them before she approached Liam. "Well, that was a train wreck. Media reports haven't been kind to Auger, and I suspect he's feeling the heat from above. No excuse for his rudeness, though."

"You smoothing things over?" He tilted his head toward the two women.

"Neither has done anything wrong. I wanted them to know we appreciate their efforts."

"This murder investigation is unfolding like all the others. Auger's anger is misplaced."

"I know, Hunter. Auger's being an arse. He never got around to asking for our reports about the Grady family. One would almost believe all his talk about getting results is empty. Boots, Jingles, and I've been digging. Let's find a vacant room and compare notes."

"And let's hope Auger forgets he's put me in charge by the end of the day."

"We've got your back. Don't let his bad mood affect your peace of mind." She patted him on the shoulder before crossing over to her desk.

Liam thought about how much better Quade had been as staff sergeant compared with Auger. She'd replaced Greta Warner as acting but lost the permanent spot to Auger, who managed much like Greta — bully-ing, playing politics, blaming others. Quade had proven to be a real leader, and he and the team had felt supported, but that was gone now. Morale had dropped, and he feared their cases would be negatively impacted. Quade caught his eye and motioned toward the door. He picked up his laptop and followed her to a meeting room down the hall. It was time to set office politics aside, block out the noise from Auger, and get down to work. They still had a killer to catch.

CHAPTER 30

Today would be Cassie's second last full day in Ottawa before flying home to Vancouver. Mick had permission from the police to return to Kingston but hadn't confirmed when he'd be leaving, although it would be soon. The family could return to their regular lives, even if she wasn't certain her father would ever recover from this tragedy. He seemed diminished, a man with nothing left to live for anymore. The thought worried her.

She took a quick shower and dressed warmly in jeans and a cable-knit sweater. A walk after breakfast would start the day nicely. At the head of the stairs, she paused with her hand on the banister and looked toward her dad's closed bedroom door. If she was going to get him alone for a talk, now was the best moment. It would be easier simply to avoid this conversation, but she'd live with the regret once back home. She straightened her shoulders, walked the length of the hall, and rapped on his door. Her dad yanked it open seconds later. Much to her surprise, he was fully dressed, his hair combed back, and eyes clear.

"I was coming downstairs to join you for breakfast," he said, taking her by the arm. "It's your last day, isn't it?"

"No, my flight is early Thursday morning. You have to put up with me for two more days."

"Then let's make the most of our time together." They began walking toward the stairs. "Your brothers and their wives will be joining us for dinner. I convinced Mick to stay one more night so we could gather as a family. I also spoke with Wilma and asked her to come with us to Riviera on Sparks Street. Have you eaten there before?"

"No, I haven't. That's thoughtful of you to include Wilma, Dad."

"Not at all. She works hard and deserves to be treated as one of the family."

Cassie had always liked this about her father. He hadn't let his wealth blind him to the plight of less fortunate people. Mick could take a lesson. She knew her dad contributed generously to several charities, never taking his good fortune for granted. Her own bank account had benefitted from many infusions over the years while she got her acting career underway.

Wilma fussed over them after Cassie let her know there'd be two for breakfast in the dining room. Omelettes and sausage, fruit salad, and fresh croissants. Rich, dark coffee with thick cream. Her dad asked Wilma to join them, but she waved him away. "I'll just leave the two of you to chat," she said before disappearing into the kitchen.

Peter stared at the last place she'd been standing. "I

was willing to let Wilma leave us. She told me before the wedding that she planned to retire after I married Marnie."

"And now, Dad?"

He turned his gaze on her. "Says she'll stay as long as she's needed."

"That's good, then." Cassie wondered what her dad wasn't saying — that he'd chosen Marnie over his life-long employee and regretted the decision? Or maybe he would prefer Wilma to retire after all. She phrased her question carefully. "Do you think she should retire anyway?"

"She hasn't given me a choice in the matter. I've left her openings to leave over the years, but she's never taken me up on them, probably because she has nowhere else to go. We're her family, when it comes down to it."

"She's always felt like family to me." Cassie watched her father's bowed head as he began eating. He seemed so vulnerable, and for the first time she saw him as an old man, one who might need care in a handful of years. The idea brought a lump to her throat that she worked to control. She took a swallow of coffee followed by a deep, cleansing breath. He looked up and caught the expression on her face before she had a chance to look away.

"I'm going to be all right, my dearest," he said. "You don't need to fret. I'm not as confused as your brothers would have you believe. I've been feeling under the weather, sure, but that comes and goes. I'm looking after myself. Exercising, vitamins, nutritious diet. I plan to live a good long while yet, and with my marbles intact."

"Dad—"

"No, I understand everyone thought I'd been taken in by Marnie's youth and beauty, but that's not how it was. I wanted to give her a safe home. She hadn't had that in her life."

"She confided in you about her past, Dad? You have to tell the police if you know something."

"What she told me has nothing to do with her murder."

"How can you be certain? The police believe someone she knew before meeting you might be involved in her death. What did she tell you?"

"Marnie made me aware that she'd had a difficult time growing up, but she never spelled out the details. She asked me to meet up late last Thursday afternoon away from the house and the family. She wanted me to know everything before we got married so that I had a chance to change my mind if I couldn't accept her life before me."

"Did you go to meet her?"

"I did, but she never showed up and didn't answer her phone. I went home and waited, all the time knowing something was wrong. That was the longest night of my life."

"Did you tell the police this?"

He shrugged, a delicate lifting of his shoulders. "No. It would only make me look culpable. I didn't meet anyone I knew at the bar and sat at a table by myself. My alibi is nonexistent. The thing is, Cassie, Marnie wasn't a gold digger or trying to trick me into marrying her. She had a conscience. She was a good person who never had any breaks. I went into our relationship with my eyes wide open." He nodded, lowered his head, and resumed his meal as if this ended the discussion.

Cassie had so many more questions, but he finished eating and called for Wilma before the time felt right to continue probing.

"I'm heading out for a meeting at the club and won't be home until midafternoon. We can drive to dinner together. Drinks here at six, and Wilma, remember I won't take no for an answer. It'll be the last chance for all of us to gather before Mick returns to university and Cassie leaves in a couple of days. Who knows when we'll all be together again?" He stood and smiled at them both before striding out of the room. He appeared back to his old self, confident and unruffled.

"I'm not altogether comfortable attending your family dinner," Wilma said, "but your father's being insistent."

"You should come. We all want you with us."

Cassie stood and picked up her plate. She'd only managed to eat half, but her stomach was unsettled. She'd take a cup of coffee to her room and check messages before putting in a load of laundry. It would give her time to decide whether she should call the detective to relay what her father had told her about Marnie. The problem was that she couldn't be anonymous, and her dad would find out. He'd be hurt and angry and might never confide in her again. On the other hand, the police needed to be made aware of Marnie's last movements to help find her killer. Perhaps the detective could get her dad to reveal everything he knew, because she had a sneaking suspicion that he'd held out on her. His right eye had twitched like it did when he wasn't telling the truth. She'd learned the tell from those times in her childhood when he'd hidden things from her until she was old enough to handle them. Things like where babies came from and how the family dog had really died.

The little her father had shared was a terrible quandary to weigh on her conscience and ruin this glorious day. She would speak with her brothers about the problem when they checked in. Maybe they could come up with a solution if they put their heads together. There was strength in numbers.

———

SARA OPENED her eyes and stared at the ceiling. It took a few seconds to remember that she was in Jeremy's room and Nikki was gone. She turned her head on the pillow and looked across to the other bed. Jeremy slept on his side, facing the opposite wall. It was comforting having him with her. She eased out from under the blankets and dressed quickly in the same clothes she'd worn the day before. She was about to put on her jacket and boots when Jeremy rolled over and looked at her. He sat up and rubbed his eyes. "Good morning. Where are you going?"

"Home to my dad's. I've got to check out the damage and get that dealt with. It'll be fine now that it's daylight. Whoever broke in is long gone."

"I could come with you. Ride shotgun."

"That's okay. I'm sure you have better things to do." She slipped her arms into her jacket. "Thanks for everything, Jeremy. You helped a lot. I'm sorry Nikki didn't stick around."

"Yeah, I hope she's okay. Anytime you need an accomplice, I'm available."

"Good to know."

The morning was cold, with a biting wind that whirled gusts of snow into her face as she trudged across campus to her car. She passed several students going to class. The parking lot had been ploughed, and her car sat forlornly off by itself with a ridge of snow encircling it. She prayed as she put the key into the ignition. Three turns and the engine caught. "Thank you, Jeremy," she said aloud. He and his friend had boosted her car and taken it for a spin the evening before after he and Sara returned from their fruitless search for Nikki. She waited for the heater to warm up and pulled out of the lot. She decided to take Carling Avenue to her dad's and give the battery time to recharge. She flicked on the radio. Five minutes to the news at the top of the hour.

She idled at a red light at Bronson and Fifth. The Glebe neighbourhood stretched off to her right. She tapped her fingertips on the steering wheel and thought about how close she was to Ella Tate's apartment. She'd seen messages from Ella on her phone but hadn't called back yet. All she had to do was turn right on Fifth and left on Percy, and a few blocks farther on she'd be there. Ella was resourceful and had contacts all over the city. She might be able to figure out where someone in Nikki's position would go for help. The light changed to green, and Sara put on her right-turn signal. Hopefully, Ella was still home and would be okay with an unexpected visitor this early in the day.

CHAPTER 31

Ella had spent most of the night wrapped in a blanket, editing a podcast. She stumbled into bed and fell asleep around 3:00 a.m., awakened by Tony at eight thirty with an invitation to join him and Decker for breakfast when she finally opened her door.

"Sorry, were you still sleeping, girl?" he asked as he took in her flannel pajamas and wild hair. Her eyes were barely open slits.

"Whatever gave you that idea?" Already, the cold was seeping into her bones, the hardwood floor icy under her bare feet. The thought of spending another morning shivering in a blanket at her computer decided her. "Give me ten minutes and I'll be down."

"The coffee will be hot and ready."

She skipped the shower and pulled on warm sweatpants, a wool undershirt, and socks, sweater, and hoodie. After a quick trip to the bathroom, she happily left her apartment and jumped down the stairs to the second floor. The heat accumulated in Tony's place, for some unknown reason, although she was convinced he'd jerry-rigged the system somehow. After all, didn't hot air rise, and shouldn't the top floor be the warmest spot in the house?

She found them in the kitchen. Decker grinned at her as he stood cooking at the stove. He was dressed in denim cut-offs and a short-sleeved black t-shirt. Tony handed her the promised cup of hot coffee. "Sip on this and your blue lips should rosy up in no time. You might soon find yourself a bit overdressed."

"I should at least get a reduction in my rent," she grumbled.

"You say that every time." Tony laughed as if she was being delightfully funny. "Let's go sit at the table, and Decker will serve us. He's the only one I let in my kitchen, he's that good."

"Well, you are brothers for all intents and purposes."

Ella's eyes widened as Decker set a plate of French toast speckled with icing sugar and smothered in whipped cream and berries in front of her with a side of sausage. He returned with flutes of orange juice and Prosecco that he distributed before sitting down with his own plate. "I see the family resemblance now," she said, picking up her fork. She took a bite and moaned. "So good. How did you both come to be such wonderful chefs?"

"Decker's mom. She couldn't cook a lick, so if we wanted a decent meal, we had to figure it out."

Decker laughed. "She could burn water. A heart the size of the ocean, but don't wrap her in an apron."

"She sure made me feel like part of your family." Tony smiled at a memory.

"Because you were … are." The two men exchanged a look.

"Decker also saved me from the bullies. Life had been hellish before he took me under his wing."

"And look at you now. More friends than there are days in a year. Which brings me to repeat my question, Ella Tate. Tony and I are going south for a week, and would you like to join us? This is my treat." Decker studied her over the rim of his coffee mug while Tony clapped his hands.

"Warmth, sun, piña coladas. Dancing the night away under a Caribbean moon. You have to come, girl."

"I'm not sure … I have work—"

"Nonsense. One week away won't end your career, and you can always leave an out-of-office message. You're entitled to a holiday."

"I've booked the rooms in a resort in the Bahamas and the flights already. Don't make me have to cancel your tickets." Decker grinned. "Tony said you needed this as much as we do."

"Come fly away with us." Tony toasted her with his drink. "Be spontaneous and live a little."

Ella shook her head at both of them. "When are you leaving?"

"Friday morning. Our flight to paradise takes off at eight," Tony said.

"Let me think on it until this evening."

"I can't imagine what there is to think about, but all right, take the rest of the day, as long as you agree to come with us. Decker and I will show you a good time, no doubt about that."

She inwardly balked at the idea of a handout, which essentially was what this trip would be. Decker was a stranger, even if he did grow up with Tony, and she'd owe him, maybe not right away, but sometime down the road. She finished eating and excused herself as soon as it seemed polite. Tony walked her to the door.

"Think how jealous the good detective will be if he knows you're flying off with Decker. Might change the tides, if you get my drift."

"Still working that dead horse, are you?"

"They don't call me never-give-up Tony without reason."

"Well, this time you should cut your losses, my friend, and stop speaking in clichés. And to be honest, trying to make Hunter jealous so he'll come running is very high school."

The doorbell rang, giving her a reason to say good-bye. She hurried down the stairs and pushed the door open to find Sara McGowan standing on the stoop with the familiar scowl on her face.

"I hope you remember me, because I need your help," Sara said. "A friend of mine is in trouble, and there's nobody else I can turn to."

Ella reached across the space and pulled Sara out of the cold and into a hug. "Of course I remember you, Sara McGowan. And I'll help your friend in any way I can. Let's go upstairs, and you can tell me all about it. Then we'll decide the best way forward."

———

"So, in a nutshell, your friend Nikki has fled a trafficking situation and has no money and nowhere to stay. She's scared to contact her family because the traffickers threatened to kill her mother." Ella waited for Sara to nod. "This sounds like a police matter. I'd like to bring in Detective Hunter."

"No, we can't. Nikki was adamant we not involve them."

"But she's in trouble, and they're best placed to help, especially to prosecute her traffickers and protect her family. They need to be stopped from doing this to anybody else, not to mention saving the other girls."

"Please, Ella. If we can find her, then I'll … we can talk her into going to the police."

"Let me think for a minute." Ella's instincts tilted toward contacting Hunter immediately, but to tell him what? This girl Nikki was gone, and Sara had no names or locations. She didn't even know Nikki's surname, only that she came from a small town out west. "If Nikki doesn't know anybody in the city, and she has twenty dollars in her pocket, no cell phone or other device, then there are only a few places she could go. To get there, she'll have to walk, which is unlikely for long in this frigid weather, or take public transit. I think we should check out shelters and churches."

Sara sat up straighter. "She mentioned a hostel or motel, but she can't afford those. I floated the shelter idea, but not seriously. I didn't say the exact name or address of any of them, but Nikki's resourceful and kind of desperate."

"Cornerstone provides emergency shelter for women, and it's downtown. I wrote an article about the work they do last year. Let's start there. Give me a sec to get ready. We can take my car in case the men that broke into your dad's house ID'd yours."

"You're thinking like a PI. I knew you were the right person to help us." Sara grinned.

"Once we find her, we'll bring in the police," Ella said. She studied Sara to make certain she was in agreement. She planned to contact Hunter with or without Nikki's approval but would prefer to have her on board.

"Yup. We're on the same page. We'll convince Nikki because this is too dangerous to continue without bringing in reinforcements."

Ella went into her bedroom to change out of her sweatpants. In addition to helping Nikki return home, the idea of exposing a network of traffickers was strongly motivating. This would make exciting fodder for a podcast, but she wouldn't think about that for now. Keeping Sara and Nikki safe had to be the priority after they located her — and for that, she had Hunter on speed dial.

CHAPTER 32

Ella drove out of the Glebe on Bank Street, heading north toward the downtown. Snow-ploughs had cleared the main arteries, while some side streets remained nearly impassable with thick, drifting snow. The city staff promised they'd have the roads back to rights by nightfall, an immense feat considering the sprawl of the city and the amount of snowfall. She cruised past the Cornerstone emergency shelter, a three-storey, faded red-brick building taking up most of a city block on the corner of O'Connor and Nepean, and found a parking spot on a nearby side street. It was one of the lucky roads already visited by a snowplough.

"These places are high on privacy and won't reveal any information unless they believe it's in the woman's best interests. Even then, they'll double-check with Nikki before telling us anything. Let me do the talking," Ella said before they got out of the car.

The woman on the desk listened to Ella's query without reacting. Ella was certain she'd heard it all before and wouldn't be easily swayed. "Nikki is in danger, and we want to protect her," she said with growing desperation. Sara stood silently next to her, becoming increasingly agitated.

"And you don't know her last name?"

"I just know her as Nikki or Nicola," Sara said. "If she's here, perhaps you could tell her that Sara's still got her back." She took a pen and piece of paper out of her handbag. "Here's my phone number, if you could give this to her too. Tell her that I can get her home."

The woman's facial features softened for a moment as she accepted the note. "I can't promise anything, but rest assured that we do all we can for our residents while protecting their privacy."

Ella knew this was as good as they were going to get. "Let's keep moving, Sara."

Sara took a step closer to the desk. "I know your rules, but we're going to keep looking for her all over the city, unless you can tell us that we shouldn't."

The woman's eyes held Sara's stare. She appeared to be weighing the request against all the reasons she should say nothing. After a several-second impasse, Sara lowered her eyes and turned away from the desk. Her shoulders slumped in defeat. "Guess we should go."

The woman's voice stopped them before they reached the door. "Your friend is safe. You don't need to keep searching."

Sara spun back around. "Thank you. Please tell her to call me."

The woman nodded and gave a thumbs-up. Ella took Sara's arm, and they walked together down the hallway to the exit.

"Well done, Sara." They stepped outside. "It hasn't gotten any warmer." Ella shivered and did up her jacket.

"I'd go south if I were you," Sara said. "Get away from all this crap weather."

Ella stopped. "What did you say?"

"Go on a holiday … what … is that the wrong thing?"

Ella resumed walking. "No, it's just Tony and a friend of his are trying to convince me to take a trip with them. Maybe the universe is conspiring to get me on the plane."

"There are worse things."

They got into Ella's car and waited for the engine to warm up and melt the coating of frost on the windshield. Sara pulled the hood of her jacket over her head and huddled closer to the air vent.

"Just cold air coming out of that," Ella said. "It'll take a minute."

"I know, but I can pretend." Her face turned serious. "Do you think we should try again to get that woman to tell us where Nikki is? I felt like she wanted to help."

"She has to follow the rules, which are in place to protect some very vulnerable women."

"I know, but Nikki needs us."

"As soon as you hear from Nikki, call me and we can visit her together."

"If she gets in touch with me."

Ella patted Sara's shoulder before putting the car in gear.

"Wait, wait," Sara said, pulling out her phone. "It's Cornerstone." She listened for a moment. "Yes, we can come back. I understand." She signed off and half-turned to face Ella. "Nikki said for us to return this evening around seven. She's got something going on now, but she'll be free then."

"Terrific. What will you do in the meantime?"

"I'll get my car and go to Dad's to check out the house. I'll have to call a locksmith or somebody to fix the front door."

"Are you safe to go back there?"

"Yeah, whoever broke in is long gone. I'll come pick you up around six thirty, if you're free and still want to help."

"I'll be waiting at the front door."

———

QUADE TURNED AWAY from Liam and spoke quietly into her phone. He could see the tension in her body, but she managed to keep her voice low and calm. He'd caught glimpses before into her antagonistic relationship with her ex-husband. Most arguments centred around their two children and her long hours or his latest girlfriend. To Liam, it seemed like a never-ending loop of woe. He tuned out Quade's voice and kept his attention on the road, driving onto Sussex Drive on his way to the Grady home in Rockcliffe. A wind had come up since he entered HQ that morning and buffeted the car whenever he drove into stretches of road unprotected by buildings. The flurries blowing in across the Ottawa River swept pockets of snow across his path, bringing with them limited visibility. He heard a snort before Quade jammed the phone into her pocket and cursed.

"He's leaving the kids alone at my house and said it's my problem if something bad happens before I get home."

"Why doesn't he keep them another couple of hours until you pick them up?"

"Right? What a turd." She sighed deeply. "He says he's on the way to the airport. A sudden emergency that only he can solve at his parents' home in Saskatoon."

"Are they okay?"

"Apparently. This has to do with protecting his inheritance." She sighed again. "I'm being a bitch. He seemed genuinely concerned about them. His dad suffered a fall a few months back and uses a walker." She stared out the side window. "I keep promising myself that I won't burden you with my home life, but here I go again."

"I don't mind."

"Seriously, I can't see how you can enjoy my grumbling. The good news is the kids are older and nearly of an age to be left alone." She pulled the phone out of her pocket. "I'm going to call and remind them of the house rules. Please ignore me for the next few minutes."

"Done."

He pulled onto Blenheim Drive and counted three cars in the Grady driveway. There was room for one more, but he parked on the street, not wanting to box anybody in. Quade was the first out of the car, still speaking into her phone. She shoved it into her pocket before they arrived at the front door and reached up to ring the doorbell. "Let's see what the Grady family's gotten themselves up to," she said, smiling at him.

Liam stood shivering inside his parka, the frostiness of the air a sharp contrast with the dry heat in the car. The sun had already begun its descent, and a peachy-rose strip of light glowed under a pale blue sky. It was a pretty street, lined with cedar hedges, oaks, and conifers.

The housekeeper Wilma opened the door, her back rigid and face devoid of emotion. "Can I help you?" she asked without a hint of irony.

"We have more questions," Quade said, pushing forward so that Wilma had to step back and let them inside. "Looks like the entire family has gathered."

"We're about to leave for dinner at a restaurant." Wilma's voice was frostier than the temperature outside. Liam noted she'd included herself in the family's outing. She was wearing black pants and a green mohair sweater, make-up brightening her face.

"Then hopefully this won't take too long." Quade didn't wait for Wilma to invite them in, taking off her boots before striding past her toward the French doors that led into the living room.

Liam smiled an apology. "Please join us," he said and motioned for Wilma to lead the way after he also stepped out of his boots.

"It looks like I don't have a choice."

The family had indeed gathered. Liam made a survey of their faces. Peter Grady stood next to his eldest son Foster near the fireplace, both holding crystal tumblers. There was a strong resemblance between the two, shared by the middle son, Gordon: blond, patrician, with slightly hooked noses. Peter appeared more rested and less grief-stricken than he had on past visits. Foster's wife Deirdre, a commanding woman of generous size, sat with legs crossed in a chair close by, sipping on a flute of champagne. She and Foster had the air of a power couple, both dressed in designer labels, sparkling diamonds in Deirdre's ears along with multiple rings of some value on her fingers. Gordon, the English teacher, and his wife Khloe sat close together on the couch, dressed in less stylish clothes, but Gordon appeared equally at ease in this setting while Khloe's mannerisms struck Liam as slightly neurotic, constantly tidying her hair and straightening her clothing. Liam had spoken with their twin daughters, Bobby and Trisha, and they talked about their mom with exasperation and a certain condescension. He knew this wasn't unusual for teenage girls. Mick, youngest and Queen's student, reclined on a pillow next to Gordon, both men holding glasses of beer. Mick appeared to be playing at being a dilettante, bored with family get-togethers, too hip for the rest of them. He was darkly attractive, in the mould of his sister, Cassie.

As if on cue, Cassie stood with a rustle of silk from her midi-length dress and crossed the floor toward Liam and Quade. A worried frown creased her striking features as her eyes met his in silent connection. Liam was again cognizant of her effortless grace that translated so well to the television screen. She'd called him earlier that day to repeat the conversation she'd had with her father. Liam had promised to keep her name out of the reason for their visit. "Have you got an update, Detective?" she asked, stopping next to Wilma.

"We're glad to find you all together." Quade led the conversation as planned while Liam watched for reactions. "We have yet to unravel the mystery of Marnie Vaughan and are working diligently to piece together her movements on the last day of her life. Unfortunately, her laptop doesn't contain anything that helps us, except that she was corresponding with a local reporter named Ella Tate, and they'd made plans to meet the evening she died. However, she never showed up because she'd been murdered, as we now know. She told Ella that she wanted to share information that would implicate powerful people in an illegal enterprise but gave no details. We also know that Marnie spent an hour in a nail salon after she left home Thursday morning. The beautician told us that Marnie received a phone call while she was getting ready to pay. She spoke to somebody in a voice described as placating and agreed to meet, apparently with reluctance, although this could be the beautician's interpretation. Marnie had lunch with Khloe and Cassie at bistro Viv on Preston after leaving the nail salon. Nobody can confirm her movements after she left the restaurant at one o'clock." Quade stared around the room. Everyone had gone still as they absorbed her words. "Have any of you remembered a conversation with Marnie that might help us determine her final hours?"

Peter had been watching his family from his position next to the fireplace. His gaze came to rest on Cassie's face. He raised a hand. "We were also to meet late that afternoon between five and six for a drink in Wilfrid's at the Château Laurier. Marnie had something to tell me that she felt I should know before we wed on Saturday. I waited half an hour or so for her, called and left a couple of messages, but she didn't respond. I phoned one last time, and she still didn't pick up. I said on the voice mail that I'd meet her at home and left right afterwards. Nobody can confirm my whereabouts that afternoon."

Cassie's shoulders relaxed, and Liam realized how tense she'd been, not knowing if her father would reveal what he'd been holding back.

"This could have bearing," Quade said. "Did

Marnie give any hint about what she was going to tell you?"

"I've racked my brain to remember. When we made plans to meet, I was distracted and not giving her my full attention. She said more, but damned if I can recall."

"If she was involved in a con scheme and about to tell you the truth, the people she was working with might have silenced her."

"That has crossed my mind."

"Did you call her that morning while she was having her nails done?"

"No. We didn't connect that day after she left the house. Cassie and I spent an hour catching up over breakfast, and I worked out in our gym in the basement. I'm afraid I didn't see anybody. Wilma left midmorning to run errands, and Cassie rested in her bedroom before leaving for lunch. She was gone too when I finished showering and getting dressed. But you know this already from previous interviews."

"I had a lot to do before the wedding," Wilma said.

"Dad, you're … we're not on trial," Foster said.

"I feel as if I missed something—" Peter's voice trailed off. He kept his head lowered, not meeting anybody's eyes.

"What do you mean, Dad?" Cassie put a hand on his forearm.

"I've been so upset. Marnie said things that didn't make sense at the time. I need time to organize my thoughts."

Mick jumped to his feet. "I don't think you should push my father any more. He's suffered enough."

"I can handle myself," Peter said. "But thanks for your concern, everyone."

"Mick is returning to Queen's, and I'm flying home Thursday, if that's okay, detectives," Cassie said. "I believe Mick previously received clearance to leave Ottawa?"

"I've already missed classes," Mick added. "And I'm sure Gordon and Khloe want their house back."

"We've enjoyed having you," Khloe said. "The twins adore their Uncle Mick."

Quade shifted next to Liam. He sensed her patience waning. They weren't gaining any useful information to further the case, and her kids were home alone.

Her tone turned brusque. "As I've already told Mick, we can reach you both if necessary, so please carry on with your lives. We're available anytime, Mr. Grady, if you recall your conversations with Marnie. Any detail, no matter how trivial it seems, could lead us to finding out more about her identity. So, has anyone something more to add? No?" Quade turned toward Liam. "Well, we won't hold you up any longer. Enjoy your evening."

Liam glanced around the room, certain they'd let Peter off too easily. Cassie was watching her father with a quizzical expression, as if she didn't quite believe him. Wilma motioned for Quade and Liam to follow her out of the room, and he decided to regroup and return when he could get Peter alone. His intuition told him Peter Grady was hiding something.

They put on their boots and zipped up their coats before stepping outside into the early dusk. He counted six mature trees in the Grady front yard, all laden with snow and ghostly in the dimming light.

"Not getting any balmier," Quade said. "Hard to believe in global warming this week."

"Nice to see a normal cold winter forecast like in days gone by, though." Liam did what he could for the environment — recycled, walked instead of driving when time allowed, brought tote bags to the store, looked into purchasing an electric vehicle. He promised himself that once the price came down a bit, he'd bite the bullet. He tried not to worry about the state of the world, but the increasingly dire news was hard to ignore. They got into the car, and he let the engine idle while they both stared at the Grady house. "They're rallying around the dad," Liam said. "Getting protective."

"Normal after what he's been through."

"It seems more than that." He raised a hand to wipe the coating of moisture off the side window. "The way they look at him … it's as if they wonder about his mental state. How old is he again?"

"Sixty-four."

"Within the normal age range for dementia, albeit the younger end. They must have been mighty concerned when he took up with Marnie. The age difference and him with all that money they planned to inherit."

"We found nothing out of the ordinary in their backgrounds."

Liam eased out of the parking spot, but the rear tires spun on a patch of ice before gaining traction. "I'll run a check on his statement that he spent time in Wilfrid's. Somebody on staff will surely recognize him."

"Maybe Marnie did show up for their rendezvous, he didn't like what he heard, and he strangled her. Drove her to Shirley's Bay in his car and left hers to be stolen. Lord knows it wouldn't take long for a new BMW to disappear in this city."

"He owns three vehicles. We'd have to show probable cause to get a warrant to search them and get GPS information on his phones."

"There was no question about how his first wife died?"

"Boots said nothing came up." Liam had asked him to check as a precaution. "She died of cancer."

"The three sons are different in temperament. The older two look like their old man. Foster took over running Peter's architecture company, and his wife is a university recruiter. On the ballsy side. Gordon became a teacher with a stay-at-home wife raising two kids. One family making loads of money, the other scraping by on a teacher's salary. Mick and Cassie have a strong resemblance, I imagine, to their late mother. Attractive people all. Cassie's talented, with a television career taking off. Saw her show once, and she's the obvious star. Mick is brash. Comes off as entitled. Wilma appears to be more of a family member than employee. There's an edge to the woman."

She was thinking out loud, slotting facts and observations into place. Liam knew she worked this way, and he listened carefully without interrupting as he drove to the end of the street. She finally ended her monologue. "I'm heading straight home when you drop me off at HQ. Do you have plans this evening?"

"I'll input a report about this visit into the system and then head home too. It's been a long week."

"Still seeing that woman, Georgina, is it?"

"Yes, but we're casual." A wave of guilt washed over

him as soon as the words were out of his mouth. Georgina would have been offended if she'd heard him.

"I liked her the one time we met, although she seemed more into you than the reverse."

Liam inwardly cringed but said, "She's a good person. Likely, I don't deserve her interest."

"It could simply be that you aren't that much alike. Opposites might attract, as they say, but that doesn't mean the other person understands you. My marriage could serve as a flashing red warning sign for what not to look for in a relationship. My advice would be not to get in too deep if you aren't certain she's the one. For sure, don't get her pregnant, marry, have another kid, and then realize you hate the person. Believe me, that will not end well. Oh no, it won't end well at all."

CHAPTER 33

The room held two single beds, but the second remained empty for now. Michelle, the worker on the front desk who'd completed her intake, had told her to enjoy the privacy while it lasted. There'd likely be a roommate by the next day. Nicola took full advantage and spent most of the afternoon sleeping. She needed a day to let her body recover and her mind settle.

When she rose from the bed at four o'clock to take a shower, she remembered Michelle knocking on the door and telling her that somebody named Sara and another woman had stopped by, looking for her. Nicola had replied that she'd see Sara at seven that night if she came back. She'd been half-asleep and barely registered the exchange until now. In hindsight, it was surprising that Sara had bothered to track her down yet disturbing at how easily she'd been found. Then she remembered how resourceful and tenacious Sara was. They'd talked about shelters at one point when they discussed options, but Sara hadn't been specific and had glossed over the idea. Well, seeing her would be an opportunity to thank her for everything and to tell her to stand down. She also needed to return the clothes Sara had lent her and would organize that after Michelle helped find her some second-hand stuff tomorrow.

A different woman was on the phone with her back turned when Nicola walked past the desk to the main door. Michelle had been sympathetic and said they'd work on solutions once Nicola had a chance to get her bearings. It had been good not to be judged after all the awful things she'd done to survive. The shame she felt was making her reluctant to act. Her mother might be better off not knowing about her life since she left home. Nicola hated the thought of adding to her pain. Maybe it would be kinder if she never found out.

She waited inside the door and peeked through the side window, watching for Sara. It didn't take long for a car to pull up and Sara to step out onto the sidewalk. Nicola hurried outside to waylay her. The cold air shocked after the warmth of being inside.

"There you are," Sara said and grinned. "Get in the front seat, and we'll go somewhere to chat."

"Are you certain—"

"Ella's cool. I trust her."

"If you're sure, then okay."

She climbed into the car, and the woman smiled at her. She looked to be in her early thirties, with startling green eyes in a narrow face. Tufts of blonde hair stuck out from underneath a black wool cap. Her smile seemed warm and genuine. "I'm Ella Tate. Good to meet you, Nikki."

"Likewise." She pulled on the seatbelt and snapped the buckle into place. "How do you know Sara?"

"Her family was in the news last year when her half-brother went missing. I'm a freelance reporter and covered the story. We helped bring him home. Sara and I bonded." She took her eyes off the road and shot Nikki a grin. "How's Italian sound?"

"As in food?"

"Yeah. We'll pick up a pizza on the way to my place. You'll be safe there."

"Okay." Nicola felt herself relax. She'd worried about being in a public place. Too many eyes watching for her. "Thanks."

Ella used her hands-free to place a pizza order and stopped in front of the restaurant to run in and get it. Her apartment wasn't far. She parked in the driveway, and they entered a red-brick house on a narrow lot. Nicola heard a baby crying in the ground floor apartment as they trooped upstairs to the third floor. Ella's place was small, with well worn furniture, except for a leather chair and floor lamp, their quality and newness making them appear out of place. The striped couch looked as if it had been pulled out of somebody's trash. A computer, microphone, and other equipment covered the top of an ancient oak desk. Above the desk, Bart Simpson smiled cheekily down on the living room. The rest of the walls were bare. A chill in the air made her shiver, and she kept her coat on.

"Take the good chair, Nikki," Sara said before she plopped down on the couch.

Ella went into another room and returned a minute later with pizza slices on three plates. She made a second trip and handed each of them a can of sparkling water before swinging around her desk chair to face them. "Sorry for how cold it is in here. The space heater should warm it up in a bit. Use the blankets on the back of the furniture if you want."

When they were done eating, Ella set her plate on the desk and leaned forward, elbows resting on her knees. "Tell us your story, Nikki," she said. "Don't leave anything out, so we can figure out the best way to help you."

"I'm scared the information could put you in danger too."

"I've found that most people only have power if you keep their bad deeds a secret. Once they're exposed and the truth comes out, they have nothing. Are you okay if I record this?"

"Yeah, I guess."

Ella turned on a tape recorder. "Start whenever you're ready."

"As I already told Sara, I flew to Thunder Bay for work last summer, thinking it was a legitimate job in a summer camp. A man and a woman met my plane and drove me to a place in Sudbury, where they locked me in an apartment and took away my phone. The man raped me, and then I was taken to Windsor for a few months before they moved me to Toronto. They kept me in a motel and different men came. There were parties — do I have to talk about what they did?" She had tried to keep her voice a monotone, but her words rose on the question. She didn't want to share those memories with anyone, least of all Sara, who would look at her differently once she knew.

"No, we don't need those details. I know what you experienced must have been horrible." Ella's voice had softened, but her eyes glittered with anger. "You have nothing to be ashamed about, but now is not the time to relive what they did to you. I think you're going to need a therapist to help process what happened, but we'll get to that in time."

"Maybe." Nicola shrugged. "Anyhow, they moved me to Ottawa next, where a guy set me up in another condo downtown. It was like he'd chosen me for his own use, although sometimes he brought a friend. I was using heroin by then. I'm not sure what kept me going."

"Your strength," Sara said. "You have incredible strength."

Nicola smiled at her. "I watched and waited. There was an alarm system and a video camera in the hallway leading to the door. I learned the code and got out a few times. It was a risk, but one I had to take. I figured they weren't watching the video feed every minute, since they believed I was high most of the time. I went to a free clinic, and the doctor helped me get clean."

"You could have escaped then." Ella seemed to be making an observation, not a judgement, and Nicola nodded her agreement.

"I needed to be clean and to have a plan. The man said he'd kill me if I ever left. I'd been told by the others that they'd kill my mother. I had to be ready."

"So, what made you decide to finally leave the condo and not go back?"

"The man … I overheard him on his cell telling somebody he was looking for a new, younger whore and to put me back in circulation."

"You also had somebody who was going to help you," Sara added.

Nicola took a second to remember who she was talking about. "I met Veronica at a party in Toronto a couple of times. She wanted to get away as bad as I did, but she had a plan, because we both figured we were being trafficked to Ottawa next, and she knew the city well. She said if I ever got free, to leave a message for her at a restaurant in the Market, and we could meet at a Tim Hortons in the east end that she thought was far enough away from the downtown to be safe. She even gave me the address, so I know she'd given the plan some thought. The restaurant set-up sounded like an urban legend, but word had gotten around how this guy would help refugees and street people. Veronica said she'd make contact with him after she escaped, because she planned to help other girls get away too and set up new lives. She said that she'd run away from home because she hated her stepfather and would never go back there, but she'd figure things out once she got away from these men. The last time out of the condo before I left for good, I wrote a note to her and left it at the restaurant."

"What restaurant?"

"Gleason's. I guess Veronica never got my message, because she didn't show, even though I waited all day. Luckily, Sara was working at the coffee shop where Veronica said to meet if I got free and took pity on me."

Ella blinked, but not in time to hide the surprise in her eyes. "This is helpful," she said after a pause. "Do you know Veronica's last name?"

"Maisonneuve."

"How about the name of the man in the condo?"

"He was careful not to say it, but I looked through his wallet once. I'm not sure if I should tell—" Her gaze swivelled over to Sara as she began speaking.

"Two biker-looking guys came in looking for Nikki that day, but I lied and said I hadn't seen her. I guess they didn't believe me because they showed up at my mom's house and then broke into Dad's on Locke Isle Road. I had a friend Jeremy with me, and we got away and spent the night in his dorm room at Carleton U." Sara's face reddened, as if she was embarrassed by the admission. Her gaze shifted from Ella to Nicola. "But why did you run, Nikki? We were going to help you."

The terror filled Nicola again, and her entire body began trembling. She was vaguely aware of Ella crossing the space and crouching down in front of her. Ella grabbed both her hands. "Whatever happened, we'll deal with it. You are not alone."

Nicola breathed in and out, in and out, calming her heart rate. She looked across the room at Sara, and the panic eased. She nodded. "I watched TV in the common room while you and Jeremy were in class. The news was on. The dead woman, the one found strangled in the woods last week…" Nicola's voice choked as she struggled to hold back tears. "It was Veronica Maison-neuve. She got away from them, and they killed her. And that's what's going to happen to me too if I don't keep running."

CHAPTER 34

Veronica Maisonneuve was both Marnie Vaughn, Peter Grady's fiancée, and Sally, Ella's deep throat. Of this, there could be no doubt. Ella now knew that Veronica/Marnie/Sally had wanted to share information to blow this trafficking racket wide open and to point the finger at men in important places. Ella's first instinct was to call Hunter and help with the police investigation. Her second was to contact the Canadian Centre to End Human Trafficking and put Nikki in touch with people who could help her recover. They should also be involved in locating the people who'd trafficked her and rescue the other girls. She raised both ideas, but Nikki began trembling and broke down sobbing each time, refusing to listen further to either suggestion.

Sara walked over to Ella after Nikki went to the washroom at the back of the apartment and bent over the desk, her mouth close to Ella's ear. "She's traumatized. The news story that her friend was murdered has shaken her, because she was a lot more pulled together when I first met her. I promised her that you'd help, but maybe she needs a bit more time?"

"We have to get her professional counselling, and the police need to be involved. Think about the other girls being trafficked. The men could be moving them as we speak."

"She knows that, but she's scared."

Sara straightened as Nikki entered the living room on silent stocking feet. She'd scrubbed her face, and her eyes were red but dry. "I know you're right, Ella. I'll have to speak with somebody in case I can help the others. But how do I know who to trust?"

"I have a friend on the police force. A detective. His name is Liam Hunter, and we've worked on cases together. I would trust him with my life. We can start there and let him guide you and keep you safe."

Nikki considered her words before nodding. "I'll talk to him but nobody else … yet."

"That's good. I'll call—"

"Maybe text him instead. Don't tell him about me, though. Just say you need to see him about something important. You can't let him talk to anybody else about me. Not until I speak with him."

Ella studied Nikki and saw evasion in her eyes. *What aren't you telling me?* she thought. "Okay, if that makes you comfortable." She typed a message into her phone and showed it to Nikki before hitting send. *Slow and careful. Gain her trust,* she thought.

Hunter's reply came ten minutes later. *It's late. Can't come this evening but can stop by tomorrow morning on my way to HQ. Coffee?*

Ella looked at Nikki. "I could call him. Tell him I need to speak with him right away?"

Nikki shook her head. "I want to wait for him to come here tomorrow."

Ella hesitated but typed, *I'll have it on. Thx.*

She looked at Sara. "Then maybe it's best if you both stay here tonight until we have a chance to fill in Detective Hunter." There wasn't much that could be done at this time of night anyway.

Sara looked around. "Not sure where you plan to put us."

Ella laughed. "Yeah, not the most spacious of places. If you don't mind sharing a queen bed, I'll take the couch. It's old but comfy." She was usually awake half the night anyway.

"I can go to my dad's and come back first thing," Sara said.

"Night is not the time to go back there," Nikki said. "If you insist, I'm going with you."

"Your dad's place is half an hour away, and you might miss Hunter in the morning," Ella said.

"All right. All right. I'll stay." Sara crossed to the couch and sat down. "What'll we do until bedtime? Play charades? Say, is that Celine Dion coming up through the floorboards? Tony must be home."

"Who's Tony?" Nikki asked.

"Just the coolest guy ever. Can we go see him, Ella?"

"Sure. He's got a friend here from Vancouver, but they're both chill. Nikki, maybe use my phone to call the shelter to let them know you're fine, and then we can all go warm up downstairs."

"Okay."

Five minutes later, Tony greeted Sara with open arms and a big hug. He looked over her head at Nikki and Ella. "Who have we here?" he asked, grinning widely.

"This is Nikki," Ella said. "A friend of Sara's."

Tony stared quizzically at Ella for a moment before inviting them all into the living room. Lena staggered toward them, Luvy following close behind. "Lala," she said. "Up."

"Sweet girl." Ella scooped her into her arms and inhaled her baby scent. She looked over at Tony. "Where's Finn?"

"In a meeting with equipment distributors. They've gone out for dinner."

"Not exactly a social life, but an evening off. At least a step forward." She and Tony moved closer to the kitchen. "And Decker?"

"Montreal, finishing up a deal." He raised his voice. "Get comfortable, girls. I'll just rustle us up a snack." He turned back to Ella. "Finn never stops working at that gym. Did you hear how his coffee date went with Adele?"

"No. You?"

"She wants a separation. Finn didn't say more than that."

"Damn. He was hoping she'd decide to come home."

"I worry she's going to try for full custody of Lena."

Ella squeezed Lena more tightly. "Surely, that would never happen?"

"She *is* the mother."

"But one who abandoned her child the first year of her life. That has to count for something."

"I'm not convinced it will in the end."

Tony left her and went into the kitchen. She

returned to Sara and Nikki, who were making themselves comfortable on the couch and flipping through fashion and hair style magazines that Tony had left on the coffee table. Luvy had found her way to the space between them. Lena squirmed until Ella set her down on the floor. She staggered over to the couch and grabbed on to Nikki's knee. "Up."

Nikki reached down and helped Lena climb into her lap. For the first time since Ella met her, Nikki smiled, and her eyes shone as the baby settled into the curve of her body.

"She loves you," Sara said.

Tony returned with a tray loaded with cheeses, French bread, crackers, pate, almonds, and dried apricots. A second trip to the kitchen and the tray was restocked with glasses of white wine. "You girls are up for a glass?" he asked Sara.

"Twist my arm."

Ella didn't question their ages. They'd more than earned the right to have a drink.

Tony waved his glass at Nikki. "So how do you know our girl, Sara?"

"I'm leaving an abusive situation. Sara saved me."

"Oh my gawd." Tony clutched his chest. "Are you okay?"

"No, but I will be."

"Hunter is coming first thing tomorrow, and we're going to tell him everything." Ella still had difficulty getting her head around the horror from which this girl had escaped. The same horror that others were still enduring. She wanted to move on this tonight, but Nikki was fragile, and pushing her too hard could have dire results. "Say, if Decker is away overnight, do you have a spare bed? We're staying together until Hunter gets involved tomorrow. Your apartment is a lot warmer than mine."

"Of course they can stay here. I'll change the sheets, and you girls can take the spare room and my room. I'll sleep on the couch."

"We don't want to put you out," Nikki said.

"Nonsense. I love sleepovers." He looked directly at Nikki. "You're in good hands. Ella, Hunter, and Sara are the most caring and resourceful people you'll ever meet."

"Count yourself in there too, my friend." Ella smiled at him.

"Why don't you take the couch, Ella, and I'll pull out my sleeping bag? The shag carpet is like being on a cloud. Believe me, I've spent many a drunken night passed out on it."

"Well, if you insist." She'd had an uneasy feeling at the thought of leaving Sara and Nikki, even if it was only a one-floor separation. There was too much she couldn't control in this situation.

"Sara and I can change the sheets if you let us know where they are," Nikki said.

"Aren't you the perfect houseguests? Look in the cupboard next to the bathroom. Leave the ones you take off the beds in the hamper."

Ella watched the girls go with Luvy scampering behind. Tony scooped up Lena before she could toddle after them and settled her in the playpen. She picked up a puzzle piece and became instantly absorbed. "Sometimes I swear you're the kid's mother. Her self-reliance and fascination with whatever is at hand is are a chip off your block."

"Well, I'm definitely not her mother, so don't even whisper that rumour outside these four walls." Ella motioned him closer. "There are men after Nikki. It was more than an abusive relationship — she was being trafficked, Tony. They know she's being helped by Sara and have been to her mom's and broken into her father's house in Rocky Point."

"Good lord. This is serious."

"You should know that anyone who comes in contact with her is in potential danger. These are vile, violent people. If you prefer that we stay upstairs—"

"Not a chance."

"I figured, but you deserve to know."

There was a knock at the apartment door, and they both jumped. "I'll get it," Ella said.

"Over my dead body. Whose apartment are we in?" Tony edged past her, but she kept pace, and they arrived at the door together.

"Who is it?" Tony called with his hand on the knob."

"Finn. Who else would it be?"

Tony opened the door. Finn looked beyond him to Ella. "Does it take two of you to answer a knock?"

"I'll let Ella explain while I get Lena," Tony said.

Ella hugged Finn. "I hear Adele wants to separate." There was no easier way to say it. "How're you doing?"

"Been better, but it's early days. I still hold out hope she'll come around."

Ella stepped back and studied his face. "She could, but maybe don't bank on it. You need to make certain Lena is protected."

"From her own mother? Adele would never hurt her

child. We'll work things out." He stepped inside. "What was Tony talking about just now?"

She wanted to ask more about Adele and her state of mind but realized this was not the right moment. Finn needed time to reconcile that his marriage was all but over. "Sara — remember her from last year — came by with a young woman she met who is in the process of escaping an abusive situation. The guy is looking for her, so we have to be careful who we let into our building."

"The two girls are here?"

"We're having a sleepover. Detective Hunter will be by in the morning, and we've convinced Nikki to speak with him. She's in a bad way and skittish about talking to the authorities, as you can imagine. We're trying to make her feel safe, although I'd feel better if Hunter had been able to come tonight."

"If I can help, come get me."

"Thanks, Finn."

Tony reappeared with Lena, who reached for her dad. Finn smiled as he hefted her onto his hip. "I'm not far if you need me. I'll keep an eye out for anybody suspicious outside."

"These people have no idea Nikki is here, so we should be okay tonight, but it's good to know you're watching out."

Tony stood still for a moment after Finn and Lena left, staring at the closed door. "He's too good a man to be going through this bullshit."

"Adele is going through her own hell."

"She's lucky that Finn — and you — are so understanding. I land on the sceptical side of things. I worry she hasn't shown the selflessness needed to be a good parent, or partner for that matter."

"I worry about that too, Tony, but Adele and I got off to a rocky start, so I'm attempting to give her the benefit of the doubt."

"You put me to shame, Tate." He took her by the arm. "I'll be more sympathetic as long as Lena doesn't become the monkey in the middle of a tug of war. Let's go check in on our guests and get them settled. There will be a busy day ahead on the morrow."

CHAPTER 35

Nicola woke up frightened in the unfamiliar bed. Her mind scrambled to remember where she was as her eyes skittered around the room, trying to recognize shapes in the dim light. Her heart rate settled as she realized she wasn't locked up in the condo but was safe inside an apartment with Sara and her friends. The man hadn't found her in the night.

She lay in place, thinking about the day ahead. The detective would be here soon, and she needed to decide how much to tell him. She supposed this would depend on whether she trusted him or not. She'd figure that out once they met, once she had a chance to size him up. She hoped he turned out to be the man Sara and Ella described. It would be good to share the truth and ease the lump of fear in her chest. She breathed deeply in and out to calm herself before she stepped out of bed.

A toilet flushed, and someone was walking past her door. They stopped and knocked lightly. Sara entered after she called to come in. She was still dressed in flannel pajamas lent to her by Ella and held two cups of coffee. "I remembered you like cream and one sugar."

"Come sit." Nicola patted the spot next to her. Tony had a king-size bed, and there was plenty of room.

Sara handed her a cup of coffee and settled against the pillows next to her. "Isn't Tony the best? He's cooking us breakfast after the carrot muffins finish baking. Ella's gone upstairs to shower and change. You can have a shower when she's done if you want."

"That would be great." The coffee smelled and tasted delicious. "Have you updated Jeremy?"

"No, should I?"

"I'm sure he'd like to hear from you."

"Maybe. He's probably busy. Have you contacted that neighbour or your mother yet?"

"I will today if it goes well with the detective." Nicola stared at her. "Seriously, send Jeremy a text."

There was a knock at the door, and Tony poked his head into the room. "Fifteen minutes to brekkie, so shower up, get dressed, and join me at the dining room table."

Nicola thought how easily she could have missed out on being here, how close she'd come to giving up. The idea of speaking with her mom for the first time both terrified and excited her. The terrible things she'd done to survive, the men, the drugs — she wasn't the same innocent girl who'd set off for that summer job halfway across the country. Her mother had led a simple life, not straying from her hometown, marrying the boy she'd dated in high school, and never being with anybody else even after he died. The church had filled the gap in her life, and while religion preached forgiveness, Nicola couldn't predict if the truth would destroy their bond.

She longed to see her mother while at the same time dreading her rejection.

Sara pushed herself off the bed and gazed down at her, eyes blazing with conviction. "No matter how things turn out, you aren't alone anymore. We're all here for you."

"I've seen … and done things I can never undo. I'm not sure I can ever get back who I was before."

"You had no choice, and that's shitty. Those things you did — that they forced you to do — will never take away your soul. We can all see that you're a good person. And for me, that's the only thing that counts."

***

ELLA WAITED in her apartment until she received a text from Hunter at seven thirty that he was at the front door. She hurried downstairs and let him in, a cold blast of air accompanying him into the hallway. "I wanted to let you know what's going on before we join the others."

"Is everyone okay?"

"Sara McGowan stopped by yesterday. She met a young woman who'd escaped from an abusive situation and took her home to her dad's. Two men broke in, but Sara and Nikki — the girl's name is Nikki or Nicola — got away. They spent last night here." Ella grabbed onto his arm. "She was being trafficked. We haven't pressed for any details because she seems to be teetering on the edge of a breakdown. I believe she's going to need counselling, but for now, she said she'd speak with you. There are other young women in her situation. And Hunter, Nikki knew Marnie Vaughan as Veronica because they were both being trafficked by the same men. Nikki said they were at the same parties in Toronto."

"I should call Quade."

"Not a good idea. Nikki's agreed to speak only with you."

Hunter glanced up the stairwell. "I can do a preliminary interview but will need to get the team involved."

"Maybe don't say that right away. She's reluctant enough to talk as it is. She wouldn't even let me tell you about her in my text last night. She worries for her mother's safety. I think there's more going on than she's revealed."

"Understood."

"You can talk in my apartment, and the rest of us will stay in Tony's place until you call us."

They climbed the stairs and found everyone gathered around the table, eating. Tony had prepared omelettes and sausage to go with the carrot muffins. "I've left you both plates in the oven on warm," Tony said, leaping up from his chair.

"Hey, Sara," Hunter said before taking the seat across from her.

Sara raised a hand. "This is my friend Nikki."

Hunter nodded and directed his gaze on Nikki. "I understand you have a story to tell me. Ella has offered her apartment after we're done eating. If you'd like Ella or Sara to sit in, that would be fine. Whatever makes you the most comfortable."

Nikki had been studying Hunter from the moment he entered the room. "I prefer talking to you alone."

"Then we can do that." He met Ella's eyes, and she signalled that he'd handled the interaction well. She wondered what Nikki was going to tell him that she refused to share with anybody else. Was she being extremely careful, or were the things she'd revealed to her and Sara only the tip of an iceberg?

———

THEY WAITED at the dining room table, eating muffins and drinking coffee. Sara kept scrolling through her phone while Ella and Tony filled in the time doing a crossword. After half an hour, Tony threw down his pen. "Time for hair trims," he announced, ignoring Sara's and Ella's groans. "Which one of you wants to go first?"

"After you, Sara," Ella said. With any luck, Hunter and Nikki would finish their talk before it was her turn.

Tony worked his scissors magic on both of them, and still Hunter and Nikki remained upstairs in Ella's apartment. Ella began pacing. Every ounce of her reporter body wanted to be with them, hearing Nikki's story and working it into a feature article. She wasn't proud of this instinct but acknowledged that this drive made her a relentless investigator into injustice.

"Do you think it's going well?" Sara asked, looking up from her phone on one of Ella's passes. "Nikki seemed so scared."

"We had to bring in the authorities to move forward. Hunter is the right person."

"I just hope Nikki's going to be okay."

Another half hour passed before footsteps descended from the third floor. Hunter and Nikki entered Tony's apartment, and Ella tried to read their moods. Nikki's eyes were red from crying; Hunter's jaw was set in a grim line. "Everything okay?" she asked.

"Would it be possible for Nicola to stay with you for the day?" Hunter asked.

"Of course. I planned to work from home, so I'll be here." Ella smiled at Nikki.

"Great. I need to get to HQ. Nicola and I have discussed a path forward, and I'll set that in motion. Everyone, please keep her location a secret until I get things under control." He half-turned and patted Nikki's shoulder. "We've got this."

"We've got this," she repeated.

"All of you take care," Hunter said and left them none the wiser about what had been discussed upstairs.

Nikki stood still for a moment after Hunter left, her eyes focused on a painting hanging on the far wall. Finally, her gaze shifted and landed on Tony. "Any more muffins? I could eat now."

Tony grinned at her, and the tension in the room dropped several notches. He took her by the arm as he began leading her toward the kitchen. "You got it, sweet girl. Then I can give your hair a trim so you keep up with the other ladies."

CHAPTER 36

Liam scraped frost off the windshield, all the while making a thorough inspection of the cars parked on Percy Street near Ella's building. Everything looked in order, nobody watching her house or sitting for long in an idling car. He got inside his sedan and cranked up the heat.

He stared outside at the people hurrying past on the sidewalk while he reviewed his conversation with Nicola Larsen. He remembered now where he'd seen Veronica Maisonneuve before. Her photo had been circulated when she first ran away from home, but she'd been younger then, a teenager with long brown hair. He'd searched for her face whenever he was on a call as he had for other missing children, but eventually her image had faded in his memory. He pulled up the photos that Peter Grady had forwarded to him of Marnie Vaughan, whom he now knew was the missing Veronica Maisonneuve. Traces of the teenage girl he'd searched for years ago could be found in her adult face. He closed the photo app. Her family would need to be told.

The snowbanks crowded the street and cramped the parking spaces. Grey cloud cover had blown in while he was inside the house, and it hung low above the rooftops. Scattered flakes melted quickly on the windshield. Heavier snow was expected by nightfall. He watched two children walk past with their mother on their way to school, and his heart ached at the evil that Nicola had described. The evil that these people had forced upon her after they'd stolen her freedom. He struggled to control the anger that coursed through his body, not allowing it to consume him. This was a time for a clear head. Nicola was depending on him to keep her safe and to rescue the others. He looked at his cell phone screen and hit Quade's number on speed dial.

"Where are you?" he asked.

"Just parked my car at HQ. Why, Hunter? Is something the matter?"

"I'm going to be late. I need to speak with someone. Cover for me?"

"Of course." There was a pause while she opened the car door. "Anything I should know about, Hunter?"

"Yes, but once I make it in."

"I'll be waiting."

———

PETER GRADY WOKE with a pounding headache. A wave of nausea roiled through his stomach when he sat up, and he feared the flu had found its way into his body. He hadn't felt like himself for a while now, moments of forgetfulness, stomach aches for no reason, light-headed. He'd ignored the symptoms, deciding to outwait them until his internal system settled itself. He told himself mind over matter, because he couldn't be ill today. Perhaps it was something he ate at dinner the night before. He'd ordered the prawns in cream sauce, and that might have been a mistake. Seafood out of season could be iffy.

He shuffled across the bedroom to the ensuite and stepped into the shower. A long, cool soaping helped him to feel slightly more human. He got dressed in jeans, turtleneck, and pullover sweater before sitting on the bed to take his vitamins. He glanced over at the clock. Only six thirty. He'd slip silently down the stairs past Wilma's constant hovering and take a walk to the nature trail to watch the sunrise. He was sick of being monitored and discussed like a child. It was time to take back his rightful place as head of the family.

He managed to creep downstairs without his feet landing on any creaking boards. The sun was beginning its slow ascent over the pines when he finally stepped outside into the brisk January morning. He'd remembered to dress warmly in ski pants and parka with a woollen scarf wrapped around his neck inside the jacket. Wilma had bought him a red and black chequered hat with earflaps that he wore whenever the temperature dropped below zero, and he was thankful for its warmth today.

He took a moment to orient himself at the bottom of the driveway. He even turned and walked a few steps before recalling the path through the woods was in the opposite direction. He checked the windows of the house to make certain nobody was peering out, watching his confusion to file away as ammunition later in support of their hare-brained theories about his mental state.

Grief was a funny thing. It consumed all one's energy, leaving a man wrung out and empty as a broken promise. Marnie had misrepresented herself to him from the get-go. He'd known she hadn't approached him that afternoon in the gym because of his rippling biceps or toned physique. He'd played along with her flirting, surprised when she waited for him outside the change room. Once seated at the table in the coffeeshop waiting for their drinks, she'd continued with the banter and come-ons while he waited for the real Marnie to emerge. She hadn't shown herself then. It took two more coffee dates and a dinner before she relaxed enough to be herself. He progressed from intrigued and flattered to smitten, but initially not in a romantic way. It was her vulnerability, her tortured childhood, her alone-ness that reeled him in. She'd run away from home at fifteen to escape her stepfather. Done things she wasn't proud of to make money. Survived by her wits. She wanted to help other young women in equally bad situa-tions. He'd liked her immediately, even when he believed she had ulterior motives.

He reached the opening to the trail. The snow had been nicely tamped down by cross-country skiers, dog walkers, sleds, and whatever else journeyed along the track into the woods. Soft morning light filtered through the trees, the sky a blush of rose and pink to the east, although a bank of clouds was visible on the far horizon. He trudged along the path, wishing he'd thought to bring a flask. A sip of Scotch would have made this early-morning walk perfect and calmed his stomach, still teetering on the edge of nausea. He tilted his head to gaze over the pines and balsam trees at the patch of sky. After navigating the small bridge, he carried on to the large pond, rimmed by trees with rooftops visible in the far distance, smoke from the chimneys hanging suspended like cotton candy in the air. Weak sunbeams sparkled on the sheet of ice spread out in front of him where the snow had blown away, and he wondered if he should chance walking down the slope and across the pond. The ice would bear his weight, but the thought of slipping and falling kept him rooted in place.

Marnie had been the one who moved their friendship from platonic to physical. He'd been satisfied with being in her company, but she reawakened the part of him that had fallen dormant when his wife died. At first, he'd been uncomfortable with Marnie's youth, his aging body, the impropriety, but she hadn't cared. She'd won him over with her generosity of spirit, and he'd come to love her in a fashion, knowing he wouldn't be enough for her ten years from now. "Don't think about the future," she'd said once after he shared his doubts. He wondered now if she'd had a premonition. He'd naturally believed he'd be the one to die first.

He spotted movement out of the corner of his eye. A deer had bounded out of the wood and was leaping through a snowbank onto the ice several metres away. Transfixed by the beauty of the animal in the gilded stillness of the morning, he watched the doe make her way in the opposite direction along the shoreline.

A flood of sadness washed over him as he contemplated what he now knew needed to be done. He hadn't been entirely honest with the police about his last conversation with Marnie the morning of the day she went missing. Hell, he hadn't really told them anything that she'd shared with him over the past few months. It was all so raw. He'd said he couldn't remember everything she'd told him, but that was a lie. He simply hadn't been ready to share the damning words. They'd planned to meet that afternoon at the Château so she could fill in the details and they could find a way forward, if that was what he wanted. She'd said if he went through with the marriage, they would have a good life.

Peace filled him as he stared at the disappearing doe. Was Marnie sending a sign to him from beyond? It was time to share her confession with the detective. He owed her that. What was it Cordelia said to her father, King Lear? *Time shall unfold what plighted cunning hides.* It was the secrecy that gave him pause. The planning. *Such cunning.* He could barely bring himself to think about it. The evil had been lying at his feet like a snake in the grass, and he'd been oblivious until that last morning. He still struggled to believe her words.

He turned back toward the opening to the woods. The sun was nearly up, but the cold had begun to sting his cheeks and forehead and make his eyes watery. He'd lingered longer than he had intended, and it was time to return to the house before his absence was noticed and the inclement weather scudded in. Wilma would have the coffee on, and he fancied a cup.

Expecting to meet a dog walker or two on his return trek, he kept an ear out for an approaching canine romping along the path. The wind had already begun gusting in the fresh cloud cover, and tree branches cracked as boughs bent under their burden of ice and snow. He plodded on and nearly reached the bridge over the frozen trickle of water when he thought he heard the crunch of a footfall behind him. He half-turned but saw nobody and self-consciously chuckled at his jumpiness. He set foot on the icy wooden bridge, careful to find solid purchase before lifting his other foot. He stopped in the middle and closed his eyes, taking in the warm smell of conifers and feeling the dampness of errant snowflakes on his face. It was time to face that which he'd been loath to contemplate. He'd hesitated because revealing what he knew to be true would destroy so many lives, least of all his own. If only there'd been another way. But he knew there wasn't. Already he'd let things go on too long.

This time, the footsteps coming behind him were unmistakable. He opened his eyes to turn, but a rush of motion, a hand on his back, and he was over the rail and flying through the air. *I've miscalculated*, he thought before the ground knocked the air out of him. *Forgive me, Marnie.*

Somehow, his side took the brunt of the impact, and his head was spared. He closed his eyes and lay still, knowing with certainty that the person was bent over the railing, staring down at him. When enough time had passed, he looked upward and saw an empty bridge framed by a row of trees with grey sky overhead. Flakes of snow had begun swirling, making the scene bucolic if but for the pain in his leg, twisted at an odd angle. He tried to push himself up, but a stab of fire shot from his knee into his thigh and hip. There was no way he'd be able to crawl up the hill to the path. He'd landed on a bare patch of ice and heard it cracking under his weight. The cold and wet had begun seeping through his clothes. His spirit grieved.

Surely somebody will be along soon.

His feet and hands hurt from the biting cold. He knew numbness would eventually replace the pain. He flexed his fingers and toes, willing them not to succumb to frostbite. He shifted his weight and cried out. Tears slipped unbidden down his cheeks as the rush of pain overwhelmed his defences.

Where the hell are all the dog walkers this morning?

The snow was picking up, coating his parka in a white film and soaking his face. He closed his eyes as black dots blurred his vision. The light-headedness could be a result of his blood sugar level dropping, the frigid temperature, or the stabbing pain rippling up and down his body. Likely a combination of the three. He wondered how much time he had left before he'd fall into an unconscious state. Part of him would welcome the release, but he admonished himself even for thinking about giving up. Somebody would be along soon. He had to hang on for Marnie's sake. His beloved Cassie would be heartbroken. He would not die mere steps from his house in the woods surrounded by neighbours. Somebody would be along soon to save him.

I will not die this way. I'll face my failings and accept what needs to be done. I will not die this way.

THIS IS my last day in Ottawa before I fly home, Cassie thought as she rolled onto her back and stared at the ceiling. Weak morning light filtered through the window, and she scowled at the idea of another cold, grey day. One part of her couldn't wait to resume her life in Vancouver, where snow was a rarity; the other part dreaded the return to an empty apartment. She'd received two texts the evening before from the show's producer to let her know that a package with her latest lines would be arriving by courier early this morning for some "light" reading on the plane. She'd mentally shift back into work mode on the four-hour flight tomorrow, barring delays.

She made a trip to the washroom down the hall, showered quickly, and got dressed warmly for the day ahead. Her flight was early the following morning, giving her plenty of time to visit family, finish packing, and get in one last walk. She glanced at the clock on the dresser. It was going on eight thirty, and she'd slept longer than intended. She hurried downstairs, hoping her dad hadn't begun eating without her. She was surprised not to find him at the dining room table drinking a cup of coffee and reading the paper.

"Good morning, Wilma," she said as she opened the kitchen door. "Isn't Dad up?" She didn't have to say that he rarely slept in, because Wilma knew this as well as anybody.

Wilma stopped stirring a fruit salad at the counter and swivelled to face Cassie. "I haven't seen him yet. If you sit, I'll scramble some eggs. Coffee is in a carafe on the hutch."

"Thanks." Cassie stood in the dining room and looked at her father's empty chair. He'd spoken about eating with her before she went upstairs to bed the evening before. Surely he'd want to spend this last full morning with her?

She checked that Wilma was still in the kitchen before taking the stairs two at a time and hurrying to the end of the hall. She rapped lightly on her dad's door, paused when he didn't call for her to enter, and knocked harder. Not hearing any movement within, she turned the door handle and called good morning as she poked her head into his room. She looked toward the bed, surprised to find it empty, the blankets pulled up and straightened. She crossed the carpeted floor and stepped inside the ensuite since the door was wide open. Her father's bathrobe lay on the chair next to the shower, but he was nowhere in sight. He must have slipped outdoors without anybody knowing, resuming his schedule of early morning walks. Cassie smiled. He was getting back to his active routine. A good sign.

She climbed down the stairs and returned to the front hall. Checking inside the closet, she noticed that his warm coat and boots were missing. She hesitated for only a moment before deciding to go after him. Breakfast could wait a few more minutes while she walked him home.

She returned to the kitchen to let Wilma know to keep the eggs warming in the oven while she went in search of her dad. He'd likely have gone to the pond to watch the birds. She didn't wait for Wilma's response but hastened to the front hall and put on her outdoor clothes, invigorated by the idea of some fresh air and exercise before sitting down to eat.

Snow was softly falling in large, wet flakes, making her feel like a kid again. After she'd walked two blocks and turned the corner, she was startled to see a crowd gathered on the street near the opening into the wood and an ambulance idling across from them. A police car eased past her as she rushed toward the people, fear propelling her forward. She searched faces for her dad, becoming increasingly agitated. "What's going on?" she asked Wesley Saunders, who was standing slightly apart from the others with his dog.

"I was going to come get you. It's your father. He fell

off the bridge and appeared unconscious. Lucky I had my cell phone with me."

"No. It can't be my dad."

"I'm sorry, Cassie. Nova found him. Good thing we came by when we did."

Cassie stopped hearing his words as she struggled to comprehend what had happened. Her father knew the path intimately and had crossed that bridge more times than she could count. He was an experienced hiker and would never have been careless enough to take a tumble, even if the boards had iced over. She spotted a police officer standing alone and bolted across the street to intercept him.

"Is he going to be okay?"

"I'm sorry, but you'll have to stay back."

"It's my father. I'm Cassie Grady." Emotion made her voice ragged. "I need to be with him."

The officer's eyes held hers, and his expression relented. "We're bringing your dad out of the woods any second. You can ride with him to the hospital."

Cassie nodded, not trusting her voice. This nightmare of a trip home seemed never-ending. She checked that she had her phone in her pocket and pulled it out to call Wilma. The family would need to gather again.

CHAPTER 37

Late that morning, Liam gathered with Quade, Boots, and Jingles in a basement meeting room, away from Major Crimes on the second floor. By complicit agreement, none had let Auger know what they were up to. "We'll include him soon enough," Liam said as they took seats. He shot the others a grim smile before relaying his conversation with Nicola Larsen and the steps he'd taken to keep her safe.

"Then it's all set up?" Quade asked. She somehow kept the rage he saw in her eyes out of her voice.

"I believe so. I don't see other options, unless anyone has a better idea?"

"Nope." Boots spoke for the three of them.

"If Nicola's story is fabricated—"

"But to what end?" Quade interrupted. "If you want to know whether or not I'm on board with the plan and recognize the personal risks, you don't need to ask. Woman and girls do not lie about sexual abuse, except in rare cases. It takes a lot to come forward."

"I believe her," Liam said.

"Right then. Goes for us too," Jingles said after Boots nodded his agreement.

"Alrighty then." Liam put his palms on the desk and pushed himself to his feet. "I'm heading upstairs to inform Auger."

"Should one of us come with you?"

"I can handle it."

He left the room alone and climbed the steps, pulling out his phone as he went. None of the team would take the fall if he was wrong. He'd make certain of that. He scrolled through messages as he reached the second floor. No new emails or texts of import. He was still holding the phone in his hand when he knocked on Auger's office door. Auger called for him to enter.

"Take a seat. Any developments?" Auger removed his reading glasses and rubbed the bridge of his nose before leaning back in his chair.

Liam set the cell phone on his knee and took a pen and notebook from his pocket. He read from the first page. "We've located a woman named Nicola Larsen. Have you ever heard of her?"

"No, why, should I?"

"She's an eighteen-year-old young woman from a small town in Western Canada who arrived in Thunder Bay two summers ago to work. The job offer was bogus, and she was forced into prostitution, first in Windsor, then Toronto, and finally here. She managed to escape her captor a few days ago, and I met with her this morning."

"How did you get involved? I don't recall anything coming through the front desk." Auger frowned and began drumming the arm of the chair with his fingertips.

"A phone call from reporter Ella Tate. She had Nicola in a safe location. We met and I listened to the girl's story. The important information that came out of our conversation is that Nicola knew Marnie Vaughan, although not by this name when they met."

"That's a breakthrough. What was Marnie Vaughan's other name?" Auger leaned closer to the desk and reached for a notebook. He picked up a pen, keeping his head down.

"Veronica Maisonneuve. They met at parties in Toronto and managed to speak with each other privately. They both wanted to get away. Veronica escaped first, but before that, she promised to help Nicola if she ever made it to freedom."

Auger's hand on the pen went still. He seemed to be working something out in his head. His voice had a trace of uncertainty. "So you believe these thugs found Veronica Maisonneuve and murdered her?"

"It's a viable line of enquiry."

"Did she give you any names?" His expression was difficult to read, but Liam thought he saw tension in his jaw, a flicker of panic in his eyes when he lifted his head.

"Nicola remembered some first names of her captors and johns. It's early days, though. She needs time to recover from the trauma. I want to have our police artist make sketches when she's up to it."

Auger rubbed his forehead. "So next steps? Will you be bringing … Nicola Larsen, is it … to HQ to get her statement on the record?"

"I don't see the need yet. She's in a safe location for now, and this will give her a chance to decompress. I'll be visiting this evening to bring her some dinner. In the meantime, we're going to see if we can track down more information about Veronica Maisonneuve, her associates and movements."

"Agreed." Auger appeared to be thinking. "Should we be deploying some officers to protect Nicola? Where did you say she's staying again?"

"I never said, but she's alone for now in an out-of-the-way motel and knows not to contact anyone. She'll be fine."

"Good, good. Tell me the name of this motel. I'll need to brief up." He reached again for the notepad and pen.

"The Sleepy Time Motel off Heron Road. It's in the middle of nowhere, not close to any stores, restaurants, or transit. Even the residential neighbourhoods are a mile or two away on the same side of the highway."

"Sounds safe enough. Anybody else in on this?"

"Only the team." He didn't specify, and Auger didn't press. Liam bent to retrieve his pen that had rolled off his notebook. He grabbed for the pen after tucking his cell phone on the floor under the desk. He straightened and nodded at Auger. "Well, if that's all for now, I should get back at it."

"Of course. Keep me in the loop." Auger began to turn away and stopped. "Is anyone from the team with her at the motel?"

"No. She didn't want police."

"Okay, well, when you know something, I'll be your first point of contact."

"You got it."

Liam walked to the door and turned back to Auger. "Open or closed?"

"Closed, please."

Liam smiled and pulled the door shut before striding

back to his desk. Quade looked at him with questioning eyes.

"Now we wait," he said.

"In the meantime, we've got a development. Peter Grady fell while he was out for a morning walk and has been taken to the hospital. He's unconscious."

Liam blinked. "Are they certain it was an accident?"

"No. In fact, his daughter Cassie claims it couldn't have been."

"This family is a moving target. Can you take Boots and get over there? Jingles and I will keep things under control here."

"Gotcha."

Liam looked toward Auger's closed door. "I'll give him a bit more time before I retrieve my phone." He didn't need to add that the following few minutes were critical. They could be the difference between him keeping or losing his job. If he was wrong, he intended to take the full brunt of the punishment. The worst part would be having to issue an apology to a man who disgusted the hell out of him.

———

LIAM DUCKED into the hallway to check his phone soon after retrieving it from Auger's office, and relief flooded over him after listening to the recording. He hadn't been wrong. He forwarded the tape to the senior officer in Human Trafficking and returned to his desk. He glanced at Auger's closed door before settling in to work.

Quade and Boots returned after lunch with an update on Peter Grady's condition, and it didn't look promising. Boots reported that Grady had broken his knee and hip when he fell. He was also being treated for frostbite in his hands, feet, and face. If the neighbour hadn't found Peter when he did, he'd surely have frozen to death.

"Is he conscious?" Liam asked.

"He slips in and out." Quade swivelled in her desk chair to face Liam. "The doctor sedated him. His daughter Cassie is distraught and won't leave his side. She was supposed to fly home tomorrow morning but cancelled her flight. She insists her dad knows that path like the back of his hand and would never have been so careless. One of the sons — Foster, I believe — said that they've been worried about Peter's memory. He's not as convinced as his sister that their dad didn't make an error in judgement."

"Interesting." Liam regretted not making it back to the Gradys to interview Peter again. His gut instinct had told him the man was holding back. Could his fall have something to do with the secrets he was keeping?

"Well, it's likely an accident, especially since we appear to have other suspects for Marnie Vaughan's murder. Or should I say Veronica Maisonneuve?" Quade started typing on her laptop. She paused and looked up. "Are you going to update Auger on Grady's fall?"

"I am, but I'll suggest we're considering it to have been deliberate. Keep the waters muddied. I'm leaving now to bring Nicola Larsen her dinner."

"Let me know how it goes. I'll be eager for an update."

"You'll be the first one I call."

———

Liam picked up a couple of burgers, fries, and milkshakes at a drive-through window and arrived at the Sleepy Time Motel just after four o'clock. He'd periodically checked in his rearview mirror as he travelled the route and hadn't spotted anybody on his tail. Once in the motel parking lot, he took a space near the office and walked the length of the building to the end unit. He knocked and waited until the door opened. He stepped inside.

"I won't stay long."

"Thanks for the meal. Chocolate shake? You're a prince."

Liam recognized her from the special task force. Last name Baron, as he recalled. Two other officers in full gear, holding weapons, stood near the door. "I should have brought more food."

"Might have been nice. I like chocolate," the taller of the two men said, and everyone laughed.

"Did anybody follow you?" Baron asked.

"Not that I noticed. I expect they're waiting for nightfall."

"I'll call when it's over." Baron checked her watch. "Let's give it five more minutes to be safe, and then you can skedaddle."

"I'll be circling back once it's dark if I haven't heard from you. I'll keep a watch from the parking lot."

"We likely won't need you, but good to know."

Liam drove a distance to a mall where he backed into a parking spot. He opened the second bag containing a hamburger, fries, and shake and devoured the meal while he watched traffic and people getting out of their vehicles. The interior of the car cooled along with the darkening sky. Dusk arrived quickly, just as the cold cancelled out any residual heat. *Showtime*, he thought, turning on the car and putting on his seatbelt.

He drove back the way he'd come and turned into the motel lot, easing his car into a location farthest from the end unit. He shut off the engine and slumped deeper into the seat. There were others positioned outside the motel room as well. A van looked empty near the other exit, but he knew a team was inside waiting. Baron had texted him earlier that she'd warned everyone he'd be returning, so he needn't worry about being on the receiving end of a shakedown. He'd dressed warmly, including putting on a heated vest and hand and foot warmers that he activated. There were blankets on hand in case it got too chilly.

The minutes and hours ticked past without any unusual activity. Liam answered texts while keeping an eye on the cars coming and going. A couple checked in, and he watched them filling in a form and paying with a card at the desk, the lighted office like a movie set on a darkened stage. They parked their SUV several doors down from the end unit, and each rolled a suitcase into the room before closing the door. Several other rooms were occupied as far as Liam could tell. All were a distance from the last unit where Baron and her friends were holed up, the owners' vehicles parked outside their motel room doors or a short distance away in the lot. A couple of work trucks indicated out-of-town crews bunking down for the night.

At 11:00 p.m., all of the occupied rooms were in darkness, and silence had settled over the property. Liam ran the engine every so often to heat up the interior of the car. Midnight came and went, and he found himself yawning. His phone signalled a text.

You may as well go home. We've got this covered.
I'll give it another hour, he typed.
Your call. Hope you're managing to stay warm.

Liam settled back and surveyed the landscape. Piles of snow had been pushed to the edges of the tree line, and pockets of woodland surrounded the perimeter of the property. There were two entrances off the roadway, with a large parking area in front of the motel. The office was in the far right corner of the low-slung building with twenty rooms stretching south in a straight line. The establishment had been well maintained, almost pretty with new white siding and black shutters. The business website called this a family-run operation.

At one thirty, he considered going home to get some shuteye. He needed to feed Lucky and check in with his sister. Hannah had sent a text earlier inviting him and Georgina for dinner on the weekend. He thought about going alone, needing time to think over their relationship. If they moved forward, he should tell Georgina about his night spent sleeping in Ella Tate's bed. The problem was he couldn't lie about his feelings for Ella. He couldn't lie to Georgina, and it was becoming more and more difficult to lie to himself.

The battery life for the heated vest had run out, and the night's chill had worked its way into his bones. He surveyed the property one last time and was about to turn the key in the ignition when he caught the flash of headlights as a car turned off the highway at the far entrance before the vehicle's lights were extinguished. The driver drove at a steady clip, guided by the well-lit office and the outdoor lights next to each motel room door. Liam remained still, adrenaline pulsing through him as the car stopped in front of the end unit, the room entirely in darkness. He'd updated Auger with the room number where he'd supposedly hidden Nicola Larsen before leaving HQ to buy her dinner.

Two men got out of the car, one from the back seat and one from the front passenger side. A third man remained inside with the engine running. They broke into the locked motel door with impressive speed. Liam turned on his car, leaving the headlights off but putting the vehicle into drive with his foot on the brake. Moments later, gun shots, shouting and commotion filled the air from the end unit. Liam drove toward the closest exit with his lights off. The police van began moving into position at the other exit.

The driver of the car idling in front of the motel room must have realized the plan had gone horribly wrong because the getaway car's headlights snapped on and the car rocketed forward, pulling a tight turn to get out of the parking lot. Liam angled his vehicle so that the path to the highway was cut off. The car sped directly toward him, only veering away at the last moment. Liam's heart slowed, but not for long as the car zipped toward the police van, now blocking the second exit. The cornered driver hit the gas and rammed into the side of the van, attempting to clear the path, without success. He backed up to take another run at it. Two officers in full gear leapt out of the back of the van and aimed guns at the driver, screaming at him to get out of the car. Just when it looked as if the driver was going to ignore them, he swung his door open and stepped out with his hands raised, palms facing outward. The officers grabbed him and shoved him to the ground.

Liam backed his car into a parking spot and started walking toward the end unit. Lights in the neighbouring rooms had snapped on, and someone from the office was making their way toward him. The two of them stopped a short distance from the room to take in the action. The night clerk lit a cigarette, and they stood watching while the police marched two men in hand-cuffs onto the sidewalk and into another police vehicle that had pulled into the lot after the arrests. Baron had kept her backup idling out of sight. Liam told the night clerk all would be over soon and walked over to meet Baron, who'd also exited the motel room and was standing on the sidewalk shaking her head at the men in the back of the police car.

"Nasty couple of boys," she said. "They fired a round into the bed, believing Nicola was asleep under the covers. Imagine their surprise when we emerged from the shadows." She grinned. "Good work, Detective. Your staff sergeant is being taken in for questioning as we speak. I've already updated mine. I'll be interested to hear the full story once Auger gives his version."

"You and me both. Auger's the only one in Major Crimes besides me who knew Nicola Larsen was holed up in the end unit, so that's a nugget for your arsenal."

Baron sighed and shook her head. "I hate corrupt cops. Makes us all look bad. Well, we'll see if these three thugs spill their guts after some divide-and-conquer. One usually sees the light. Hopefully we'll get more young women out of their clutches and into safety."

"That's Nicola's hope too."

"Tell her ... tell Nicola we're damn proud of her. Not everyone would have the guts."

"I'll be sure to let her know."

Baron paused and stared intently into his eyes. "Keep her somewhere safe, Hunter, because rats like these will do whatever it takes to stay out of prison. We've lost witnesses before after they were threatened or through misadventure. This is a dirty, dirty world."

"Get those guys to talk, whatever it takes. We need names." He nodded in the direction of the car before taking out his phone to call Quade.

CHAPTER 38

It was Nicola's second night sleeping in Tony's cloud-bed. She took her time waking up, not wanting to face another day of waiting for something bad to happen. That's all she'd come to expect since the summer when those people had met her plane in Thunder Bay, the city where her innocence went to die. She rolled onto her side and stared at a giant picture of Marilyn Monroe above Tony's dresser. The movie star stood posed in high heels over a hot air grate, attempting to hold down her white pleated dress with a huge smile on her perfect lips. She knew Marilyn had been a sex symbol and unhappy enough at the end to take her own life. She understood now how life could beat you down enough to want out, but she swore that wouldn't happen to her. She'd fight to the end, no matter what. At least this past year had shown her that she might be bent, but she couldn't be broken.

Tony called from the other side of the door, "Breakfast in ten if you want a shower now."

"Coming." She lay there a few seconds longer and

thought about the detective who'd listened so attentively to her story. He had the kindest, bluest eyes, and she'd found herself trusting him. He'd flinched when she told him that the cop named Kurt Auger, whom she'd seen on the news asking for information about Veronica, had been at the parties in Toronto. She hadn't had sex with him, but Veronica had more than once. She'd believed at that moment in the university residence common room when she saw his face on TV that she'd never escape the men chasing her. She'd known nobody around her would be safe either. Detective Hunter said he would make sure those people paid for what they did to her and the others, no matter who they were or what power they held. She'd nodded while fighting back tears, because he'd been so certain.

She took longer than planned in the shower but felt better for it. While she was in the bathroom, Tony had placed clean clothes on the bed — she had no idea where from — but the leggings and oversized sweatshirt felt right. Warm and comfortable. She could hardly believe the skimpy clothes she'd been forced to wear for the past almost two years. Already those days were fading into a bad dream.

"Coffee's in the carafe. Help yourself," Tony called from the kitchen. "I'll be there in a sec."

She poured two cups and waited for him. He arrived with two plates of waffles and strawberries with local maple syrup and sat across from her. "Ella will be joining us later this morning. She had an errand, so you're stuck with me."

"I'm not complaining." She smiled at him and picked up a fork. "Thanks for looking after me. I know I'm an inconvenience."

Tony rested his chin on his hand and stared until she met his eyes. "Oh my, girl. You are not an inconvenience. I love having your sweet company."

She nodded and ducked her head, brushing away a tear before it rolled down her cheek. What was wrong with her? A kind word and she fell to pieces.

"Eat up before it gets cold."

"You're the best cook—" She set down the fork, and her shoulders began heaving. Tony rounded the table and pulled her up from the chair. She pressed her face into his shirt, and he didn't let her go until her sobs subsided into hiccups. "I'm sorry," she whispered. "It just hits me sometimes."

"You need to go through these feelings if you're going to heal. Know we're here for you for as long as it takes. You never need to apologize."

She rubbed her eyes and stepped back. "Is it okay if I say that I love you, Tony?"

"I'd want nothing less."

They finished eating, and Tony poured them each another cup of coffee that they took into the living room. Luvy settled next to Nicola on the couch. "Is there something going on between Ella and Detective Hunter?" she asked, hands wrapped around the mug as she brought it to her lips.

"My, aren't you the intuitive one. I'm sorry to say they have yet to acknowledge any attraction."

"They see things the same way. I mean, they both have a way of looking at you, like they're assessing what's going on inside, not just on the surface."

"Right?" He turned his face toward the hall. "Listen, somebody's climbing the stairs. I'll go see who it is. Stay here."

Nicola heard voices outside the apartment door. Tony's and someone else's. They didn't seem threatening, so she stood and walked over to the window to look out at the snow-covered world. The sky was a deep azure, shafts of sunlight streaming through the dark tree branches heavy with sparkling snow. Footsteps entered the room and stopped. Nicola turned and froze. "Mama," she whispered.

"It really is you." Her mother opened her arms wide and started toward her.

Nicola rushed to meet her halfway, and they clung to each other while her mom peppered the top of her head with kisses. "I've waited so long for this day," she said into Nicola's ear. "I never gave up hope."

Nicola stepped back. "Did they tell you—"

"Detective Hunter gave me the main points when he phoned and today shared more details when he drove me here from the airport. He's waiting to tell you what happened last evening."

Her mom had aged. Deep worry lines were etched into her forehead and around her mouth and eyes. She seemed shrunken, diminished from the vibrant woman Nicola remembered. Her part in bringing about this change made her want to weep again. "I had to make sure you were safe before I contacted you." She hugged her mom harder. "I'm sorry I've kept you waiting even one minute longer than I did, but I was scared."

"Shush. You've done nothing wrong. None of what happened is your fault. The detective will look after us. We've lost so much time." Her mother drew her over to the couch, and they sat, legs touching and hands clasped. "If you agree, Ella Tate has arranged for us to stay with her mother in Winnipeg. Her mom volunteers at a shelter working with abused women and is offering us a refuge for as long as we want or need. Nobody would know where we are while things get sorted out."

"As long as we're together."

"We will be. Wild horses won't pull me away from you." Her mom squeezed her hand.

"The money to fly here and to Winnipeg … I don't have any right now, and I know you don't have extra, but I'll pay you back, Mom."

"Your friends are looking after us. They paid for me to come here."

There was a rap on the wall, and Detective Hunter entered. "I'm sorry to interrupt, but Nicola, it's time to go to the station and make a formal statement. We've arrested three men, and Staff Sergeant Auger is being questioned. We need to formalize what you told me yesterday."

"Am I allowed to stay with her?" her mother asked.

"Of course."

"Then we'll face this together, Nicola." Her mother rubbed her cheek gently with her fingertips. "Neither of us has to be alone anymore."

———

THIS TIME, Quade led Nicola through her interview with her mother present. Liam wasn't allowed to be part of Auger's questioning but watched the video feed in another room. Auger progressed from defensive and outraged to sullen over the course of half an hour. The staff sergeant from the Trafficking Unit played the recording Liam had forwarded from his phone in which Auger spoke on his cell phone, telling somebody that

Nicola Larsen was staying at the Sleepy Time Motel. He wanted to ensure that she'd be taken care of as soon as possible. Auger and Liam's phones had already been taken into evidence.

"Got him dead to rights," Boots said. "He's going on the offensive, but that recording is about as damning as it gets."

"I've also testified that he was the only one besides me who knew the motel room number. We'll get one of the three men to talk, and Auger's career will be over."

"Couldn't have happened to a more deserving S.O.B. I'm guessing the chief of police is watching the same feed?"

"That's my understanding."

"Did Auger kill Marnie Vaughan? I realize we should start calling her Veronica Maisonneuve."

"I know who you're talking about either way. Everyone knew her as Marnie, and it'll be difficult for them to make the switch. My guess is no, he didn't kill her, but he likely knows who did."

"I realized the guy's underhanded and chauvinistic but never would have guessed he's also corrupt. I hope this means Quade will get the staff sergeant job that should have been hers."

"That would be a good outcome." Liam was reluctant to wade into these waters, careful not to sound vindictive. Auger hadn't been convicted of anything yet.

"So what's up for you now, Hunter?"

"I'm going to make a run to the hospital to visit Peter Grady and his daughter. Something feels off about his accident."

"How so?"

"His fiancée is murdered and then he suffers a fall

on a trail he knows well. Cassie says no way he'd be that careless. I'd like to speak with her before deciding if there's an issue."

"Perhaps she's not accepting the truth. Her father's getting up there in age."

"Certainly a consideration, although I'd argue sixty-four isn't all that old."

Liam sent a message to Quade about his trip to the hospital and zipped up his parka. While he'd be in a heated car for the most part, it always paid to be dressed for the weather in case something unforeseen arose along the way.

Parking always proved a challenge at the Civic Hospital, but he found an empty spot second time circling the lot. Reception sent him to intensive care, where he spoke with a nurse about Peter Grady's condition before entering the single room where he was being monitored by a heart machine with fluid dripping into his arm and an oxygen tube in his nose. Cassie started to rise from her chair near the head of the bed, but Liam motioned for her to remain seated. He moved to stand near her and looked down at Peter.

"The nurse said he's doing well," he said.

"Still unconscious, but yeah, his vitals are improving." She was holding his hand. Her eyes filled with tears. "I don't know what to do." She stared into her father's face and bit her bottom lip. "I'm needed back in Vancouver, but I don't dare to leave him alone."

"He has your brothers and Wilma."

Cassie's eyes darkened for a moment before she looked away. "Things just seem so ... uncertain."

"You said that you can't believe he slipped and fell from the bridge. Do you have evidence otherwise?"

She shook her head and looked past him. Liam turned to find Mick and Gordon standing in the door-way. The silence felt awkward as the brothers looked from him to Cassie.

"How's he doing?" Mick asked, taking a step into the room.

"Better." Cassie gave them a shaky smile. "Although the doctor isn't certain how cognizant Dad will be when he wakes up. The trauma could affect his memory."

"And he was having lapses before this happened." Gordon crossed the space and rested a hand on Cassie's shoulder. "You should go home and rest."

She ignored him and looked across at Mick. "When are you returning to university?"

"This evening, if Dad's all right. I was halfway to Kingston when I got the call about his accident."

"It's good you weren't too far away." She looked up at Gordon. "Where's Foster?"

"He's getting coffee with Deirdre and Khloe. I need to return to work tomorrow too. My supply teacher could only give me today, and I've depleted my days off to almost nothing." His eyes darted from Liam to his dad and back as he spoke. "Is there a reason you're here, Detective?"

Cassie's face whitened, and Liam sent her a reas-suring smile. He wouldn't tell anyone that she'd come to him with her concerns about the fall. "Only to check on your dad's condition and to give an update on Marnie's murder case. Are you okay if I call her by her real name, Veronica Maisonneuve?"

"Yes, please do."

"Once the others are here, we could find a quiet

space where I can brief everyone at once. I'll go check with a nurse to see if she can help."

The same nurse he'd spoken with earlier pointed to a small meeting room and told him that he was free to use it. She'd let the rest of the staff know. By the time he returned to Peter's room, the entire family had gathered. They followed him down the hall and settled in the chairs and on the couch while Liam leaned against the window ledge. "Last night we arrested three men whom we believe are part of the operation that trafficked Veronica. They were attempting to kill another young woman who escaped last week. This woman knew Veronica from the time they were both being forced into sex work."

"They killed Marnie … Veronica then?" Foster asked. Liam noted that not for the first time, he took on the role of family spokesman.

"It's too early to say for certain, but we're working on this premise."

"Dad hasn't been himself since Marnie arrived on the scene. We've been worried about his mental acuity, and now it turns out with reason. We'd hoped Wilma would be able to monitor him, but Deirdre and I have begun looking into senior residences with different levels of care."

"What the hell are you talking about?" Cassie jumped up from her chair. "You're not putting Dad in a home. He's far from incompetent."

Liam noticed the three brothers exchange glances. So they'd discussed their dad's future without her input. Was Cassie the difficult sibling, or was something else at play? Liam stayed silent and waited.

"You're not in a position to make these decisions,

Cass," Deirdre said, her voice striking a reasonable tone. "We're the ones who see your dad almost daily and have been noticing his decline. It's been difficult at times."

"We didn't want to worry you," Khloe added. "Gordon's been especially concerned. You know he and your dad have breakfast at a diner every Sunday, and they belong to the same gym, so he's tracked your dad's cognitive issues."

Cassie stared at each of them in turn with what Liam could only call incredulity. "You've all gotten together and decided this already, haven't you? Was it Marnie? Is that why you've ganged up on him?"

"Nobody ganged up on Dad. We all want what's best for him," Gordon said, putting his arm around Khloe as if to emphasize their united front.

Cassie focused her gaze on Mick. "Where do you stand on this, little brother? Do you think Dad belongs in a home?"

Mick shifted in the chair and looked at Foster. "I'm not in Ottawa enough to know."

"Great. That's just great." Cassie sat down and slumped against the chair back. She crossed her arms and legs and stared into space.

Foster broke the awkward silence. "So where do we go from here with the case, Detective?"

"You carry on with your lives while we continue to investigate behind the scenes. If anything arises, we'll inform you."

"Like when these three scumbags get charged."

"If charges are laid, you will be told."

"Then it looks like we can finish up here and get back to Dad." Foster stood and walked over to shake Liam's hand. The rest of the family took their cue and filed out of the room behind him. Cassie was the last to leave, her steps slowing as she reached the door. "Please don't let my dad's fall go into a report without looking into how it happened. I have to return to Vancouver because a lot of people are counting on me to film the next episode of the TV series. I've changed to a Friday evening flight but would stay here another week if I had a choice. You're the only one who can find out the truth."

"It could well have been an accident, Cassie." There was no point in giving her false hope.

She nodded. "I get that, but I need to know one way or the other."

"And I'll do my best to find out the truth."

CHAPTER 39

He should have gone directly home. Lucky would love some attention, and he could call Georgina and meet her somewhere for a drink and dinner. That's what he should have done. Instead, Liam found himself turning into the Glebe neighbourhood and searching for a parking spot near Percy and Third.

He trudged the two blocks to Ella's front door, rang the bell, and waited. A chilly breeze found the exposed skin on his face, and he shivered inside his parka. Tony or Finn might let him in if she didn't hear the doorbell. He hoped they'd do it soon. Footsteps pounded on the stairs and down the hall, and a moment later Ella swung the door open, her expression turning guarded when she saw him. He soaked in the sight of her. Tousled blonde hair, thoughtful eyes that seemed too green to be real, oversized sweater, black leggings, and moccasins — unconcerned with her appearance yet effortlessly attractive. She was a watcher, like him, content to be in her own head. "Do you have a minute to talk?" he asked before the silence lengthened into the uncomfortable range.

"Sure, come in out of the cold."

He followed her up the two flights of stairs into her apartment, which was marginally warmer than the outdoors. She led him into her cramped living room, where a space heater under the desk kept the frost off. "My landlord Alex said last summer that he was going to get insulation blown into the attic but never did. I'm not even certain that's possible in this old brick house." She shrugged. "Good thing the cold snaps don't last too long. The temperature in my apartment's better than last week anyway. Here, take the good chair and I'll move the heater closer."

He sat and watched her fiddle with the heater. She straightened and caught him staring. He smiled. "I don't know anybody else who'd put up with this place as long as you have."

"I like it here." She returned his smile. "Yeah, it's quirky and has its issues, but this is all I need, really. I'm able to put away some money too, which is important, since who knows when my work will dry up again."

"I can't see that happening. Your podcast alone has a huge following."

"I admit it's getting lucrative." She shrugged. "This place suits me for now. So what brought you to my door this evening?"

He unzipped his jacket. "We've arrested the three men who were after Veronica."

"I heard. She and her mom are at the airport as we speak. Thank you for sending Jingles to take them. Why do you call him that, by the way?"

"Jingles? His real surname is Jorgenson, but he used

to have all these lucky charms in his pocket when he was a beat cop, and he kind of jingled when he walked. His partner at the time started calling him Jingles, and the name stuck."

"And his current partner, Boots?"

"His surname is Bottes, which is—"

"French for boots."

"Yeah, not too original."

"It kind of suits him." Ella's face turned sombre. "My mom works with abused women and will be a huge asset for Nicola and her mother."

Liam knew the two had a long road ahead. This support would be a crucial piece of Nicola's recovery. "We're questioning Kurt Auger."

"Your staff sergeant? Why?"

"Nicola identified him as being at parties in Toronto. She said he had sex with Veronica."

"My God, your unit must be reeling." Ella paused. "I wish I could say that I'm surprised."

"Why aren't you?"

"I did some digging. Auger had two female officers in Toronto bring sexual allegations against him that were eventually dropped. He also instigated Rosie Thorburn's transfer out of Major Crimes after trying the same on her and being rebuffed."

"Thorburn never made a complaint."

"No, she didn't want to take him on and possibly ruin her career."

"I wish she'd come to me."

"You were her partner. She didn't want you involved."

"I could have helped."

"Maybe. She knew that you'd try but didn't want more people dragged down with her."

Liam took a moment to relive Rosie's reactions to her transfer out of his unit. She'd been upset, could barely look at Auger when he was in the same room. He'd known there was animosity between the two. This information made him look at all their interactions through a new lens. "Well, Auger is getting his comeuppance now. Nicola said she'd testify if it comes to that. She's already signed a statement. We have other proof he was trying to silence her."

"He could be behind Veronica Maisonneuve's murder."

"In all likelihood, but that thread is still dangling." He voiced his concerns for the first time. "Something is going on in the Grady family. The dad had a bad fall out walking, and his daughter Cassie insists he was too experienced to be that careless. She seems ... on edge around her family, if that makes sense."

"What are you going to do?"

"Not sure." He rested his elbows on his knees and leaned toward her. "Ella, I've been thinking about you since the other night—"

She waved a hand in the air. "It was a mistake. Too much alcohol and not enough food. You don't need to dwell on what happened, and I certainly don't want an apology. I was as much at fault as you."

"What if I *want* to dwell on it?" He forged ahead. "We could go out for dinner."

"Like a real date?"

"Yeah, see where things lead."

She studied him, her green eyes attentive and soft. When she spoke, her voice held a note of regret. "You mean too much to me, Liam. I don't want to jeopardize our friendship for a few rolls in the hay. Neither of us appears made for the long haul in relationships — at least I'm not, if you look at my track record. I want to avoid losing you from my life."

"Fear isn't a good reason not to act on whatever is between us. We could both regret never giving it a chance."

A knock at her apartment door broke the moment. Ella gave him an apologetic smile before tearing her gaze from his and getting up to answer. She returned a few seconds later with Decker in tow.

"Detective Hunter." Decker nodded before swinging his attention back to Ella. She stood near her desk as if uncertain what to say. Decker smiled at her. "I came to update you on our trip. The cab to the airport arrives at five tomorrow morning. Tony plans to be upstairs in an hour to help you pack."

"Tell him not to bother. I'll be ready."

"Funny, he told me you'd say that and to let you know he won't be deterred. Anyway, tomorrow at this time, we'll be sipping piña coladas by the pool, basking in the heat and forgetting all about this insufferable northern climate."

Liam watched their interaction. Ella appeared ill at ease, but she was going along with the trip, which said a lot. Decker had shown his interest in her, and they'd be spending a week together in a party environment. Liam didn't believe he was jumping to conclusions when he saw where this was heading. He stood. "I'll be on my way. Enjoy your trip and safe travels."

Ella took a step toward him and hesitated. "We can talk when I get back."

"Sure, but no need to worry about the idea any longer."

"I want ... we should talk about it more. I don't want to leave things this way."

He walked down the hallway and opened her apartment door without responding. He regretted stopping at Ella's house, weary from a day at work, unsettled by all he'd learned about Auger. One thing had become clear to him, however, as he attempted to put forth a case for dinner with Ella. He needed to break things off with Georgina and not waste her time any longer. He liked her immensely but didn't feel what he should to take their relationship deeper. Perhaps he was as Ella said, incapable of a long-term commitment with any woman. The thought saddened him as he trudged the two blocks to his car through the snowy streets. His phone rang as he turned on the engine, and moments later his personal problems disappeared as he concentrated on Coroner Brigette Green's voice.

———

QUADE PULLED in behind him across the street from the Grady house. Liam waited until she turned off her car before stepping out of his vehicle and walking back to open her door.

"Hell of a night to be working. Seems like this has become our pattern." She glowered at him before leaving the warmth of her car and standing next to him. Both stared toward the Grady front door as flakes of snow began falling from the leaden sky. "Another storm coming." She pulled up the hood of her parka. "Damn this weather."

"We agree Wilma was the one most likely poisoning Veronica with arsenic?" Liam wanted Quade's assurance that they were on the same wavelength before entering the house.

"Wilma had reason to be upset. Peter was bringing a young woman into what had become her home. Wilma also prepared the meals and was in the best position to doctor the food. Who else?"

"It couldn't have been Mick or Cassie. The poisoning had been going on a while, and they didn't live here. Foster, Deirdre, Gordon, or Khloe had more opportunity."

"I'm still liking Wilma for it. A strong motivation and the best access. Now the trick will be getting her to talk. She's a tough customer from what I've seen. Have you ordered a tox screen on Peter Grady's blood too?"

"I did. It'll take a week at least." He thought about the family's comments concerning Peter's mental lapses and general ill health. They'd even talked about putting him into assisted living. Slow poisoning, if proven, had affected him more strongly than Veronica, possibly because of his age. He might have been given a larger dose. Liam voiced another misgiving. "That Wilma would poison both defies logic if she wanted Peter to herself."

"Ah, but she was angry, and revenge isn't always logical. The woman gave up the better part of her life serving him and raising his kids."

"Maybe."

They crossed the street, and Liam rang the doorbell. He could hear the chimes pealing throughout the house before taking a step back to stand next to Quade.

Wilma opened the door only far enough to look

outside. She wore a flowered apron over a black sweater and slacks and was drying her hands on a tea towel. "Back again, are you? The family isn't at home, if you're looking for someone in particular."

"We're actually here to speak with you." Liam moved forward and pulled the door wider open so that she had no choice but to step back and let them in.

"Has Cassie left?" he asked.

"She's upstairs packing. Her flight is tomorrow morning. This is her second time rescheduling."

Liam wondered if she'd be at the airport the same time as Ella. "Is there a place we can sit and talk?"

"Remove your boots and follow me into the kitchen. I'll make a pot of tea, and you can take chairs at the island."

Quade glanced at Liam, and he nodded. Better to have Wilma in a place she felt comfortable as they began the questioning.

He noted Wilma's hair was pulled back into a severe bun at the nape of her neck, with a lack of make up or any jewellery to break up the plainness of her appearance. She'd put more effort into how she looked when Peter was home. They settled on stools and watched her prepare the tea with shaky hands. She waved off Quade's offer of help. At last, Wilma took a stool across from them after filling three mugs and setting out cream and sugar in china dishes. By silent agreement, he and Quade refrained from adding anything to their tea.

"You've been working for the Gradys for a long time," Liam said.

"I raised Mick after Mrs. Grady died. Peter … Mr. Grady didn't get over his grieving easily."

"The family owes you a lot."

"I was happy to be of service. The kids became like family to me."

"But they aren't — family, that is," Quade said, drawing Wilma's attention away from Liam. Quade gave a sad smile, as if commiserating. "That became evident when Peter decided to remarry without any regard for your feelings. I understand you planned to retire after their marriage."

"My feelings weren't important one way or the other. I'm simply an employee." Her even tone conflicted with the pain in her eyes. "It seemed time for me to take my leave."

"You'd be superhuman not to resent his choice of a new mate. Marnie was barely older than Cassie."

"She wasn't the woman I would have picked for him." Wilma pursed her lips so that they formed a tight, prim line. "We got along, though. I made an effort."

"Foster, Gordon, and Mick weren't happy with his choice either."

"No."

"Did they come to you with their concerns?"

"They did."

Liam heard a note of pride in her voice. He imagined she'd revelled in being their confidante. She may have called herself an employee, but she'd dedicated her life to them. It would be only natural that she considered herself one of the family. They might have thought differently about her role, especially as the children grew to be adults. He experienced a pang of sympathy for her. The life she must have wanted was never attainable. He forced himself to put the feeling aside. "A lab report showed elevated levels of a toxic substance in Marnie's system. She was being slowly poisoned by small doses of arsenic."

Wilma's eyes widened before she looked down at her hands grasping the mug. "That's impossible. She ate most of her meals here, and I did the cooking."

"That was our understanding." He waited until she raised her head and looked at him. Her gaze sharpened as realization took hold. "What were you adding to her food, Wilma?" he asked softly.

"Nothing. I wouldn't—" She closed her mouth and sighed. A look of relief mixed with frustration crossed her features. "That foolish, foolish man."

"What do you mean?"

"Peter and Foster took a trip to China in the spring for work, and Peter returned with super vitamins. He convinced Marnie to take them too. I warned him they could be laced with anything, but he laughed. The pills supposedly contained shark fin or some such nonsense that he said made him stronger and more virile. He was into fitness. Thought he could turn back time."

Quade's expression was sceptical. "Where are these pills?"

"On his bedside table. The two of them popped them every morning before exercising. He ordered a new batch last autumn via his Chinese contact. I'd say dealer, but that might be a step too judgemental. You're welcome to take the pills to analyze. You can search my things and the kitchen, whatever you like. I have nothing to hide. Peter will confirm all this when he recovers."

"Did he or Marnie experience any symptoms?"

"Peter was fine with the first lot of vitamins, but he mentioned lately that they both had diarrhea a few times and believed it was contaminated food at restaurants. He complained that the skin on his hands and feet was drying out and had me buy a special cream. He was also having difficulty concentrating and remembering things. I might add that Marnie wasn't as committed to the vitamin regime as he was after the second batch arrived. She only took the vitamins when Peter reminded her."

"We'd like to check out his bedroom now, if you can lead the way."

"Of course."

The master bedroom was on the second floor and took up the east wing above the living room. Large casement windows lined the south-facing wall and would let in a great deal of light during the day. The king-size bed was covered in pale blue satin sheets and a burgundy duvet. It was flanked by large walnut end tables that held hurricane lamps, carafes, and crystal water glasses. The vitamin pill bottles were next to a stack of architectural magazines on Peter's side of the bed. Quade put on a glove and slipped the bottles into a plastic baggie.

Cassie stood waiting for them on the landing when they exited the room. "What's going on, Detective Hunter?" she asked.

"It's possible the vitamins your father and Marnie were taking contained a poisonous substance. We'll be testing the pills to be certain. Do you know where he got them?"

"He said he found a distributor when he and Foster were on a business trip to China last spring. Dad tried to get me to take them as well, but I declined. Could this explain his mental confusion?"

"We're not doctors, but this could be the cause."

Liam met Quade's eyes. Cassie effectively had backed up Wilma's story.

Cassie's relieved expression disappeared. "The pills didn't kill Marnie, though. Sorry, I can't get my head around her real name, Veronica."

"The vitamins are simply an avenue of enquiry."

"Then whatever was going on with Dad wasn't intentional and should be easily cured if he stops taking the vitamins. That at least is one good piece of news."

She led them downstairs and made certain Liam had her contact information in Vancouver before they stepped outside. The snow was falling in steady silence, their car coated in a thick layer.

"Well, that didn't play out like we thought," Quade said. She read her cell phone screen as she walked.

"I'm okay with that." Liam preferred this outcome. "I can take the pills to lockup if you'd like to head home."

"It's been a long day. I'll owe you one." She stopped halfway down the sidewalk and turned her face up toward the sky. "The universe works in mysterious ways, Hunter. Boots sent an update. Auger's sleazy past has caught up with him, and he's going down. The three men arrested at the motel are talking, each one blaming the other. They're naming names and have pointed fingers at Auger. I wish I could say I was sorry, but that would be a lie."

"Trafficking Division will be making raids to save more victims. They'll move quickly."

"Let's hope we've figured this out in time."

CHAPTER 40

"I'm going out for a bit," Cassie called to Wilma. "I have my key, so no need to wait up."

"It's been snowing. Are you taking one of your father's cars?" Wilma strode out of the kitchen, wiping her hands on a dishtowel.

"I am, but I'm not driving far." She didn't mean to sound mysterious, but she was tired of telling Wilma where she was going. The woman was always hovering. Cassie would be glad to fly home tomorrow morning and get back her life now that her dad was expected to make a long, slow recovery. He was in good hands, and she'd plan a daily Zoom call to keep his spirits up. Thank goodness for technology.

Wilma seemed to read her mood. "I'm calling it an early night. I'll be up to make you a filling breakfast in the morning."

"Thanks, Wilma. It'll have to be early. I've got a cab booked to take me to the airport around eight o'clock."

Her dad's Beamer was parked in the heated garage, for which she gave silent thanks. Snow coated the driveway, but she easily drove through the drifts to the road. The streets had been cleared before this last snowfall and were passable. By morning, the ploughs would be out, shifting the latest accumulation.

She drove south on Bank, past Foster and Deirdre's home in Old Ottawa South into the less affluent, more diverse neighbourhoods in South Keys. Gordon and Khloe's townhouse farther south and east on Cahill was in a high-density neighbourhood lined with row housing of seventies vintage. The front porch light was on at Gordon's, and the living room was also lit up. Nobody had drawn the curtains, and she could see the back of Gordon's head above his chair. He liked to watch television in the evenings after dinner. Mick had already returned to residence in Kingston. She noted that Khloe's car wasn't in its usual spot in the driveway. Cassie hoped she'd taken the twins so she could speak with her brother without anyone else around. He'd avoided being alone with her so far, whether by circumstance or design, and she needed to make certain everything was okay with him before she left. She had to clear up an unsettling concern.

She parked on the street, getting as close to the bank of snow as possible without getting the tires stuck, careful not to block the laneway of any of the townhouses. Gordon would wait for this snowfall to end before bringing out the snow blower and cleaning his drive and walkway.

He didn't answer the doorbell or her knocks, and she felt the first ripple of unease until it came to her that he probably was wearing earbuds and unable to hear. *Don't think the worst.* She tried the handle, and the door swung open into the short hallway, crammed with shoes and boots piled near the wall with coats and scarves hanging on hooks. A book bag had been tossed carelessly on the floor, and the contents of a pencil case lay strewn across its surface, drawing her eye downward. The wooden planks needed a fresh varnishing, but she thought the house cozy and lived-in. Khloe didn't like to invite company over, preferring to meet at the Grady family house or in a restaurant. It couldn't be easy for Gordon to know his wife was embarrassed by their home. Khloe had come from old money, and living on his salary was quite a step — if not drop — down. Gordon had agreed in the early days when the twins were born that he would be the sole provider, so that Khloe could stay home with them. Cassie knew Khloe had no intention of going to work now, even though Gordon wanted her to help with their debt load. She'd come to enjoy the freedom and said that the bills would get paid eventually, and it was Gordon's responsibility to look after their finances. No wonder he needed to earn the vice principal job to make ends meet.

Gordon turned his head to look at Cassie as she stood in the doorway, surveying the living room. The television was turned off, which surprised her, and he wasn't wearing headphones. "Why didn't you answer the door?" she asked, moving toward the couch wedged against the far wall. Somebody, likely one of the twins, had left an empty glass and plate on the coffee table with crumbs scattered across its surface.

He ignored her question. "This isn't a good time."

"Where are Khloe and the girls?"

"Gone to her mother's. Khloe and I had a fight, and she needs her space." He mimicked her voice and said the last three words as if putting them in quotation marks.

"Nothing serious?"

"It's been building."

"I wanted to tell you that Dad and Marnie were taking vitamins that he purchased in China and online. Apparently, they were laced with arsenic, and that's why he seemed so confused. He was slowly poisoning the pair of them. How nuts is that?"

"Ironic, since she died anyway."

It was only then that she spotted the rifle leaning up against her brother's leg. She realized he hadn't met her eyes since she entered the room. She took a step toward him. "Are you okay, Gordon? You seem upset."

The fingers resting on his thigh began tapping. "I'm actually at peace for the first time in a long while."

"Well, I must confess that I was worried for a bit before I found out about the vitamins. I saw your car near the path into the woods the morning of Dad's accident. You passed by me with your head turned away. I thought … well, it doesn't matter now."

"You thought I pushed him over the bridge."

She laughed. "Preposterous, right? I know you wouldn't be capable of anything so heinous, but this has been such a strange time."

He looked at her then, and his eyes held an expression she hadn't seen before. A mixture of sadness, guilt, and regret, each emotion fighting for supremacy. "What if I tell you I did push him? Sure, it was without forethought, but I was capable enough."

"I don't believe you."

"Cassie the good." The words came out sarcastic, not complimentary. "Veronica or Marnie or whatever the hell she called herself told Dad enough the day she died for him to figure out I had reason to kill her. I wanted to stop him from talking, like I stopped her."

"But why? What could she possibly have said about you?"

"Marnie was a hooker, did you know that? I paid her pimp for a number of encounters. We became an item of sorts because I requested her exclusively after the first time."

"But she and Dad were engaged." Cassie's mind was having trouble keeping pace with what he was saying. "You have a good marriage." None of this added up.

"I'm not sure what you mean by good, exactly. Khloe considered me and our lifestyle a disappointment. She excluded me from raising our daughters. We've rarely had sex since they were born. It was easy enough to meet another woman, since Khloe thought I was working all the time."

"She loves you."

"Not really. Not the way she did once. I thought about leaving, but it wasn't financially feasible. Khloe wouldn't even get a job, so I'd have to support her, the girls, two residences — and she'd get half my pension."

"You were seeing Marnie?"

"Long before Dad, but I knew her as Veronica. She acted like she cared and was so easy to talk to. I thought we meant something … that I meant something. All the loneliness disappeared when we were together." He ran a hand across his forehead and made a disgusted sound. "I convinced myself that paying her to be with me wasn't important when it came to our feelings for each other. You cannot imagine how it felt when I realized she'd sought out our father and started up with him to get his money. It wasn't me at all that she cared about. Keeping that secret made me crazy."

"Does Khloe know——"

"About my extracurricular hobby? No, although lately she believes I've been having an affair. Hence our latest argument. I helped Veronica escape from her pimp, thinking — not thinking. Even found her a place to live and put up the rent money. Next thing I know, she's gone to my gym and is sleeping with our father and calling herself Marnie Vaughn. She begged me to keep her secret because she said her pimp and his business partners would kill her, ironic as that seems now. She thought Dad was the perfect cover. They'd never look for her in Rockcliffe, married to a wealthy businessman. I didn't want her pimp to find her, God help me, just like I didn't want her to blow up my marriage and career. Our unholy pact was based on mutual blackmail." He moaned. "Knowing she was with him was driving me crazy. You cannot even begin to understand my jealousy."

Cassie felt as if she was standing on the edge of a cliff and the earth under her feet had begun to crumble. "So what happened? How did she die?"

"I asked her to meet me. I wanted to stop the marriage before she got her hands on our money, before she became my stepmother. She said that she'd grown fond of Dad and was going to tell him the truth about us and the lies she'd told when they first met so he could back out if he wanted to. She'd already given him the basics of her past life. I said none of that mattered, and it wasn't too late. I asked her to run away with me, and she laughed. Can you believe it? She laughed. I strangled the life out of her then. I told myself it was to save the family." He rubbed his forehead vigorously this time. "I thought I could live with erasing her from our lives, but if anything it's worse than before. I can barely stand being here. I hurt all the time. Khloe said I was scaring her."

"Oh, Gordon." Sadness threatened to spill out of Cassie in uncontrollable sobs, but once started, she wouldn't be able to stop. Gordon, her gentle, supportive brother, had committed adultery and murder, put their father in the hospital. The enormity of what he'd done overwhelmed her. Yet the sorrow she felt for him couldn't erase his sins or make this right. "You didn't plan to kill her. That means something."

"Yeah, manslaughter instead of first degree. Either way is bad. Khloe will never get over the shame."

"What are you going to do? Let me help you."

"You need to leave. This is my problem to handle."

"I don't want you to use that rifle. Promise me you won't harm yourself."

"Tell Dad I'm sorry. I wasn't myself."

"Gordon—"

"I wanted to say that you're right to break up with Heath. A man who cheats isn't worth your trust. You deserve better. You're a star, sweet sister. I'll always love you, even if I'm not worthy of saying that." His face crumpled for a moment before he regained control. "Now see yourself out."

"Don't do this, Gordon. I love you. Khloe and the girls need you."

"The sad truth is they're better off without me. Leave me now, Cassie, and don't look back." His voice had hardened into a command.

Tears blurred her vision, but somehow she made it

to the hallway and outside onto the snowy stoop, leaving the door open so that she could see inside. Her heart pounded, and she let out a cry as she scrolled through her phone with a shaking hand until she found the number for Detective Hunter saved in contacts. He answered on the second ring, and she identified herself and recited Gordon's address just before a gunshot blasted through the quiet, echoing off the walls and deafening her for as many seconds. She sagged back against the wall and lurched into the hallway, telling herself to pretend this was television and she could act her way out of the scene. She drew in a deep breath and focused on the shadows stretching into the darkness outside the pool of porch light, trying to remember her lines. Detective Hunter's voice was speaking urgently into her ear, asking if she was all right, drawing her back to the present and to her grief.

"There's no rush now," she said as calmly as she might be talking to a friend who'd been held up and was apologizing for their tardiness. She paused and ran her tongue across her lips. The night was carrying on, a normal evening that swallowed up tragedies without sentimentality or judgement. Her brother's death didn't stop the snow from falling or light up the sky with fireworks. The universe didn't care about the well of grief that made her slide down the wall until she huddled a broken woman amidst the boots and shoes. "I'll keep watch until you come," she promised before dropping the phone and burying her face in her knees. She waited for Hunter there, not moving until he arrived before the others, crouched down and gathered her into his arms as if he was holding a lost child who couldn't find her way home.

CHAPTER 41

Sara skipped class Friday and the entire next week to catch up on the essays and the assigned readings she'd neglected to finish. After Nikki left town, she'd returned to the sanctuary of her father's house and had it refitted with a new front door lock, one of better quality than its predecessor.

Detective Hunter had come to visit the day she moved back, and he'd done a walk-through to make sure all was secure while she made tea. Afterward, he'd sat for an hour in the kitchen, talking to her about the charges being laid against the three men who'd been arrested. They'd turned on each other, and eventually, each had made a confession, although not for the murder of Veronica Maisonneuve. Based on their interviews, two girls had been rescued from the trafficking ring — one seventeen and the other sixteen — but the others had been moved before the police could reach them. The three arrested men were lower-level and hadn't known the names of those in charge behind the operation ... or so they claimed. However, because of the two rescued girls' testimony, a senator and two men in the business community had been charged. Liam's own staff sergeant was in deep trouble for his part in the attempted murder of Nicola in the motel, not to mention his sexual activities with trafficked girls. He said that he hadn't remembered or recognized Veronica until Hunter talked about parties in Toronto and said her name in his office. Auger's career was all but finished; his wife had moved out and had asked for a divorce.

"Nikki is safe and getting counselling," Hunter said, draining the last of his tea. "She wanted me to pass along her love and thanks to you, Jeremy, Ella, and Tony. She said that she wouldn't have made it without everyone's help, especially yours, Sara. Not many would have risked what you did for a stranger."

"I'm just glad she's okay." Sara lowered her mug and grinned. "I could get used to the excitement, saving someone from the bad guys."

"Well, don't go looking for trouble. You have a bright future ahead of you in law enforcement or as a private investigator once you're done your education. There's still lots to learn about the law and keeping yourself safe."

"I get it. Do you believe one of those men killed Veronica?"

"No. Gordon Grady, the son of the man who planned to marry her, confessed before he took his own life. The case is closed. You can read about it in the news, I imagine."

"That's tragic." Sara wanted to ask him about Ella, but he set down his mug and stood. "I've got someone making supper for me, so I'd best be on my way. You take good care, Sara."

"I always do."

———

Monday morning, Sara left her father's house and drove to her eleven o'clock class. She'd dressed with unusual attention to her outfit and had applied mascara and lip gloss, leaving fifteen minutes early so that she could sit next to Jeremy and catch up on all that had been going on. Nikki had told her to text him, but she hadn't gotten up the nerve since that last morning in his room in residence. Enough time had passed that he wouldn't think she was stalking him. She could barely admit to herself how excited she was at the thought of seeing him again.

The frigid temperatures had eased, and the radio announcer promised an above average thaw, not uncommon for late January. Sara unzipped her parka and tucked her toque into her pocket as she walked across campus. The sun warmed her hair, and she stopped to raise her face with eyes closed before entering the building. Hard to believe they'd lived through a deep freeze the rest of the month. Three girls she recognized from her class walked past her without saying hello, but Sara wasn't as bothered as she'd once been. Her self-worth didn't depend on these people liking or even noticing her.

The class was in an amphitheatre, and students streamed past as Sara stood at the top of the set of steps, looking for Jeremy. She spotted him in his usual seat, but he wasn't alone. A pretty girl was beside him where Sara had once sat, speaking animatedly and gesturing with her hands as she told him a story.

Jeremy laughed at something she said, and she punched him playfully on the shoulder. Red-faced, Sara turned and walked an aisle over, slipping into one of the few remaining seats halfway to the front. She pulled up the desk table from its slot and set down her laptop, forcing herself not to look across at Jeremy. She had no intention of adding to her humiliation. Luckily, only she knew how delusional she'd been to think he'd want anything more to do with her now that Nikki was gone.

She filed away her disappointment with all the other hurts and slights accumulated over her lifetime and waited for the psychology lecture to begin. She told herself that she was happier in the long run keeping herself closed off from caring enough to be hurt. She'd let her guard down and allowed herself to be distracted by the idea of friendship, but it was only a reminder that she needed to count on herself. Her aloneness in a crowd of people was her super power.

She focused on the prof, who'd started strutting around the stage and gesticulating with his hands as he pontificated. She began typing notes into a file and pondered the information as he spoke. The professor ended his talk, and Sara took a few minutes to add her impressions of his arguments. The debate on nature versus nurture seemed too absolute for her liking. Both had an impact, and in her mind the answer was not an either/or, as he'd suggested. She finished typing and started to pack up her bag. She jumped when Jeremy plunked down in the seat next to her.

"I was watching for you."

"You had company. I didn't want to intrude."

"Who, Sheila? I've known her since kindergarten.

Neither of us realized we're in the same class again. You skipped last week?"

"I needed to catch up on work."

"So fill me in on Nikki. Is she part of that trafficking scandal reported in the news?"

"Yes. She's somewhere safe."

"I knew it." He raised the palm of his hand toward her, and she awkwardly slapped it in a high five. "You did it, McGowan. Do you have time for coffee? We can grab a cup, and you can tell me everything that happened since I last saw you." He turned as his name was called. His two friends were standing at the end of the aisle, waiting. He swung back to look at Sara.

"Go ahead," she said. "It's okay."

"One sec." He got up and talked to his friends while Sara put on her jacket. She'd go to the library as planned and finish working on an essay due Friday. Jeremy motioned for her to join him. "Sara, these are my buddies, Ryan and Pascal."

"Hi. Nice to meet you." She smiled at them, and they nodded at her. "Guess I'll see you around," she said to Jeremy.

He took her arm. "I told the guys I'd meet up with them later. Let's go get that coffee."

Sara followed him up the steps. She couldn't believe he'd turn down his friends to spend time with her. Then she remembered Nikki. He must want to know how to contact her.

He did up his jacket before pulling the door open for her. "What a change in the weather. My room okay? I have instant. Or we could go to the cafeteria if—"

"I like instant."

His room was as she remembered it, a bit messy,

smelling of Old Spice and oranges. He got busy boiling water in a kettle and spooning coffee granules into mugs. A pint of milk sat chilling on the window ledge. He offered her his desk chair and sat on the bed while she filled him in on all she knew. She ended by saying she had no idea why Gordon Grady had killed Veronica Maisonneuve but expected the police would tell the public eventually. He'd apparently confessed to his sister before taking his own life.

Jeremy waited until she finished her coffee and reached for her mug. "I have another class and need to get going."

Sara nodded and shrugged back into her parka. He hadn't asked how he could reach Nikki, which surprised her.

"Do you think we could go for dinner this Friday?" He studied her face while he waited for her to answer.

"Like, you and me?"

"That's what I was thinking."

"Isn't there someone else you'd rather ask?"

"Not particularly." He smiled. "If you're going to be a PI, McGowan, you have to learn to read the signs. I like you and want to get to know you better. I'm asking you out on a date."

"I wasn't sure."

They stood at the same time, and he asked, "Is it okay if I kiss you … just so there's no question about my interest going forward?"

She nodded, and his lips were on hers before she had time to think it through. When he finally pulled away, she opened her eyes and thought that kissing Jeremy might be something she could do a lot more of given half a chance. Her second thought was that she wasn't going to die without being kissed, as she'd previously believed.

"So is that a yes to dinner?" His face was very close, and his eyes were hazel with golden flecks. She took a moment to make her voice work properly.

"It's a yes," she said finally.

He kissed her again before pulling away and opening the door. They walked hand in hand down the hallway and into the sunny winter afternoon, and she thought if she died that moment, she'd go to Heaven a happy girl.

———

"WELL, THAT DOES IT FOR ME." Liam closed his laptop and leaned back in his chair. "Try not to miss me."

"It won't be the same without your big ol', serious mug looking across the desk at me." Quade grinned at him. "So what plans for your week off?"

"I'm taking my sister Hannah's boys skiing at Mt. Tremblant."

"No Hannah?"

"Nope. Guys' weekend."

"You're one brave uncle. As I recall, her sons are only six and eight."

"Hugh turned nine, but yeah, Jack is still six. We won't be spending much time in the bars. Before I leave, what's the news on the staff sergeant position?"

"They offered, and I refused."

"Quade, no. I thought you wanted the job… We all wanted you to have the job." Liam tried to read her expression.

"Flatterer. No, my kids had to come first at this stage

in our lives. I know we work long hours as detectives, but my stint as acting made me realize the job demanded being constantly on call. There's no counting on my ex to pick up the slack, and they don't deserve to be in the middle of our bickering. I'm afraid you're stuck with me as your partner for the time being."

"Then I come out the winner." He stood and grabbed his parka from the hook on the wall behind him.

"Ella's podcast on Auger didn't spare any punches," Quade said. She stood too and stretched. "Have you seen her since she returned from that tropical island?"

Liam paused with one arm in the sleeve. "No."

"Funny. I thought you two were tight. She called for my take on him, but I said no comment. She had a couple of anonymous sources, though. The alleged sexual assault victims paint an ugly picture." Quade reached for her coat.

He nodded but stayed silent. Ella had sent him a text, but he hadn't followed up. He and Georgina were taking a break, and he needed time to think.

"Don't waste a minute on this place while you're away, Hunter. You've more than earned a change of scene and some fun."

A shadow passed over him as he thought about Veronica Maisonneuve and her terrible death. Nicola Larsen and the two other girls they'd reunited with their families had been to hell and back; their trauma would be difficult to work through, if it ever could be. Then there were all the young women they hadn't been able to save — but his mind couldn't go there for long. Cassie Grady and her family had their own burden of grief to carry. Cassie's tortured face the night he found her with her dead brother steps away in the living room continued to haunt his dreams. It was going to be difficult not to think about all of them for some time to come, but he didn't say this out loud.

Instead, he gave Quade a thumbs-up and followed her out of the office to begin his first real holiday since joining Major Crimes. A week spent with two of his favourite people, seeing the world through their innocent eyes, was just what he needed to get his life back on an even keel. And since a week wasn't near enough time to clear away all the ugliness and trauma from the past year, he'd booked a solo month in Ireland in the summer. This frigid winter with its record-breaking amount of snow would one day be a memory, and with any luck, his peace of mind would return with longer days and healing sunshine as he retraced his childhood footsteps in Dublin and along the Irish coast. He'd use the time to clear his mind and heart of Ella Tate and return to his life refreshed and ready to take on a new workload, maybe even commit to moving in with Georgina.

And thank God the world will keep on turning, he thought, *because this has been one hell of a winter, and spring can't get here soon enough.*

ACKNOWLEDGMENTS

This story is completely fictitious, and all of the characters come out of my imagination. While many of the locations are real, I sometimes include a building or address that is not. The odd time, as in my real life, I get a direction wrong (just ask my husband). This is a work of fiction after all.

The issue of human trafficking sadly is all too real. The Canadian Centre to End Human Trafficking has valuable information, including the link to a national 24-hour hotline. This resource can be easily accessed through the web.

I would like to again thank my beta readers, Darlene Cole, Derick Nighbor and Carol Gage as well as my editors Allister Thompson and Susan Rothery. Another warm thank you to Laura Boyle for again designing the cover, which reflects the theme so beautifully.

Thank you to John Delacourt and Don Butler for reading advance copies and providing such lovely recommendations.

We all need people who believe in us. I've been blessed to receive support from so many readers, authors, and people in the book industry. A special thank you to Jim Sherman of Perfect Books and all the store managers who've championed my books and invited me for signings. Love and thanks to my good friends Dawn Rayner, Kathryn Anthonison, Wendy Pell,

Jan Yemensky and Kathleen Schiemann. A shout out to Fred Taylor for photographing my launches and for our years of friendship. And to each of my readers and the book clubs who continue to buy my books, send me notes and messages, and help to spread the word. Writing is a solitary endeavour, but it helps to know the pack has your back.

Finally, to my family near and far, thank you for your continued love and support. To my husband Ted, daughters Lisa and Julia, sons-in-law, Robin and Shane — the journey would be a lot less fun and exciting without you.

ABOUT THE AUTHOR

Brenda Chapman is a crime writer who has published twenty-five books, including the lauded Stonechild and Rouleau series, the Anna Sweet mysteries for adult literacy, and the Jennifer Bannon mysteries for middle grade readers. Brenda's work has been short-listed for several awards, including four Crime Writers of Canada Awards of Excellence. A former teacher and senior communications advisor in the federal government, she makes her home in Ottawa.